GHOSTS OF THE PROVENCE

Parisian Ghosts

Janna Ruth

Janna Ruth

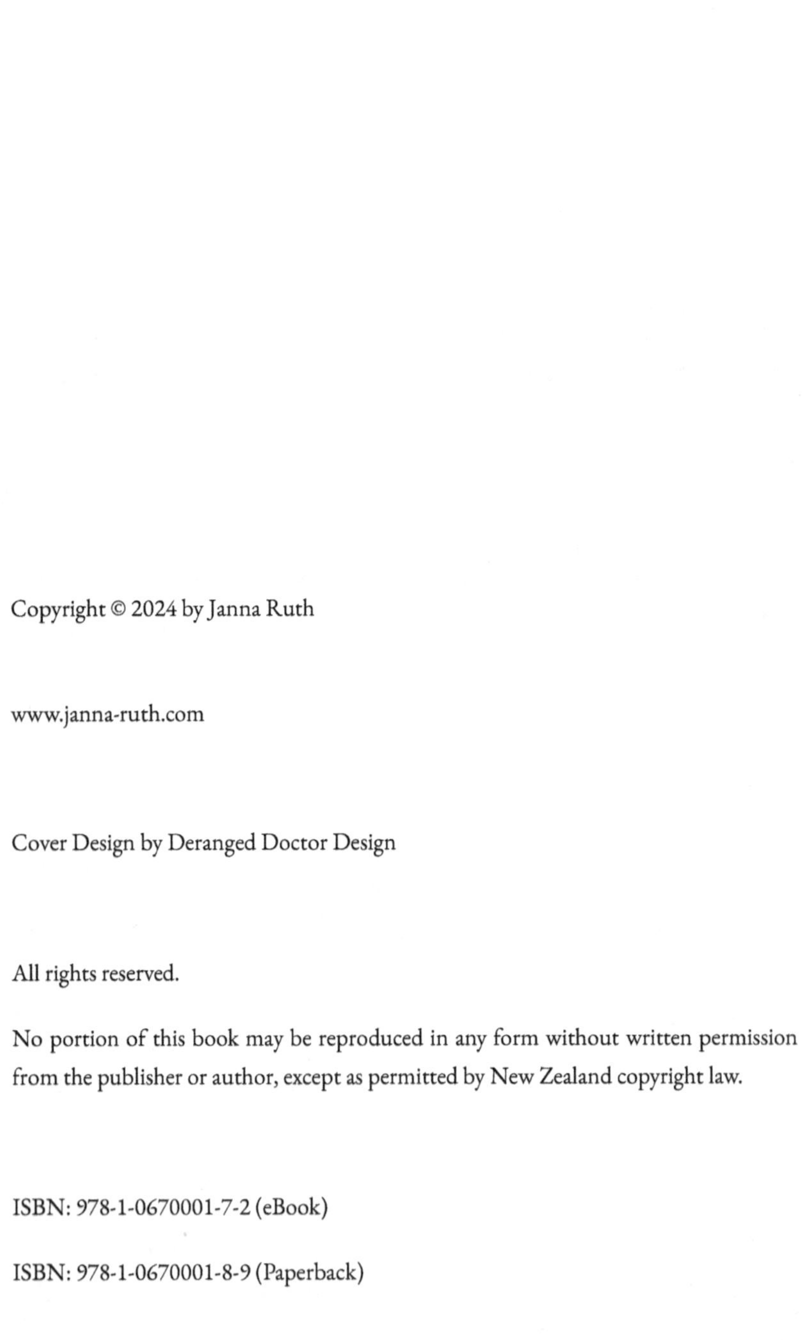

PARISIAN GHOSTS 5

GHOSTS OF THE PROVENCE

JANNA RUTH

Grab your free copy

When an undead movie star asks you for a small favour, you know you're gonna be in deep trouble.

Seeing ghosts is just something I've learnt to live with. They're everywhere I go, especially since I chose to study history at the Sorbonne, one of the oldest universities in the world. While on a class trip to the Pantheon, where France's great men—and women!—reside, I get introduced to the fabulous Josephine Baker! One of her war medals has gone missing, and she wants me to find its whereabouts.

Who could say no to a flapper girl turned movie star turned war hero? Little do I know agreeing to do so will send me on a wild-goose chase across the country with a ghostly pet cheetah, hidden walkways, and a murder attempt.

.

Follow Alix on her first big ghost adventure two years prior to the events of Parisian Ghosts.

.

Sign up to my Story Seeker mailing list at www.janna-ruth.com/newsletter and grab the prequel for free

A Note on Sensitive Topics

Dear Reader,

This is a book about ghosts, so naturally death plays a rather large part in it. If you don't like spoilers and you're cool with everything, skip this note and start the book. If you want to be prepared, read on. I'm writing this because reading should be fun, not a nasty surprise.

There will be a few triggers in this book. First of all, there will be two deaths. One is an accidental suicide, the other is a murder with some potentially gory details. There are also several death threats, and a gun is brandished.

Furthermore, there are discussions of human and ghost experiments, and serious child neglect. You already know Sébastien was practically killed by his father at the age of seventeen. In this book we learn a bit more about the details. Things are looking pretty bleak for him, but sometimes things have to get worse before they can get better.

Speaking of things getting worse: a beloved relationship is put to the test, and some scenes may remind you of domestic violence. That's because it is, even if our heroine refuses to see it for the longest time. It's a real thing all too often, and I wanted to depict that kind of struggle. It's not the end of the story, though, and our heroine will get through it with the same love and empathy she's shown before.

This series has physical and mental confrontations between the living and the dead, but our heroine is scrappy and will gain some strong supporters along the way.

Happy to tag along? Then join Alix in this new ghostly adventure as she travels to beautiful Provence.

.

Love, Janna

CHAPTER 1

A million thoughts run through my head as Sébastien, Gaspar, and I arrive at Sébastien's apartment. The three of us look an absolute mess after escaping from under the opera, especially after having taken an involuntary bath in the underground lake when C-Trente attacked us.

As for Gaspar, he looks as if he's been living in a hole in the ground for two months, which seems frighteningly accurate—except for the *living* part. Apart from his initial greeting, he's barely said a word, but he's agreed to come with us to a safer place. The whole time on the way here, I was fighting an enormous sense of guilt. Every time my joy over his return bubbled up, it was crushed again by what happened while he was gone.

The truth is something has changed. He feels different. Like a ticking time bomb waiting to explode in my face.

Which I probably deserve. I don't even know why I kissed Sébastien. Something about the exhilaration of being alive, flooded with gratitude when he turned on his father's whisper ghost and eliminated him, and a sense of commonality—we're both traitors to GoPol now. Part of me wants to defend myself, to say I'd thought Gaspar had gone for good, but another part calls me a liar. Another part knows why the mysterious music I heard at the opera went straight to my heart.

I'm still struggling to understand, though. If Gaspar was still around, why was he hiding under the opera? Why play games with me by inviting me to performances where people were going to be murdered? The music showed me a message about the murder, it didn't lead me to him until the very end. Why would he leave and hide from me, after promising to always watch over me?

Sébastien leads us into the living room and offers us the couch, while he lights the vervain candles scattered around the room to avoid other ghosts listening in. I want to sit, but Gaspar keeps standing there, looking at the sofa and the glass table with disgust, so I stay on my feet, too.

When Sébastien notices, he sighs. "I'll get the first-aid kit."

It's safe to assume he'll have trouble finding it quickly.

"I'm sorry," I whisper, almost afraid.

"Are you?" Gaspar drawls.

My heart almost bursts out of my chest it's pounding that hard. A tear runs down my cheek and soon another follows. "I thought you were gone."

"So you moved on." His voice is so hard and unforgiving. It's not the voice I remember. Nothing about him is the way it should be.

I try to take his hand, but he jerks it away. "What happened?"

"What happened?" His eyes are burning. He looks more like C-Trente or Nat than my sweet hedgehog boy. Is it really just because of the kiss? "You have no idea what I've been through. For us. And you're running around with Sébastien, going on one date after another, and kissing him."

I swallow hard. Put like that, I really sound the worst. "It was just an act. Sébastien and I aren't dating. We only did it to throw off GoPol and my sisters and—"

"And how did that work out for you?" Gaspar interrupts me rudely.

"Not so well," I say in a small voice. My throat still hurts from being squeezed twice in a few days, and my forehead is throbbing with pain. Our act hadn't fooled C-Trente at all.

I try to take Gaspar's hand again, and this time he lets me, though his grip is feeble at best. "I'm sorry, Gaspar. I got carried away. There's no excuse, I know, but I really thought I'd lost you forever. Your bones were gone." His grave was empty when I visited with Gaby and Marie.

He tears his hand from my grip and takes a step away. "Of course they were gone."

"Of course?"

I try not to be hurt by his actions or the coldness in his voice, but it's starting to get to me. My clothes are still wet, my body aches in a dozen different places, and only an hour ago, I'd thought I was going to die.

His blazing eyes meet mine again. "While you were fooling around with Sébastien, I went to the Chevalier and asked him to try his whole resurrection thing. He dug up my bones, took them to his laboratory, and we've been working on them ever since."

Shock roots me in place. "You're alive?"

I remember the Chevalier's creepy experiments: the skeleton squirrel, the crushed hedgehog, and the living mouse. When Gaspar and I were introduced to them, the Chevalier offered to make Gaspar his first human experiment, but we both agreed not to mess with it.

Gaspar picks up an abandoned glass of water from the coffee table, lifts it into the air and lets it fall back down. A deafening crack tears through the living room as glass meets glass. I jump as shards of glass shoot knee-high across the room. At least one buries itself in my exposed hand.

In an instant, Sébastien is back in the room. His eyes land on me, then Gaspar, then on the broken coffee table. "What's going on in here?"

"He's alive," I cry.

My knees buckle and I fall to the couch. More splinters pierce my legs, but I can't deal with them. The horrors and revelations of the last two hours have finally caught up with me. I should be overflowing with joy. Instead, I burst into tears.

"Don't you want to comfort her?" Sébastien asks in horror when neither of them hurries to my side.

"Isn't that your job now?"

Neither of them hold me. I cry and cry until my sobs turn into hiccups and I'm gasping for breath. Slowly, bit by bit, I regain some semblance of control, taking deep breaths to shake off the tears.

When I finally do, Sébastien is at my side. He gently takes my hand and pulls out the two shards buried there. Methodically, he tends to the small wounds first, then the larger one on my forehead. Finally, he gets me to my feet so he can move me to a safer place.

The entire time Gaspar just watches us grimly. I notice he's not hurt, even though he was much closer to the glass, but I have no idea what to make of that. Maybe he just got lucky.

"Is someone going to tell me what happened?" Sébastien asks, looking from Gaspar to me.

In a soft little voice, I tell him about the Chevalier's experiments and what Gaspar did to be with me.

When I finish, Gaspar adds: "I thought she wouldn't be able to see me again, so I figured I didn't have much to lose." For the first time since we found him, his voice has softened. But then he snorts. "As it turns out, I was going to lose her anyway."

Sébastien takes a step back. "Look, I'm not planning to come between you. The kiss was… accidental. It didn't mean anything."

I want to agree, but the sting in my heart betrays me. I have no idea what it meant, but it meant *something*.

"She loves you, Gaspar," Sébastien continues, "only you. You should have seen how heartbroken she was when she thought she'd lost you. And to have you back alive…" He laughs in disbelief. "That's brilliant." He looks at me with a warm smile that cuts through my heart like a knife. "I'm happy for you."

"It's not perfect," Gaspar says with an eye roll. "I'm alive, but I'm also dead. I can't just go out there and resume my life. Why do you think I was staying in the catacombs?"

"We'll figure it out," I say quietly. Slowly, I approach him again. "Together?"

Gaspar looks at me thoughtfully. There's still some resentment in his eyes, but he's softening. "I only did it to be with you. Romain said it remains to be seen if the experiment was truly successful."

I take his hands in mine and smile. "I'm just glad to have you back. I don't care in what form."

He snorts, but there's a flicker of his old smile. "So, you're still mine?"

"I always was."

With a soft sigh, Gaspar pulls me closer and kisses me. He rests his forehead on mine and whispers, "I need you, Alix."

"Ghost," says Sébastien, suddenly alert.

"Relax. It's only me."

My heart leaps when I hear that cheerful voice. "Dix!"

As he enters the living room, he does a double take. "Well, that's an interesting arrangement. How long was I gone?"

Sébastien stares as if his teenage whisper ghost has grown three heads in his absence. "Where have you been?"

"Me? I just got back from Marseille." He drops onto the sofa and puts his feet on the frame of the broken coffee table, ignoring the glass. "I've been on a bit of a quest, you know?" Dix grins at us all. "You'll never guess who I found."

"Who?"

"Maman."

CHAPTER 2

"You found Maman?" Sébastien repeats. His face has gone slack, as if after everything we've already been through today, this is just one thing too much.

Dix suddenly notices all the broken glass around him. "What happened here?"

"Maman?" Sébastien prompts.

"Oh, right. Yeah, she lives in Marseille, works for the university there. She's got her own research lab. Doing really well for herself."

As much as I usually appreciate Dix's light-hearted approach, my heart goes out to Sébastien. I know exactly how much it hurts him to hear this. But as usual, he puts it all behind a door and swallows the key. "I'm glad to hear it," he says, as if it were a distant cousin he'd lost touch with and not his mother.

Instinctively, I want to take his hand, but with Gaspar standing next to me, that's out of the question. "Did you speak to her?" I ask Dix, pushing for the details Sébastien won't.

"She's not a ghost whisperer, so no." There's the slightest crack in Dix's voice. They're both excellent at burying their shared pain. "But I did watch her work a bit. Found out where she lives. Beautiful house, windows overlooking the sea."

Suddenly, Sébastien pulls out another chair and sits at the table, rubbing his eyes with the heels of his hands. He's not crying, but he's exhausted. So terribly exhausted.

I look at Gaspar and silently ask for permission to reach out. Unlike before, there's nothing but warmth in his eyes, and he mouths, "Go on."

Grateful, I put my hand on Sébastien's shoulder. "We could go see her if you want. Or, if you like, I could snoop around when I'm in the area next month." My sister's wedding is in Provence, in a village about ten kilometres from Marseille.

Sébastien shakes his head and looks at me. "I won't let you contact my mother for me, Alix. But I'd like you to be there when I do it myself." He grimaces slightly. "Even if that means I have to go to Cédric's wedding."

"Welcome to the club." I'm going to be my sister's witness when she marries the man I hate with all my heart, but whom I'll have to learn to tolerate for my sister's sake. The wedding will be hell and will only be endured with lots of wine, frequent belly rubs for my pet hedgehog, and the presence of good friends. "We can get drunk together." I look up at Gaspar. "All of us." It's one of the many perks of being alive.

"So, is this a ménage à trois situation now?" Dix jokes from across the room. "Because if it is, I don't want to be in the room when you—"

"Oh, shut up, Dix. You're so immature." Despite his harsh words, Sébastien cracks a smile. He's missed his whisper ghost more than anything. "Alix is with Gaspar. Like always."

Gaspar slips his hand into mine as if to confirm, and I lean my head on his shoulder. I still can't believe he's not only back, but alive.

While Sébastien fills Dix in on everything he's missed, I watch Gaspar and marvel at how little difference there is between him being a ghost and being alive. But I'm a ghost whisperer. It'll be a world of difference for everyone else in my life. I can finally introduce him to Gaby and my family. I can prove the existence of ghosts to Hélène once and for all. And I don't even have to admit I haven't lost my ability to see them.

Gaspar is *alive*.

We can be together for real now. I can take him to the wedding as my date. One day, in the distant future, *we* could have a wedding. We have a future now.

"So, old C-Trente is gone?" Dix asks, stunned. "Like completely gone, poof. You removed Papa's whisper ghost?"

Sébastien shifts in his chair, wincing. "It was the only way to protect Alix. He would've never stopped trying to expose her. And now…" He seems to have an insight and his face lightens up. "Papa won't be able to see ghosts anymore. He won't be able to confirm you still can. You'll be safe. Well, *safer.*"

For a moment it looks like he's going to reach out and kiss me again, but obviously that's not going to happen. Still, I can't quite ignore the rush of endorphins inside me. I'll still have to keep it a secret, but I'm no longer under the constant threat of Charles Roubert finding out he's failed to subdue me.

"Won't he be angry you took out C-Trente?" We haven't even had time to think about the consequences yet.

"Who's going to tell him?" Despite his bravado, I see Sébastien's throat tighten slightly. He knows he'll be in big trouble if his father ever finds out what happened under the opera.

He took that risk willingly for my sake, and I want to reassure him right away that I won't forget it. "Not me."

His gaze moves over my shoulder to Gaspar. I turn my head, too. "Please."

Gaspar snorts. "I have no interest in getting involved with GoPol. I wouldn't do anything to hurt Alix, but you'd better make sure she's really safe from your father, or I can't guarantee anything."

I frown at his slightly threatening tone. It's unusually confrontational, but I guess it's to be expected after he found me in Sébastien's arms. Sympathetically, I rub his hand and smile. "Whatever danger is out there, we'll face it together."

His face softens and he plants a kiss on my forehead. "I won't leave your side. Not again."

Sébastien clears his throat and gets up. "Anyone else want some wine? Alix? Gaspar?"

As we both nod, Dix groans. "Great, you'll all get drunk and make out, and I'll have to watch sober."

Before Sébastien and I can protest, Gaspar jokes, "Or you could turn around and close your eyes."

While Dix looks at him perplexed, Sébastien snorts and goes into the kitchen. He returns with three wineglasses and a Chardonnay. It's a surprisingly good wine, none of the cheap shit Gaby and I usually buy, and it does wonders to calm our frayed nerves.

Gaspar swirls the glass in his hand, savouring the aroma and each sip with wonder. It seems to be the first time he's had wine since he died, maybe the first time he's had anything with taste.

"So, what happens next?" I ask, when a sense of calm has settled in. "You can't go back to living under the opera. That's not... living."

He raises an eyebrow at me. "I told you, to the world, I'm still dead. Gaspar du Charbonneau has been buried. My parents and my flatmates got rid of everything I owned... or almost everything. I don't have a passport, ID card, or social security number. If I turned up at the Sorbonne for my classes, there'd be hysteria. Do you think I chose to live in the catacombs because I wanted to?"

Before Gaspar died, he'd been a pretty competent cataphile. The catacombs are second home to him, but he's right, community or not, it's no life being confined to dark corridors.

Unless you're the Chevalier. He seems to be doing just fine in his second life.

"Maybe Romain could help with that." I can't believe I'm suggesting something that could lead to forgery, but what's the alternative? "He must have contacts."

Sébastien isn't happy with the idea, but he doesn't protest either. Even at GoPol, he'd never had to deal with a ghost who was alive.

"We'll make it work. We'll have your life back on track in no time." I smile. "The important thing is that you're alive and well." A wave of giddiness rushes through me. "You're alive!" I throw myself into his arms, unable to contain my joy.

Gaspar laughs, but there's still a slight reluctance. I get it. Whatever he's been through can't have been easy, and there are all these challenges in his way, but we've faced worse. What's a bit of bureaucracy when we can have a full relationship now?

Speaking of which… "We still have to work out where you can stay. You're definitely not going back to the opera." My heart wants him to come home with me, as he did when he was a ghost, but that's not so easy anymore. I need time to explain who he is, and even then, my parents won't just let my boyfriend move in. "Maybe we can book you a hotel room for the first few days, while we find a solution…"

"Or you could stay here," Sébastien offers, as if it's the most logical solution. "I have the space and, apart from a nosy neighbour, no one who would mind. You can sleep on the couch tonight, and tomorrow we'll buy a bed and move you into my spare room."

I stare. Pointing at each of them, I ask, "The two of you? Together?"

Sébastien shrugs. "It's the easiest solution, isn't it? You can come here anytime and…" His voice trails off.

And what? I want to ask, but I'm still in shock. Before Gaspar disappeared, he and Sébastien didn't exactly see eye to eye. They're not friends. And then there's the small matter of me kissing both of them. Or, if I'm being honest, *having feelings* for both of them. If he moves in here, I won't be able to visit Gaspar without Sébastien in the other room or hang out with Sébastien without Gaspar around.

"You can stay over whenever you want," Sébastien finishes, belatedly.

Suddenly, Dix's behind my shoulders, leaning into my ear. "Told you it was a ménage à trois," he whispers.

My cheeks respond with a sudden flush of heat. "Um…"

"I can help him adjust, Alix," Sébastien offers, still oblivious to my inner turmoil. "I already know him and his delicate situation, so it's no problem. That is, if you don't mind, Gaspar."

My boyfriend studies me with interest, as if trying to read my mind—which I really hope he can't, because that mind is busy creating all sorts of absurd situations involving both men. Then he shrugs his shoulders at Sébastien. "I don't mind. Beats a dripping cave any day."

"Then it's a deal." Sébastien smiles and offers Gaspar his hand. "My apartment is your apartment."

And with that, the two guys I've kissed in the last two months move in together.

CHAPTER 3

This particular situation calls for an impromptu girl talk. After leaving Gaspar with Sébastien and Dix, I text Gaby and tell her to come over. As soon as I'm home, I jump in the shower and change my clothes. A glance in the mirror tells me I shouldn't walk around without my scarf for a while to avoid uncomfortable questions. Especially in front of my family.

Malou is waking up as I settle into my room, and I can't wait to tell her the news. "Gaspar is alive," I whisper giddily. "You know what that means. More belly rubs for you." My hedgehog boy won't miss the chance to hold Malou for real.

Gaby arrives, along with my little sister. As soon as I hear her voice in the corridor, I jump out and grab her arm. "There you are."

I don't care what she and Odile have been chatting about. All I know is *I* need to talk to my girl, so she can clear my head and tell me what to do.

Amused, Gaby stumbles into my room, giving Odile an apologetic look, as my sister stares at me sullenly. "What's going on? Has something happened?"

"Gaspar's back," I whisper, in case Odile is eavesdropping.

Her eyes widen immediately. "He's back? Alix, that's… that's incredible! Did they let him go or did he say where he went?"

"Oh no, it's even better. He's alive."

Her tone changes instantly. "What?" She looks at me as if I've hit my head, and honestly, I don't blame her.

"I know." My excitement bubbles over and I squeal. "I can't believe it either."

"Wait a minute, slow down." Gaby flaps her hands in the air. "How is Gaspar alive all of a sudden? Is he like you? Was he never really dead and they made a mistake, while you fell in love with his whisper ghost?"

I shudder at the thought of a mistake that would've resulted in him being buried alive. "No, no, it's nothing like that." Knowing this requires a more complicated explanation, I drag her over to my bed and offer her my charcuterie board of snacks.

Instead, Gaby points to the bottle of wine Sébastien gave me. "I think I need the Chardonnay for this."

"It's not a bad thing," I say, with a small eye roll, before pouring her a glass. "I promise, this is a good one." Once we've ironed out the kinks, that is.

While I've shared almost everything with Gaby, the Chevalier's experiments were not part of it. I know what she's going to think about them before I've even started to explain—exactly what I thought when I first came across them—and I decide to gloss over the gruesome details.

"The Chevalier has been experimenting with resurrection for some time. He'd offered it to Gaspar before, and we'd both decided not to risk it. But after we thought I was losing my powers, Gaspar apparently went to him and asked him to do it. And it worked. He's back!"

It's a lot to swallow. Gaby doesn't even blink as she swallows gulp after gulp until her wine glass is empty. "He brought Gaspar back from the dead?"

"He's alive," I say, eagerly. "Truly alive."

"Okay."

"Okay?" I was hoping for a little more from her.

Gaby blinks, then shakes her head, and I can practically see her mind jumping back to the present. "I mean, that's wonderful. I'm happy for you. It's just... people don't usually come back to life."

"That we know of." In a world inhabited by ghosts, whisperers, and whisper ghosts, the lines between life and death are somewhat blurred. "Believe me, I find it a bit creepy, too. Not Gaspar, just the fact that it's possible. In the wrong hands, it's a hell of a power. But in this case, it's a good thing. Gaspar is alive. We can be together. We can have a future."

Gaby's face softens. "You're right. That *is* pretty great." She tucks her legs under herself and smiles. "So, tell me, how did you find him?"

Not nearly as enthusiastically as before, I tell Gaby about the music at the opera and everything that happened when Sébastien and I went back. When I get to the part about C-Trente ambushing us in the catacombs, I'm the one who needs a drink, while Gaby gasps.

"Ma puce, are you okay?"

"Well, I'm alive." I haven't really had much time to process C-Trente's attack after Gaspar's surprise reappearance. Reluctantly, I show her the bruises on my neck. "It was close. If it hadn't been for Sébastien, I'd be dead." I feel heat in my stomach at the thought of his bravery, but my mind stutters as it tries to understand what it means. "He saved my life. And he killed… I mean, he wiped C-Trente from existence. That ghost can never hurt me again."

Gaby's eyes widen. "He destroyed his father's whisper ghost?"

I nod. "He'll be in so much trouble if his father finds out. All… for me." I hesitate in telling her the last important part of what happened today—gosh, was that only today?

But Gaby isn't my best friend for nothing. She immediately picks up on my hesitation and cocks her head. "What is it?"

"We kissed," I say, with a big rush of air.

"You kissed Gaspar?"

Helplessly, I shake my head.

"Oh."

"I know," I admit with a whimper. "It wasn't planned or anything. It was just a spur of the moment kiss. It didn't mean anything, you know. Just... Gaspar saw us."

Gaby's eyes widen even more. "Uh-oh. How did he take it?"

"Not good." His initial cold reaction still makes me cringe. I try to put myself in his place and hate myself a little more. "I'm such an asshole. One day, I don't know how to function without him, and a week later, I'm jumping on the next guy who comes my way."

"Hold up!" Gaby puts her finger in the air, stopping my rant before it really gets going. "First of all, it wasn't a week. You couldn't even get out of bed for a week. And you only went out with Sébastien to find Gaspar. You did it for him."

"I kissed Sébastien for Gaspar?"

She rolls her eyes. "Of course not. But that was two months later. You thought Gaspar was gone, and if he'd really loved you, he'd have been happy for you to move on. There was a time when even he thought you and Sébastien would've made a better couple."

"Only because we're both alive." I huff. "Pretty low bar, if you ask me."

"Is that why you kissed him? Because he's *alive*?" Gaby asks with a raised eyebrow.

I shake my head. "More because *I* was alive." Technically, Gaby's right. The kiss happened precisely because we were both alive. I almost sigh with relief. There's nothing more to it than the sheer joy of surviving certain death. "Look, he saved my life, and I got carried away. So did he. It didn't mean what you think."

Amused, Gaby snorts. "What do *I* think it is?"

My cheeks heat up. "That I... we fell for each other."

Pensively, she puts down her glass and munches on a crisp. "I have to be honest with you, Alix. I'm not quite sure how you truly feel about him, but Sébastien worships the ground you walk on."

The heat intensifies. My first instinct is to ask why he'd do such a thing, but instead I shake my head stubbornly. "That's not true. As soon as we found Gaspar, he took a step back. He even said I belong with Gaspar, so I don't think he has any interest in me."

Gaby gives me a sceptical look. "Two things. A, just because he thinks you belong with Gaspar doesn't mean he's not interested in you. And B, do you *want* him to be interested in you?"

The blush in my cheeks betrays me, though I try my best to ignore it. "Of course not. We only pretended to be a couple so we could hang out together without arousing suspicion. To find Gaspar. And we did. I love Gaspar. He means the world to me. I'm over the moon he's back and—"

Gently, Gaby clasps my shoulders, stopping me from hyperventilating. "No one doubts your love for Gaspar, ma puce. We all saw how much it hurt you to lose him."

I nod shakily. I'm glad Gaspar is back, but to say it doesn't complicate things would be a lie. As he said, the world still thinks he's dead. "Well, he's back."

Gaby smiles, then leans forward to give me a hug. "I'm so happy for you." Some of the tension in my shoulders eases as I soak in her acceptance.

When she sits down again and we've had some food, she asks, "So, where is he now? He's not still living under the opera house, is he?"

"Um... he's moved in with Sébastien."

Gaby coughs and spits out the crisp she's been chewing. "Come again?"

"Just until we've rebuilt Gaspar's life. Obviously, he can't exactly go out and tell everyone he's come back from the dead. So Sébastien offered him a place to stay while we sort everything out."

"Sébastien—who's extremely fond of you—offered Gaspar—who *you're* extremely fond of and who returns the feeling—a place to stay?"

When she puts it like that, it sounds like the worst idea ever. "Do you think it'll work out?"

"Two options, they'll either become best friends or kill each other."

"Gaby!"

She giggles. "Relax! Sébastien is a stand-up guy. He probably offered because he really wanted to help you. And from what you told me, Gaspar is a real sweetheart. It's probably not what he was hoping for, but he'll be friends with Séb in no time." A grin flashes across her face. "Oh, I can't wait to meet the guy who stole your heart." Her eyes widen. "What about Marie? Can I tell her?"

My first instinct is to keep it a secret, but then I realise I can't jealously keep Gaspar to myself. If he's going to return to the upper world, there'll be other people in his life he can't wait to be with again. People who knew him from before. Who am I to deny him that?

"If you think she can handle it, sure."

"She'll probably handle it a lot better than I did. Marie loves the occult. If it wasn't for the necessary near-death experience, she'd probably become a ghost whisperer, too."

I'm about to say something when I hear a knock on the door. Odile pokes her head in. "Hey, sorry to disturb you, but Hélène just called and wants me to confirm the numbers for the hen party and the wedding." She looks at Gaby and swallows. "Will Marie be joining us for either?"

"Both."

Only I seem to see Odile sucking in a breath. But she quickly shakes her head and looks at me. "I know you don't have any other friends for the hen party. And your plus-one at the wedding will probably be Sébastien, who isn't really a plus-one since he's invited on Cédric's side. Although I don't think he's confirmed yet." A small wrinkle appears between her eyes as she ponders this. "Is Sébastien coming?"

"He is... And I'll be bringing a plus-one."

Odile does a double take. "Who? Malou doesn't count."

"Um... You'll see."

My answer makes Odile grimace. "A surprise, eh? Hélène won't like that at all."

Just the thought of explaining Gaspar's case to Hélène makes me shudder. But leaving Gaspar here while I spend three weeks in Provence is out of the question. Hélène will just have to suck it up.

Gaby waits until Odile has closed the door. "You're bringing Gaspar to the wedding?"

"He's my boyfriend. What's the point of him being alive if I can't take him to family events?"

"True. Hélène will still kill you. And you've got Sébastien there, too." Gaby grins a little too much for my taste. "Oh, this is going to be one heck of a wedding."

Chapter 4

I spend the next day with Gaspar in Sébastien's flat, while the latter goes to work and gives us full use of his place. Gaspar seems a little calmer and more like I remember him. I bring him up to date on everything that's happened, and he tells me a little about his resurrection, but admits he doesn't really understand the details. Only one man does, and it's high time I paid him a visit.

We leave a message for Sébastien and head for the abandoned gully. On the way, I notice people are no longer ignoring Gaspar. Despite the rush hour, no one tries to sit on him or bumps into him without apologising. He's actually alive and I can barely contain my giddiness.

When we reach the gully, someone's replaced the gate. The cataflics work hard, but the cataphiles work even harder, and there's already a new entrance cut into the side. Gaspar helps me through, and we both enter the darkness, which now feels almost like home.

"So, when did you become a cataphile?" I ask on the way down.

"I went to my first rave a week after my sixteenth birthday. For the first six months or so, I went to every one I heard about. Honestly, I don't remember too much from those days."

"Your peak rebellion days?" I tease him.

It's too dark to see, but I imagine his grin. "Pretty much. Anyway, one of the guides who took us there noticed I was becoming a regular and offered to take me deeper. I lost my heart there and then."

"And here I thought it was mine."

This time I hear Gaspar chuckle. "It is."

My cheeks flush with heat and I reach for his hand. Gaspar pushes up my headlamp, plunging me into darkness, before he kisses me. I sink against him, sighing into his mouth. With no visuals to distract me, the feel of him is all that occupies my mind. His breath is mine and mine is his. Our tongues meet and his heat fills me. There's heat in his kiss now. Real body heat. It almost makes me want to rip his clothes off right there and then.

An urge he seems to share, when I hear his raspy voice in my ear. "Do you want to go to the reservoir?" It's his favourite place down here, with its magical blue light and endless expanse of water.

But water isn't really my thing these days. Not after I remembered drowning as a child and then had Jacques de Molay dry-drown me and C-Trente go for the real thing.

"Not this time."

Gaspar sighs softly and pulls back. "As you wish."

I already miss his lips, but I know it's for the better. The last thing we need is for me to have a panic attack from being too close to the water. Although now that I think about it more rationally, Paris will probably appreciate my decision not to have sex near its drinking water.

"Let's talk to the Chevalier first." I'm still holding onto his hand, reluctant to let go.

"So we can ask him for permission?" Gaspar snorts quietly. "Being alive is not a medical condition. He's not my doctor or anything."

There's an edge to his voice that makes my stomach clench. I pat his arm, trying to calm him. "I know. It's still... unusual."

Gaspar harrumphs and we continue on our way in silence. There's something to be said for not looking a gift horse in the mouth, but surely, it's okay to want more details. I couldn't bear to lose him again.

A few hours later, we reach the Banga. Although I've crossed this water lock many times before, I suddenly feel as anxious as I did the first time and almost ask Gaspar to carry me. *I can do this,* I tell myself. I know exactly where the ledge is and how deep it gets. And yet I hesitate.

What if I slip? I swim. *What if someone pushes me under?* Gaspar is at my side.

I don't realise how long I've been staring at the dark pool of water until Gaspar holds out his hand. "I've got you."

I gratefully take his hand and cling to his back as if I were his backpack, testing each step twice before putting my weight on it. Gaspar never pushes me and endures my slow progress patiently.

"I'm sorry I couldn't protect you," he says when we're finally on dry ground again. "All this time you've had to fight GoPol on your own. But not anymore. I'm here now. I'll make sure no harm comes to you."

A pedantic part of me wants to correct him on the "on your own" part. I had Sébastien by my side and he protected me when it mattered, and of course, Gaby did what she could, but the much bigger part of me swoons at his vow. I can't believe how lucky I am to have a second chance with this ghost boyfriend of mine. "Thank you, but you have to promise you won't take any unnecessary risks. You can protect me, but you're not invincible anymore."

Gaspar just snorts, and I can't quite tell if he's amused or annoyed.

"I don't want to lose you again."

"You won't," he says, with grim determination, as if nothing bad could ever happen again. "Come, let's see the Chevalier."

Our first stop is the Crossroad of the Dead. Word of Gaspar's resurrection must have spread, because the ghosts are all making way for him. He's no longer one of them, and the jury's still out on what they think of that.

When we can't find the Chevalier or anyone else from the Résistance, Gaspar confidently leads me to the ruins of Lutetia. He must've walked this route dozens of times in the last two months to know it so well, since I can barely remember the path we took the only time we were here together.

Down in the deepest parts of the catacombs, in the remains of Paris' Roman past, we find what we're looking for. I don't know if he heard us, if he has a warning system, or if he sensed Gaspar's approach, but the Chevalier meets us in his laboratory with a ghastly grin. "Long time no see, Alix. I see you've found my gift."

"Gift?" I don't like the way he seems to take away Gaspar's autonomy. It was Gaspar's decision to attempt this, even if it was the Chevalier who had the idea and means to see it through.

The Chevalier approaches and walks around us, appraising Gaspar, who looks at him sullenly. "He's my masterpiece. A true resurrection. I didn't know if it would work until it did." Finally, he addresses Gaspar: "How do you feel? Is everything working as it should?"

"As far as I know," he says, sounding displeased at this scientific treatment. He gives me a pained look and I feel sorry for having made him come here.

"How *does* it work?" I ask. Not that I plan on resurrecting anyone any time soon.

The Chevalier grins at me. "It's a complex process involving the bones of the deceased. In Gaspar's case, we were lucky enough to have access to his entire skeleton, although a significant number of bones were obviously broken, and the decomposition of soft tissue had already begun."

I get about this far before I'm overcome by an intense wave of nausea. I raise my hand and say, "Forget I asked. The details aren't important." It's bad enough we're standing in this lab, with its reanimated creatures and failed experiments. The scurrying of little feet that should be still almost drives me mad.

"Oh, but they are. When you're ready to join me full time, I can teach you the process. I think you and I could make a lot of progress."

Gaspar puts an arm around my shoulders and holds me close. "Alix isn't interested in that kind of career. She's studying History."

"Just for another year and a bit," the Chevalier says, unbothered by the protest. "And it's her deep connection to ghosts that makes her perfect for this job."

The idea I could be perfect for a job that involves experiments on animals, handling decomposing bodies, and regular grave-digging makes me feel sick again. While it's true I need to start thinking about my future, resurrecting ghosts will not be on the cards. "No, thanks."

"Really?" The Chevalier seems surprised, as if he expected me to jump for joy. "I would've thought the demonstration of my new undertaking would've inspired you."

"Inspired me to do what?"

"Bring back more."

A shiver runs down my spine. I'm over the moon Gaspar is alive again, but the thought of some grand resurrection scheme makes me very uneasy. The world isn't supposed to work that way. On the other hand, why should *I* be the only one to benefit? What about all the others who've lost loved ones? The ghosts that still cling to the world of the living, longing for what they'd lost? What makes Gaspar, and by extension me, the only one worthy of this venture into a world beyond death?

My Panthéon ghosts come to mind. Surely, if anyone deserves to come back to life, it would be them. I still have to tell them about Gaspar first, though, not a thought I relish. This is all way more complicated the longer I think about it.

"Before we... *you* do that, we should figure out how to make sure they have a life to come back to. What I mean is... Gaspar's been buried. He's officially dead. He can walk the streets, but he can't enrol, he can't rent. He can't even go to the doctor or earn money."

The Chevalier laughs. "Oh, Alix, how I wish I were as young as you again. There are many people who, for whatever reason, have to live outside the system."

I'm reminded of his own case. After serving time in prison, the Chevalier practically disappeared from the face of the earth. I don't know how he earns his money, but it's not under his legal name. Then I remember the rules Gaspar once told me about the cataphiles. Nobody exchanges money down here. It's all based on an old-fashioned barter system.

Is that Gaspar's future? Relying on others to bring him food while he stays in the catacombs?

"So, you're saying he has to stay underground?"

"Not at all." For a rare moment, the Chevalier looks at Gaspar. "In the long run, I hope to change the way things are done, but until then, a fake ID will do."

I don't know what's more alarming, the fact we're suddenly talking about forging legal documents or that a long-term plan is already in motion. The Chevalier has been a great help in the past and has proven to be more trustworthy than GoPol, but his way of doing things still scares me.

"Can you get me one?" Gaspar asks, without hesitation. He seems much more pragmatic than me. And why shouldn't he be? This is his second chance at life. No matter how it happened, he has to deal with the consequences. Not me.

"Sure. Any particular wishes regarding your name?"

Gaspar swallows. "I can't keep my own?"

"It's not advisable." The Chevalier grimaces. "We can keep Gaspar, if that makes you feel better. But you should definitely change the surname."

"What about the people who knew him when he was alive?" I ask, finding it strange how quickly he's supposed to shed a name he's been associated with for over two decades. "If he wants to re-enrol at the Sorbonne..."

"Again, not advisable." The Chevalier chuckles. "I'm afraid we're not quite there yet as a society, Alix. If we don't want this operation to be shut down by the authorities"—he gives me a look that makes it very clear which authorities we are talking about—"then I would advise your boyfriend to keep his head down. I'll get him a fake ID, and if he needs a university degree, I can provide that, too. Whatever he thinks he needs. But if he wants to live on the surface full time, he should avoid his old stomping grounds. The fewer people who recognise him, the better."

How is that better than being a ghost? I want to ask. The last thing I want is for Gaspar to move away. "That's bullshit," I mutter, crossing my arms.

"Surreau," Gaspar interjects. "Put Surreau down. It's my grandmother's maiden name. And don't worry. I'm not planning to return to my studies."

I stare at him in horror. When I met him, he didn't know what to do with his degree, but he was passionate about helping people, about doing good in the world. Has that really changed so fast? "But Gaspar..."

"I didn't ask the Chevalier to bring me back to life so I could live my old life again." He turns and his intense gaze holds me. "I came back for *you*. To be with you. I don't care if that means living in the catacombs or changing my name. As long as we can be together, I'm willing to do whatever it takes."

His declaration takes my breath away. Part of me swoons pretty hard. The other part wants to protest and ask about his own life and aspirations. Before I can utter a single word in response, the ground beneath our feet trembles. Dust trickles down from above and the walls begin to ache and shake. A pebble hits my shoulder as I cry out in alarm.

What's happening? Is this an *earthquake*? Under Paris?

Gaspar tackles me. We land on the floor, and he pulls me under the nearest table, then covers me with his body as larger rocks fall from the ceiling. My breath catches in my throat as the shaking continues. The walls are now groaning.

As quickly as it came, the quake is over. A single pebble falls before silence returns to the lab. For a moment, all I can hear is Gaspar's and my heavy breathing.

"Damn," exclaims the Chevalier. He's still standing in the middle of the room, looking more annoyed than frightened. "That's the third time it's happened in the last month."

"The *third* time?" My voice is unnaturally high. "What was that?"

Slowly, Gaspar relaxes and lets me stand up. "Yeah. Since when do we have earthquakes in the catacombs?"

The Chevalier shrugs. "Since this year, apparently. I suppose it's some construction work above us. I'll probably have to reinforce the lab walls."

"Or move it," I suggest. The thought of the lab crumbling around me makes me break out in hives. I'm not usually squeamish about the underground like Gaby, but that was before I experienced the walls shaking while I was stuck here.

The Chevalier gives me a flat stare. "And give up a place of power?" He shakes his head. "Never. Not when we're finally making progress."

His eyes almost seem to glow when he mentions "progress", and I swallow. When he speaks like that, he reminds me of Marie Curie. Even though her experiments hurt—and eventually killed her—she wouldn't stop. Not with a discovery in her hands.

The Chevalier is the same. All he cares about is his research. He may claim that Gaspar's resurrection was a gift to me, but I know he must've been exalted when Gaspar came to him. His willingness to be a guinea pig was the real gift. I'm just glad it worked.

"Give me a month and I'll get you all the relevant documents," he tells Gaspar. Then his gaze meets mine and he smiles. "I'm glad to see you again, Alix. For a moment, I was afraid we'd lost you. It would've been a tragedy."

A tragedy, no doubt. The question is whether for me or for him.

Chapter 5

Despite the Chevalier's warning, Gaspar and I decide to go ahead with his reunion program. He won't consider re-enrolling at the Sorbonne and has no interest in seeing his old flatmates or even his parents, but there's no way we're going to leave Marie out of the loop. So, the next day, we meet her and Gaby at *Chambelland.*

Now that lectures are over, the café is much quieter, which suits us just fine. In fact, Marie even abuses her authority as an employee to temporarily close the café. When Gaspar and I arrive, the 'Closed' sign is on the door and we have to knock.

Marie hurries to the door to unlock it but freezes at the sight of Gaspar. He raises his hand and gives a mocking wave, which spurs her back into action.

"Come in, come in." She holds the door open and locks it behind us.

I greet her with kisses, while Gaspar strolls into his old workplace and reacquaints himself with it. He runs his finger along the bottom of the display case and snorts, "You missed this spot."

Puzzled, Marie checks with me before approaching Gaspar. "You're welcome to clean. You know where the supplies are." Then she pulls him into an oddly one-sided embrace. "It's so good to see you," she whispers, though Gaspar barely returns the gesture.

I let them have their moment and sit next to Gaby, who's already waiting with four cups, a pot of coffee, and a plate of pain au chocolat. "So, that's him. Hmm."

"Is that all?" I laugh quietly at her lack of response.

She tears her gaze away to look at me. "I guess I expected him to be a little more... enthusiastic. Marie could hardly sleep last night when I told her. She was so excited. In disbelief, of course, but overjoyed. And the first thing he does is complain about the dust."

While I agree it wasn't the best first impression, I can't help but defend him. "It's probably an inside joke." Marie didn't seem offended, and she had the perfect response for him. "It wasn't a complaint."

"If you say so." Gaby stops scowling for my sake and takes another look. "I've only seen a picture of him. He's cute."

I grin so hard my cheeks hurt. "Yes, he is." And Gaby hasn't even seen him smile yet.

And she won't for a while. For some reason, Gaspar seems to be in a foul mood. The expression on his face as he leans in to greet her can best be described as neutral. They touch cheeks, but he doesn't even look her in the eye. I wonder what's bothering him.

Meanwhile, Marie makes up for it with a bubbly attitude. She pours coffee for us and grins at him.

"I can't believe you're really back. I mean, how is that possible?"

"With a little bone alignment and good old-fashioned blood magic," Gaspar says dryly.

"What?" Even I do a double take. There was no mention of blood magic yesterday.

His lip curls slightly, but it's a far cry from his smile. "You didn't want to hear the details, remember?"

I can't tell if he's joking, admonishing me, or simply telling the truth.

Marie laughs, making the decision for me. "I missed your dark humour. Does that mean you believe in magic now?"

Gaspar snorts, not exactly looking amused. "I came back from the dead, didn't I? Hardly possible without magic."

"Oh, but it's science," I protest. "The Chevalier uses science, doesn't he?"

To be fair, the lines between science and magic are becoming increasingly blurred. I don't know why I have such a hard time accepting magic when I've been seeing ghosts all my life, but I struggle with the concept.

"If it's pure science, why does it have to be done in a place of power? What are the candles for? The blood? Right; no details."

Okay, this time it *does* sound like he's mad at me. We hadn't talked much after our meeting with the Chevalier. I'd been too busy trying to escape the catacombs before a fourth earthquake struck and was pretty knackered. I didn't know he'd wanted to talk about the procedure. When I'd asked him before, he didn't seem to remember much.

Gaby gives me a worried look and I feel the need to say something. "I think it's one of those philosophical questions that would delight Rousseau. Magic, science. It's just magic until we find a way to explain it, isn't it?" The places of power clearly hold a lot of ghost energy. If someone were to study it further, they'd surely find an explanation.

"I think that's a bit narrow-minded. Sorry, Alix." Marie flashes me a quick smile. "I know what you mean, but I still think there are things in this world that are beyond our understanding, and always will be. I take comfort in the fact there are forces in the world that can't simply be dissected and demystified until they lose all their... magic." She chuckles at her lack of a better word.

"Well, it all sounds like magic to me," Gaby adds. "I mean, I didn't even believe in ghosts before you proved me wrong. I still find that hard to swallow. And this..." She looks at Gaspar. "Sorry, Gaspar, but this is the stuff of legends."

He doesn't seem to take offence. At least not at that. "I don't know why it matters so much whether it's science or magic or something else entirely. The important thing is I'm alive again."

I stroke his arm and snuggle into him. "Of course. We're just curious. That's all. After all, you're the first person to come back from the dead. That we know of."

"I suppose." He shakes his head and pulls away to drink his coffee.

As I shift my weight back to my seat, I catch another glance from Gaby. She's not impressed with how this is going, and I suddenly feel the pressure to prove her wrong. "For the record, I'm thrilled. I don't care about the details, because all I care about is here."

Instead of giving me that elusive smile, Gaspar says, "Not all you care about."

I'm confused. What does he mean?

"Hey, Gaspar," Gaby says and I'm already dreading the harsh tone of her voice, "do you like Alix?"

He grimaces at her, now definitely offended. "What kind of question is that?"

"I'm just wondering, because every time she opens her mouth, you attack her."

Oh no, this is not going well at all. "That's not true, Gaby. Of course Gaspar likes me. More than that. He's just having a bad—"

"Would you stop talking for me?" Gaspar snaps.

Stunned, I stare at him.

"Seriously. That's all you did yesterday, too. You *and* the Chevalier. You've talked about *my* life as if I wasn't standing right next to you. And you keep telling people what I want or don't want, as if I'm not capable of doing so myself. I'm not a ghost anymore."

Before I can process his outburst, Gaspar stands up, his chair scraping the floor. "This is bullshit. I shouldn't even be here." And with that, he marches to the door and slams it behind him with enough force to flip the 'Closed' sign over.

I'm absolutely shell-shocked. Gaspar's words swirl in my head, stabbing me over and over again. I'd noticed the Chevalier doing it enough to annoy me, but have I then gone and done the same? Have I slipped back into a ghost-whisperer routine, conveying his thoughts because no one else could hear them? Am I really that condescending?

"What a jerk." Gaby crosses her arms and leans back in her chair with a heavy scowl. "Sorry, sweetie, but when you told me about Gaspar, I was expecting someone sweet and adorable, someone who'd carry you in his hands, not a judgmental, unappreciative ass."

"He's not like that," I protest. Sure, the meeting could've gone better and I'm aghast at how badly it went, but I know Gaspar, and he is the sweet, lovable guy Gaby expected.

Marie nods and puts her hand on Gaby's. "Alix is right. He's not usually like this. I mean, I've seen him grumpy before, usually when he's had a fight with his parents, but I think in this situation it's more a case of PTS, you know. We have to take into account that he died. Probably in agony. And then he woke up as a ghost and saw us all moving on and living our lives. Now he's been resurrected, which is probably another shock to the system." She shrugs. "Frankly, it doesn't surprise me that he needs some time to get back on his feet, to readjust and recalibrate. He'll come around."

I find myself nodding along, agreeing with every word she says. At the same time, a massive wave of guilt washes over me for not having seen it myself. I've always known some ghosts struggle with their death. I've seen it. Is it really so surprising for Gaspar to struggle with being alive again?

Gaby raises her eyebrows, not really sold on this take, but I can't sit here and convince her that Gaspar is a good guy. Not when he's out there hurting. Before they can talk me out of it, I jump up and run after him.

Luckily, he hasn't gone too far, and after a quick check of all the available streets, I see him heading away from the university area.

"Gaspar!" I call, before hurrying to catch up. "Wait, please."

He takes a few more steps, shoulders hunched, before relenting and waiting for me. When I get to his side, he barks, "What?"

"I'm sorry. I didn't know what I was doing. Speaking for you, I mean." I reach out to him full of hope, tugging the sleeve of his hoodie. "I thought today would be a nice day: you'd get to meet Gaby and catch up with Marie." Maybe I can coax him back into the café to continue our date.

"Did you ask?"

"What?

Gaspar groans, then gestures in my direction to underline his point. "You *thought*! You didn't ask me if I wanted to meet Marie and your friend. The Chevalier warned us just yesterday not to do anything like this, but you'd already arranged everything with Gaby."

"I don't understand. We talked about it this morning. Together."

"No, we didn't. You told me you and Gaby had planned this, and I went along with it. I certainly didn't *want* to be paraded around for everyone to gawp at and marvel at this *miracle*."

Stunned, I take half a step back. Gaspar and I have never argued before. He's certainly never hurled so much vitriol at me or misinterpreted everything I do in a negative light. Then again, maybe I was a little insensitive, eager as I was to introduce him to my loved ones. I remember what Marie just said and feel even worse. "I'm sorry."

"Are you?"

My eyes burn with the sudden pressure of tears. I'm overwhelmed with guilt for making things worse for him, and discomfort at how angry he is with me. "Yes." I reach out again. "I didn't mean to parade you around. I was just excited to finally introduce you to Gaby. To be able to share you."

"I'm not a thing to share!" His raised voice freezes me in place. "I'm a person, Alix. My own person. With my own needs and wants." He shakes his head in disgust. "You know, sometimes you make me feel like you loved me better dead. Would you prefer if I were a ghost again?"

My heart's pounding in my chest, my head spinning. To be honest, I *did* like him a lot better when he was a ghost, but that's nonsense. Gaspar is still the same person, dead or alive. He's just gone through two traumatic transformations and all I could think about was how to introduce him to all my loved ones. Instead of helping and listening to what he needs, I've been swept up in the excitement of it all and put this burden on him.

"Of course not." Tears run down my cheeks as my emotions spill over. "I love you."

One moment, he glares at me, his mouth a thin line of discontent. The next, his face softens, and he pulls me into his arms. "Oh, Alix. I'm sorry. I didn't mean to yell at you."

My tears flow faster, as if his kindness is worse than his anger. I cling to his hoodie and sob into the fabric, so grateful he's holding me.

His arms tighten around me, and he leans his head against mine, as if he can't be close enough. "I'm so sorry. I don't know what's going through my head at the moment. You haven't done anything wrong. I'm just... I don't know what I am." He sounds so stricken, as if this is a revelation in itself. "This isn't how I thought it would be. When I went in... I dreamed of turning up at your door, surprising you. And you'd be happy to see me, and we'd kiss and..."

"I *am* happy to see you." I can't believe he'd think otherwise. "Gaspar, I'm overjoyed to have you back in my life. And although I loved you as a ghost, I'm more than happy you're getting this second chance at life. Not for me, but for yourself. You deserve it. All I want is for you to take full advantage of it. That's why I advocated for you. And I'm sorry if I overstepped. I know you can do it yourself."

Gaspar rocks me slightly, then murmurs in my ear, "I actually don't know if I can."

I turn my head to kiss his cheek. "Well, I do."

He sighs heavily, and he inhales into my hair. "Sorry for being a jerk."

"You're not." Marie is right. He's struggling to adjust, nothing more.

"I love you.

"I love you, too."

He pulls back just enough to kiss me gently. I can taste the salt of my own tears on his lips, and yet I can't think of a sweeter kiss. We can do this. Together.

My phone buzzes, interrupting our moment. "That's probably Gaby."

Gaspar snorts in amusement, letting go just enough so I can get my phone. "She hates me."

"She doesn't know you well enough to hate you." I pat his cheek and smile at him. "She'll come around. No doubt."

But the message on my phone isn't from Gaby. It's from Sébastien and it's only two words long.

He knows.

CHAPTER 6

There is no question who *he* is or *what* he knows. Sébastien's message sends me and Gaspar racing back to the apartment. I half wish I'd brought my bike, because the Métro seems too slow today. It gives me too much time to think about the consequences of the message. In short, I'm screwed. If Charles Roubert knows I can see ghosts, my days are numbered.

Gaspar holds my hand and squeezes it, despite how sweaty it gets with every station that isn't Charles de Gaulle, Étoile. "Remember, I won't let him hurt you," he says, quietly but firmly. "And neither will Sébastien."

Charles has the full force of GoPol behind him, access to the gendarmes, and probably a carte blanche from the government to do whatever he likes. As sweet as the two guys are, can they actually protect me?

My only hope is that Petite Alix is well hidden in the Panthéon. The ghosts there have power over the living, but will they be strong enough to repel all those who wish me harm? And there's no doubt Charles wishes me harm. I've been a thorn in his side ever since he met me. The demise of his whisper ghost is just the icing on the cake.

I'd hoped we'd have more time, not just a few days. I guess it must've been pretty obvious what had happened when Charles lost his whispering ability the moment C-Trente ceased to exist. Stunned, I sit a little longer with my thoughts. Charles has lost his whisper ghost. He can't see ghosts anymore. He's no longer a ghost whisperer.

"We're here," Gaspar pulls me out of my thoughts. We squeeze through the other commuters and exit the Métro, before quickly making our way up the stairs and down the streets until we arrive at Sébastien's apartment.

He must have had a spare key lying around, because Gaspar pulls one out of his back pocket and lets us in without ringing the bell. Nevertheless, Dix greets us in the hallway. "He's in the living room. Tidying up."

Tidying up?

After Gaspar's first outburst, Sébastien had to replace his coffee table. It's now a plain wooden one he picked up at the second-hand shop down the road, and it clashes a little with his otherwise sleek, modern style. I personally think it gives the whole room a bit more character. Like someone actually lives there.

It looks like he's going to have to replace a few more things now. One of his bookshelves has collapsed, smashing two vases. The certificates on the wall are hanging crooked and one has some nasty cracks in the glass. Sébastien is on the floor, picking up the books and assessing the damage.

"What happened?"

He turns and I gasp. There's a purple bruise on his left cheekbone, surrounding a nasty crescent-shaped cut. It must've bled like crazy because there's still some dried blood on the edge of his chin, and a lot more on his shirt.

"Told you. He found out."

All this time I'd been worrying about myself and what this could mean for me. I didn't spare a single thought for Sébastien who'd actually been the one who'd destroyed C-Trente and had to stand up to his father. "I'm sorry."

"For what?" Sébastien asks, amused. He puts the rest of the books on the table and stands up. "You didn't do it. You didn't tell my father." He stops in front of me, his hands half raised, but then forgotten. "You've got nothing to be sorry for."

I don't necessarily agree, but I appreciate the sentiment. Instead, I examine his cut. It's not too deep, though stitches wouldn't hurt. "Did he hit you?"

Sébastien avoids my eyes. "Something like that."

"More like pointed a gun at him," Dix chimes in.

"A *gun*?"

"I thought we agreed to keep the details to ourselves," says Sébastien, slightly annoyed. Only the flattening of his breath betrays his shock.

Dix snorts. "I didn't agree to anything. Just because you want to play the silent hero doesn't mean I have to go along with it." He looks at me. "Our father is a madman. Nothing to see. Move along."

My head is still reeling from the fact an actual gun was involved. "You need to see a doctor."

Sébastien shakes his head. "I'm fine. It looks worse than it is. Just a little cut."

The "little" cut is two centimetres long and quite thick. I have to agree with Dix. "You don't have to play at hero."

"I'm not," he promises. "Look, it stopped bleeding. What's a doctor to do?"

A massive eye roll is my response. It's such a typically male thing to say. "Fine, have it your way. Are you going to tell me what happened, at least?"

He doesn't look like he wants to, but a sigh later, he gives us the quick rundown. "Obviously, he realised he'd lost C-Trente pretty quickly and he knew who C-Trente was following, so it was either you or me."

"You told him you did it."

"I *did* do it," he insists.

He's right, of course. I was nothing more than the damsel in distress in this scenario. Still, without me, Sébastien would've never been forced to take a stand.

He sighs. "Look, it's alright. I think. He threw a tantrum, accused me of lying to him—which isn't wrong—and of protecting you... *and* Petite Alix. He's not happy about it, but he thinks I'm..." Sébastien lowers his eyes, not telling me what his father thinks of him. "I managed to convince him that you're not the danger to GoPol he thinks you are."

If it were up to me, I'd burn down GoPol and raze the foundations to the ground, but as far as being an actual danger goes, he's probably right. "You mean he's letting me stay a ghost whisperer?"

"For now."

I don't believe him. After everything that's happened between me and GoPol, I find it hard to accept that eliminating Charles' whisper ghost has brought us a truce. If that's true, I may be more dangerous to them than I thought.

I raise an eyebrow at Dix, encouraging him to tell me more. As expected, he spills the beans. "He put Séb on probation. One more slip and he'll stick a treason charge on him. But yes, he's agreed to leave you alone, so long as Séb vouches for you, because he thinks—"

"Dix."

The two of them exchange a look, which causes Dix to shut up, much to my dismay.

"He thinks you'd protect Alix with your life, if necessary," Gaspar says. "Or in this case, with your integrity."

I look back and forth between them. A picture is forming in my mind and it's not a pretty one. "I don't want you to risk your life or your integrity or whatever for me."

A crooked smile slips across Sébastien's lips. "Too late."

"Much too late," Gaspar adds.

"Yeah, that train left the station a long time ago," Dix comments dryly.

I sigh. What am I going to do with them?

Shaking my head, I walk past Sébastien, grab the empty snack bowl from the table and start picking up broken glass.

"You don't have to do that," he protests predictably, dropping to his knees beside me. "I can do it."

"Let me help you, please. You need to go to the doctor and get stitches for that cut or you'll have an ugly scar for the rest of your life." It comes out a little petulant.

Sébastien's lips curl. "Is that all you care about? How pretty my face is?"

The sight of that awkward little smile makes my stomach do a little flip.

"I can take him to the ER," Gaspar says, quickly silencing my unwarranted reaction.

"I don't need to..." Sébastien catches my glare and sighs. "Fine, if it makes you happy, I'll go to the doctor. But more importantly, we need to discuss what this means for us and how to move forward."

With a gentle smile, I pat his arm. "After you've had that wound looked at."

Sighing again, he stands. "Will you be here when I get back?"

"Of course."

He finally departs with Gaspar, leaving me alone with Dix. As soon as the door closes, I fix Dix with a glare. "Tell me everything."

Three hours later, I've cleaned up the mess in the living room as best as I can and cooked dinner. It's just a simple ratatouille with leftover vegetables from Sébastien's pantry, but it smells divine. Meanwhile, Dix has told me all the gory details of the meeting.

Apparently, Charles took Sébastien by surprise when he pushed him against the wall, hence the fallen bookcase. While Sébastien was down, he pulled a gun on him and extracted all the information he needed about C-Trente's demise. Dix had tried to attack Charles, but since he's no longer a ghost whisperer, the whisper ghost couldn't touch him, and Sébastien kept his presence quiet.

My abilities were revealed when Sébastien protested that C-Trente had tried to kill me. Then he had to admit he'd never eliminated Petite Alix as he'd been ordered, and that he'd broken

GoPol protocol to protect me against his father's orders. For that, he was struck with the gun, which explains the round cut on his cheek.

In the end, Sébastien pleaded my case, saying I was nothing more than a history student and that my interest in ghosts was purely academic. *I'm no danger and never will be*, were his exact words.

There is more, but Dix remains loyal to Sébastien and refuses to tell me what argument finally swayed Charles. Whatever it was, it's put Sébastien in his father's bad books and officially on probation. He's been removed from all active cases and has weeks, if not months, of paperwork ahead of him. And he's vouching for me. That means one slip from me and he could not only lose his job, but go to jail.

For better or worse, our fates are now tied.

The problem is, I have no idea what Charles would consider a slip on my part. Sure, stealing a classified file and a whisper ghost are pretty clear-cut cases, but sometimes I feel like my mere existence is bothering him. It wasn't my idea to get involved in the conflict between GoPol and the Résistance. Sébastien is right. I'm just a history student with a unique talent and a lot of long-dead friends. Maybe if I focus more on that, I can prove myself worthy of existing.

I snort at the thought. There's already too much bad blood between us to forget what happened. The very fact he threatened and attacked his own son makes my blood boil. A man like that shouldn't be in charge of the only agency dealing with ghosts. I'll keep as low a profile as possible to protect Sébastien, but if I have to fade into obscurity then I'll strike from the shadows when he least expects it. There's only one way to keep everyone I love safe, and that's with that man behind bars. If only we had enough power or dirt on him to put him there.

The door finally opens, and I hear Gaspar's voice in the corridor. "She once gave all my band shirts to Goodwill and replaced them with dress shirts. I was so freaking mad."

Who is he talking about?

"There wouldn't have been time in my training schedule to buy band shirts," Sébastien replies, sounding much more cheerful than his words suggest.

Gaspar laughs. "Oh boy. We'll have to make up for it. Don't fear. I've got you."

"Are they bonding over their abusive parents?" I ask Dix, not quite sure that's what I heard.

Dix just grins. "Hey, if that means we're sneaking off to a concert, I'm all in."

The two enter the room and stop talking when they see the food. "You cooked," says Sébastien, who's sporting a bandage on his cheek.

"Well, I thought you might be hungry. It's dinnertime. I hope these vegetables weren't meant for something else." Otherwise, it would have just been cheese, since there's been a surprisingly large selection in the fridge.

"Not specifically, no."

Gaspar kisses me on the cheek before sitting down. "This smells delicious. Much better than eating leftovers from the opera break room. Or whatever *you* call cooking," he says to Sébastien.

"Hey! You're welcome to take over dinner duty," Sébastien shoots back as he sits opposite me.

"I might have to if I want to *stay* alive." Gaspar plays it up with enough theatricality to make me laugh.

Sébastien rolls his eyes, but he's obviously just as amused. It's an odd look for him. Whatever Gaspar did on their trip to the E.R., it's worked wonders in loosening him up and coaxing the Dix side out of him.

As for the actual Dix, he sits on the other side of me without a plate in front of him, grinning as he watches the back and forth between his older self and the former ghost.

"Thanks for cooking," says Sébastien, a little more seriously. "It tastes really good."

"Amazing," Gaspar corrects, savouring every bite of food he puts in his mouth.

I smile at them. This little get-together is healing something in me that all the turmoil of the last few days had broken. It feels like it's doing the same for the boys, giving us a sense of normalcy that's been sorely lacking in all our lives lately—or in Gaspar's case, the afterlife.

It almost hurts I have to be the one to break this harmony. I wait for the plates to be cleared and wine be drunk before I face Sébastien. "We need to speak to your mother."

He frowns and cocks his head slightly. "Wasn't that the plan?"

"Obviously, you two need to reconnect, but apart from that, I think it's crucial we find out why she left." The flash of pain on Sébastien's face breaks my heart. He's had such a tough upbringing. "Look, I know it's going to be hard to talk about, but I don't think she simply abandoned you. Your father forced her to leave. I'm sure of it."

"And you want to know why?"

I nod. "She may have some information about him that we can use to…" I hesitate to say it out loud. Standing up to his father is a completely new experience for Sébastien. Even today, he dutifully swallowed the abuse, accepting it as the consequence of his perceived failures. But if he continues to play his cards that way, there are only two options: either he becomes the soulless tool his father wants him to be or he ends up dead.

Obviously, I won't accept either outcome. "…to build a case."

Sébastien swallows and immediately begins to shake his head. "Don't. Leave it be, Alix. Please, I need you to be safe."

"But I won't be. I'll never be safe. Not as long as I'm a ghost whisperer, and I won't give that up. Ever." But this isn't just about me. "And you won't be safe either. Nor will any other ghost whisperer—or whisper ghost," I add pointedly, with a glance at Dix—"for as long as this practice continues."

"This practice keeps us… the people of France safe," he protests meekly.

I scoff. "Last time I checked, you and I were also people of France."

"Yes, but we're individuals. In the grand scheme of things—"

"Communities are made up of individuals," Gaspar interjects. "The rhetoric of the greater good can actually be quite harmful if it ignores the needs of individuals, especially marginalised groups who don't have a voice. Like the ghosts."

There's my sociology student. I take his hand and squeeze it proudly. "What he said. In my opinion, your father is using this rhetoric to keep you in line. He's using your own moral code against you."

"That tracks," Dix says. "It's his favourite bedtime story. I… *we* don't matter. It's an honour to serve France, and we should be proud to be among the chosen. Right?" he asks Sébastien.

Besieged by all three of us, Sébastien scowls. "He never told bedtime stories." He sighs. "I hear what you're saying, but the reality—"

"The reality is your father is an abusive psychopath who shouldn't be in charge of anything, let alone people's literal lives," I snap.

Sébastien stares at me with his mouth agape. My direct words have stunned him so much it takes him a moment to remember how to breathe.

In contrast, Dix seems quite amused. He taps his fingers on the table and looks like he's about to burst. When our eyes lock, he can no longer hold it in. "Finally. Yes. Yes! One hundred per cent yes." Suddenly excited, he scoots over to Sébastien and forces him to look at him. "History Girl is right. He put a bloody gun in your face. He sent his whisper ghost to *murder* her. I don't care about France—it never did anything for the dead—but I do care about you. Us. If you won't help Alix, I will."

"Of course I'll help Alix," says Sébastien, as if it were a foregone conclusion. "I'm just... cautious."

"And I understand that. I'm not saying let's storm GoPol tomorrow." Although there is something to be said for the idea. "All I want to do is talk to your mother, hear what she has to say, and then go from there. And don't worry. I'll be an irrelevant, ditzy little history student for as long as it takes."

"You could never be ditzy or irrelevant," Sébastien says seriously. He bites his lip, then takes a deep breath. "I suppose there's no harm in gathering information. There may not even be a case."

Then we'll look for others, like the Chevalier or the defected GoPol agents in the Résistance, I think. If Sébastien's mother turns out to be a dead end, there's no shortage of others Charles and GoPol have harmed. We'll show him the power of those meaningless individuals.

61

CHAPTER 7

After all the drama with Sébastien, Gaspar, and GoPol, I need a break. Luckily, I get one the following weekend when I'm whisked away to Hélène's hen party. I feel bad that Odile had to organise it all on her own, but she thrives on stuff like that and would've hated any of my suggestions anyway.

Hélène and I had it out last week and I've been re-invited to the wedding. We're on good terms at the moment, even if the ground feels a bit shaky. My sister's important to me, but if she told me she was thinking of calling off her wedding to Cédric, I'd be her number one supporter. I'm still coming to terms with the fact he's going to be my brother-in-law after the way he exploited and betrayed me, but it's an issue between the two of us, and I'm willing to put all that aside for Hélène's happiness.

And she is extraordinarily happy today. At home, Hélène always comes across a bit snooty and stiff, bordering on cold. With her friends, she's a giggling party girl who rarely lets go of the champagne flute. The increasingly drunken behaviour is all a bit much for me, but luckily I've got support in the form of Gaby and Marie.

The hen party starts with a boat ride on the Seine, which I spend as far away from the railing as I can. Despite nearly drowning in the river as a child, I'd never developed an adversity to water. Until now.

Fortunately, we move on to a limousine tour with apparently unlimited champagne, before a drunken stroll down the Champs-Élysées, where Hélène does increasingly embarrassing tasks.

"Remind me not to let Odi anywhere near my hen party," I whisper to Gaby as I watch my sister pose with two American tourists, kissing one on the cheek.

Gaby snorts. "She'll have to fight me for it. And we'll have a museum rally."

"With or without alcohol?" Marie asks, grinning.

"With. We're not savages!" Gaby replies.

"Oh, there's a wine and paint club in my neighbourhood," Marie says excitedly. "Every third Tuesday of the month, I think. We should go."

I love the idea. Not that I can draw, but anything with wine is good. "That sounds fun."

"Did I hear fun?" Odile swoops in and almost scares me to death. "It's almost time for the big finale. You'll love it," she says.

Then she throws her arms up in the air and shouts for half the Champs-Élysées to hear: "We're going to the catacombs!"

"What?" I stare at Odile as the other women burst into drunken cheers.

Gaby immediately takes a step back. "And I'm out."

Marie cocks her head in surprise. "Really? I've always wanted to see them."

"You're welcome to go, but me and confined spaces underground... not a good match."

Marie immediately locks her arm with hers. "If that's the case, I won't abandon you."

"Neither will I," I try to say, earning a tongue click from Odile.

"Uh-uh. You're not going to leave early." She grabs my arm and squeezes it tight. "You're our guide."

My stomach almost turns, though I've hardly drunk anything. "Odi, what are you planning?"

The last thing I want to do is take a bunch of drunk girls into the catacombs to show them the Boutique of Psychosis or Crossroad of the Dead. Why don't we all just jump into the Seine and drown instead?

Odile bursts out laughing. "Your face! Don't worry. I did a little research of my own and found this party that's just perfect for us." She raises her voice. "Ladies! Let's take this party downstairs!"

Hélène stumbles towards us, already tipsy. "What's the meaning of this? We're talking about Alix's catacombs, aren't we? Did you have something to do with it?"

"This is all Odi," I defend myself.

My little sister snorts. "Thanks for the support. Last time I checked, the catacombs belonged to everyone."

"They're illegal," Hélène hisses, leaning forward a little too far.

"Relax, Lilou," one of her school friends says, wrapping an arm around her waist, though it looks more like she's steadying herself. "My brother was there, and he said it was the coolest party ever. Your party's going to be the coolest now. Let's go. You're not a police wife yet."

Hélène would've ripped my head off if I'd suggested such a thing, but to my surprise she just giggles and leans back until they both stumble, and we have to catch them before we take the party to the E.R. instead.

"Sure, let's do it!" Hélène laughs, takes another swig from her champagne flute.

"From now on, I'll only have family dinners with her after she's had a bottle of champagne," I tell Odile, which makes her giggle.

We say goodbye to Gaby and Marie and make our way across the Seine and down a few streets until we reach Odile's contact. I don't know how we manage to get down a manhole without one of Hélène's friends falling down the ladder or alerting the cataflics, but we end up with only one lost heel. In my experience, going into the catacombs drunk is a bad idea. If something happens, there's almost no chance of getting help. And a lot of things have happened to me in the catacombs. Let's just hope tonight isn't an undercover operation or gunfight day.

I can't help myself and take pictures of Hélène crawling through a narrow window in her skimpy dress. These will either be shown at the wedding or kept for blackmail, depending on my mood.

Crawling through the catacombs takes less than half an hour. When we emerge, we find ourselves in a surprisingly comfortable room. It's smaller than the one I had my first rave in and much more chic, almost like a cocktail party, which suits Hélène's style. Once again, I'm amazed at how organised the cataphiles are and how they manage to get everything they need down here, then get rid of it the next day.

There are fancy hors d'oeuvres and interesting, slightly morbid art on the walls. It takes me a moment to realise this is some kind of gallery opening. I have to admit, Odile has done a fabulous job of tailoring this party to Hélène's tastes, while at the same time offering something unique and memorable. She's impressed me.

I tell her as the music's turned up and dancing begins. Odile beams and simply says, "I know." Modesty has never been one of her strong points.

Besides Hélène's large wedding party, there are about thirty others, including the artist, a thirty-something trans woman who's happy to discuss the meaning of her bone sculpture photos. She's combined ordinary skeletons to create unique creatures, just by the way she's arranged their shadows. Her work reminds me of the Chevalier's experiments, but in a purely artistic way.

"These are all part of my 'Hidden Monsters' series," she explains. "A reflection of the darkness in the ordinary, brought to light only through death."

"It's quite spectacular." I marvel at a shadowy phoenix rising from the skeleton of a rat called 'Rotten Beauty'. Who would've thought there'd be such beauty in a sewer rat?

The artist nods. "That's my favourite." She points to another skeletal shadow, photographed through the eyes of a skull. It's called 'Look into the Beyond'. A delicious shiver runs down my spine as I step closer, feeling like a voyeur peering into the mind of someone depraved. It's uncomfortable but fascinating.

This one looks almost like a fearsome dragon—in miniature form. "Wow. What bones did you use for this?" There's so much detail in the monster lurking in the skull.

"A combination of sparrow and fish. It took me five weeks just to build the sculpture from the tiny bones."

I'm in awe but can't help shuddering as I step back. It really does feel a little too close to the Chevalier's experiments. "Marvellous."

"Oh, you'll love the last piece."

The last piece isn't a photograph like the others, but a mirror. I'm expecting just to see myself—to drive home the fact we all carry a hidden monster in us—but it's even better. Somehow, she's treated the surface with kinks and strokes of paint that are almost invisible from a distance, but distort my face when I look inside, making it seem as if there is a *literal* monster inside me, lurking just under my skin.

I'm about to compliment her on the visual representation when I notice something else. Someone's watching me from behind, a mischievous smile on his face, distorted by the mirror into a grimace.

"Gaspar?" I turn to see him standing on the other side of the room.

"Looks like you found your monster," the artist says, laughing, before moving on to someone else.

Her words give me the same uncomfortable yet exhilarating chill as some of her photographs. Gaspar isn't a monster, although I suppose he's now a kind of revenant, which, strictly speaking, falls into the monster category. I shake my head, laughing at my silly line of thought, and make my way over.

"How did you get here?"

"Heard about the party," he says, his lips close to my ear so I can hear him better. "I'm your Angel of Music, remember?" He still hasn't explained how he ended up under the opera.

Not that I care. My body tingles from the deep timbre of his voice and hot breath against my skin. Laughing, I wrap my arms around his neck and pull him close. "Remember our first date?"

He puts his hands on my hips and I sway beneath his touch. "How could I ever forget?"

"I love you." I lean in to kiss him when I'm suddenly pulled back.

"Alix!" Hélène screams in my ear. "What are you doing?"

Odile's joined her and snaps at Gaspar, "She's got a boyfriend."

Gaspar frowns slightly, before snorting. "Yeah, me." He grips my hips tighter and pulls me back into him.

"No," Odile insists. "Sorry, buddy, but it's not you."

"Her boyfriend's a policeman," Hélène slurs.

Oh my god, my sisters think they have to save me from cheating on Sébastien. I turn in Gaspar's grip and lean against him to face my sisters. "It's alright. Sébastien and I... We're not together."

"Did you break up?" Hélène asks, looking as if I just cancelled her wedding. She's still incredibly drunk.

Meanwhile, Odile folds her arms and narrows her eyes. "You were together last week."

Gaspar's fingers tighten around my hips, and I feel his anger coursing through my veins. Even though he and Sébastien seem to get on surprisingly well, he still doesn't like being reminded of our fake relationship and where it led.

I'd better sort this out quickly. "It's not what you think. Sébastien and I... This is Gaspar. *My* Gaspar."

"Gaspar is dead," Hélène points out. "You said he was your ghost boyfriend, but this isn't a ghost, because I can't see ghosts unless I... Did I die?"

"No, Léni, you didn't die." Odile pats her arm reassuringly. "I can see him, too," she says, so viciously I would've stumbled if Gaspar hadn't been there.

"Well…" I won't explain how he's alive again. Hélène may be drunk, but I can't risk it getting back to GoPol, and as for Odile, I'm *not* going to drag her into this again. "There was a mistake. Gaspar's alive. Isn't that wonderful?"

Odile's eyes narrow even more. "How? People aren't dead one day and alive the next."

"They are now," Gaspar snarls.

"That's wrong," Hélène says, though I'm not sure what exactly is bothering her. "This is just wrong. You're with Sébastien and ghosts aren't real. Not really real. Not boyfriend real."

I wince at her drunken attempt to make sense of what she's seeing. "Gaspar is real," I assure her. "And I'm not with Sébastien. I'm with Gaspar."

"Wrong," she repeats, but she staggers away, back to the safety of her friends. I can't help but think she's going for another glass of champagne to wash down the bitter aftertaste of meeting Gaspar.

"Guess I'm not invited to the wedding," Gaspar says, letting go of me so abruptly I almost lose my balance.

"Gaspar!" But before I can follow him, he's already slipped out of the room. Annoyed, I turn to Odile. My little sister's eyes are blazing. "What was that about?"

Odile huffs. "Gaspar *is* dead."

"*Was*," I say quietly.

Although she can't possibly have heard me over the music, Odile's eyes widen. "You were never actually with Sébastien, were you?"

"Odi..."

But she shakes her head angrily. "You're doing it again."

"What do you mean?" I've certainly never fake-dated someone before or hooked up with a resurrected boyfriend.

"Cutting me out." Tears well up in her eyes. "I bet Gaby knows all about it." My guilty conscience must be visible on my face because she snorts. "Of course, she does. Because you trust her and you don't trust me."

"Odi, please. I trust you, but—"

"I don't care!" she shouts in my face.

Her outburst surprises her as much as me. Embarrassed, she wipes the tears from her cheeks. "Whatever. You do you. As always." Then she turns and strides away.

Gaspar is gone, hurt by my past actions, Hélène will freak out properly as soon as she's sober, and Odile's angry at me for patronising her and cutting her out of my ghost drama.

Maybe the mirror was right, and I *am* a monster.

Chapter 8

Hélène was having fun at her party, but she's certainly not the day after. She's been texting me on and off for the last few days. Sometimes it's to tell me how absolutely wrong I am, and sometimes she accuses me of being a liar, although she can't decide whether I lied about Gaspar being dead or about my boyfriend being the same Gaspar. She also thinks I'm going through too many guys, but I've only ever had the one boyfriend.

I rarely answer and let her rant. So far, she still wants me at her wedding—probably for her perfect wedding pictures—and she hasn't told me not to bring Gaspar, either. Apparently, I have Cédric to thank for that, as he tells me at a family dinner that he can't wait to meet my beau. *Fun times.*

Hélène's tantrum is easy to handle. Meanwhile, Odile's completely ignoring me, even going so far as to leave the room when I enter. I find myself spending more and more time out with Gaspar,

Sébastien, and Dix. I haven't slept over yet, but we eat together regularly. We share the cooking, and I'm impressed by what both boys come up with. Gaspar loves rich soul food, which is a revelation, as he never ate as a ghost. Meanwhile, Sébastien's diet is much more balanced and sophisticated. We haven't talked about it, but I suppose nutrition was part of his training. He knows exactly what he needs to consume to maintain that body of his. His only weakness—and the way to his heart—is cheese, which delights me no end.

But it's not all sunshine and roses. Gaspar turns out to be terribly moody. One minute he's the sweetest boyfriend, the next he's cold and sullen. Sébastien's drowning in work, but he refuses to bring any of it home, which drives me crazy. I want to help, but they both shut me out, preferring to swallow their feelings.

By the time March arrives, I'm ready to run in circles. That's why Gaby and I decide to go to Provence a few days early.

On Friday, I inform my ghosts at the Panthéon of my plan. I'll be gone for almost three weeks, and I need them to hold down the fort. So far, no one seems to have tried to find Petite Alix, or if they have, Victor's keeping quiet about it. Meanwhile, Petite Alix has adapted well to her new surroundings. She has absolutely no idea the ghosts around her were once larger than life, and bonds with each of them without fear. I find her marching with the Napoleonic generals, taking great pleasure in their exercises, receiving dancing lessons from Josephine Baker, having great nonsense discussions with Jean-Jacques Rousseau, or helping Marie and Pierre Curie with their experiments. The latter always makes me a little nervous, but all Petite Alix radiates is joy.

After my shift, I close the office and take care of some ghostly favours, such as adding to my list of repairs for the restaurateur. Voltaire and Rousseau are having one of those days where they try to persuade me to petition for a move that would separate their resting places, which I politely ignore. I'm not going to make a fool of myself in front of my boss just because the two ghosts can't go a day without arguing.

Today's quarrel is a rather unusual one. "You shouldn't be any-where near children," fumes Voltaire, "let alone lecture others on the subject of education. Do you think the world has forgotten how you persuaded the mother of your illegitimate children to give them up to an orphanage?"

"What do *you* know about children?" Rousseau bites back. "You never had any."

"That's called being responsible."

Rousseau laughs. "Were you being responsible when you took your niece to bed? Or were you only spared the shame of that union by your infertility?"

Voltaire's head reddens in one of his famous rages. "You have some nerve, Rousseau. Didn't you sleep with your maman?"

"Um, what?" I know a lot more about these men than I care to, but Rousseau sleeping with his mother is new to me.

"I speak of his benefactor, Madame de Warens," Voltaire is eager to enlighten. "She took him in when he was only fifteen, and he speaks of her as if she were his mother, yet he had an affair with her and her steward as soon as he came of age."

"Oh, that." I wave him off at first, familiar with Rousseau's early years in the de Warens household. They weren't related, and Rousseau was too old to form a familial relationship, however much he respected her. I suppose nowadays we'd call it grooming, though it's too long ago to start any kind of investigation, and I'm certainly not going to question Rousseau in detail. But one thing sticks out in my mind. "Wait a minute. You were having an affair with her *and* her steward?"

Rousseau frowns, as if he doesn't understand why I'm asking. "There was nothing shameful about it. We both loved her very much and she loved us."

Right. It didn't last, but Rousseau *did* have a polyamorous relationship. Come to think of it, so did Voltaire. "Was it the same for you and Émilie and her husband?" He and the brilliant—and *married*—mathematician had a sixteen-year long affair.

"My relationship with her was mainly intellectual, but her husband joined us occasionally, yes. Why do you ask?"

Startled, I blink. "Oh, no reason, really. Then you two do have something in common," I say cheerfully.

A big mistake. They narrow their eyes at each other, then turn on their heels and storm off.

I sigh and make my way down to the crypt to join Victor in the writer's alcove. Petite Alix is sitting on Victor's lap as he reads 'The Hunchback of Notre Dame' to her. It's not exactly literature for a three-year-old, but she's been three for almost twenty years. She probably enjoys the act of reading more than the text itself.

When I approach, he looks up and the ghostly book on his lap disappears. "The usual trouble?"

Petite Alix climbs off his lap and jumps into my arms. While she's happy with the ghosts here, she always spends a few minutes with me, as if she needs to recharge. I almost consider taking her with me, but I know it's a bad idea. "Sometimes I think, with how far our world has come, we used to be much more open-minded." When he frowns, I explain, "Like when you had several affairs, and your wife had several affairs, and everyone was fine with it."

"Are you thinking of having an affair?" he asks, amused.

Heat rises in my cheeks, and I shake my head. "Oh, no. I'm just... Everyone here seems to have had at least one affair or lived in a ménage à trois."

"Ah." He looks at me knowingly, keeping a smile on his face. "There's nothing greater in life than love."

"It's also messy as hell."

Victor throws his head back and laughs. "True, very true." His eyes sparkle. "But that's the fun of it."

I sigh, then look at Petite Alix, who has snuggled up against my shoulder. "Hey, little one. I have to go away for a while. Can you promise to stay with Victor and the others until I'm back?"

Despite her nod, Petite Alix holds me even tighter.

Victor asks, "You're leaving Paris?"

"For my sister's wedding. We're going to spend some extra time in Provence to relax. Three weeks to be exact."

"Where in Provence?" The question doesn't come from Victor, but from one of his alcove neighbours. Émile Zola steps out of the wall in his sack coat, a book under his arm, looking a little alarmed.

Surprised, I tell him, "Rognac. Why?"

"May I speak with you in private?"

Victor shrugs and gets up to talk to one of the other ghosts. "In private" apparently includes Petite Alix, who isn't ready to let go just yet. "What is it, Émile?"

"As you know, I'm originally from Provence."

"True. You could come with me." There must be many streets, squares, and even schools named after him in the area.

Émile shakes his head quickly. "Oh no, I shouldn't. I wouldn't want to impose on anyone."

"What's going on?" He definitely sounds like someone who's about to impose himself on *me*. "What can I do for you?"

"This is probably futile, but you have a way with our kind." He struggles to meet my gaze, which tells me that this is something very personal. Something he doesn't usually talk about. "If it's not too much trouble, maybe you could take a trip to Aix. It's close and you have cars now."

"Just tell me what you want," I say, gently but firmly.

Émile deflates. "I want you to go see Paul and tell him I'm sorry."

"Paul?" Before he can clarify, my tour knowledge kicks in. "Oh, Paul Cézanne. Your friend." He's a famous painter and childhood friend of Zola's.

"Former friend," Émile corrects. "Just... he can be quite difficult. You see, he doesn't really like other people or society in general. A real hermit, that one." There's a hint of annoyance in the tone, as if he'd tried to change Paul's ways more than once. "Anyway, I've wronged him. I'm sorry. Tell him that. Please."

"Are you sure you don't want to do it yourself?" It should be easy for someone of Émile Zola's reputation to travel to the city of his youth, even if he spent most of his life in Paris.

Émile shakes his head. "It's better that I don't. Perhaps... perhaps in a few years."

"It's been over a hundred," I say, but he's already withdrawn again.

I quickly go through what I know of their friendship. They met at school, both outsiders, and formed a close bond that deeply inspired their creativity. In fact, they and a third, whose name I can't remember right now, were called Les Trois Insèparables. But they grew up. Zola went to Paris and found success as a writer, while Cézanne stayed in Provence, where he built his reputation as a painter. No longer inseparable. It's a tale as old as time.

As far as ghostly favours go, this is an easy one. I don't see how a visit to Aix-en-Provence could be a problem, and I can't wait to make Paul Cézanne's acquaintance. He was the bridge between late Impressionism and early Cubism, an inspiration to none other than Pablo Picasso, another Provençal.

Suddenly I'm even more excited about this trip. We're not only going to see the sea and enjoy the beauty of the south coast, but we're also going to meet all these interesting ghosts who left their mark on Provence. I can't wait to show Sébastien what ghost whispering should be all about.

Chapter 9

The next morning, Gaspar and I are picked up by Gaby and Marie. I don't know how Gaby managed to talk her brother out of his car for three weeks, but I love her for it. We manage to squeeze all our luggage into the back and lift Malou's travel cage onto the back seat between Gaspar and me. Sébastien will make his own way to Provence on his motorbike, with Dix following wherever he goes.

We have a lot of fun singing loudly to the music on Gaby's special playlist and telling stories about our youth. That is, Gaby, Marie, and I chat all day, while Gaspar becomes increasingly quiet. I guess a car full of girls is a bit intimidating.

Marie tries to draw him back into the conversation when we're talking about exes. "You've had a boyfriend before, Gaspar, haven't you?"

That's certainly news to me. I look at Gaspar expectantly.

He crosses his arms and rolls his eyes. "I made out with a guy. He wasn't a boyfriend."

"Was it Gustave?" I ask.

Gaspar looks at me in bewilderment. "No, we were just friends." He sighs. "It was another cataphile. We went to a few raves, smoked some weed, and made out. It wasn't serious."

"I wouldn't mind if it was serious," I assure him.

"You want me to go back to him?" he asks aggressively, making me inhale sharply.

I catch Gaby's concerned gaze in the mirror and know it's better for all of us if I change the subject. Ignoring Gaspar, I lean forward and rest my arms on Gaby's seat. "I've taken on another ghostly favour. Don't worry, it's nothing serious."

Gaby snorts. "The last time you accepted a ghost favour, you almost got killed. And before that, the ghost tried to kill you. And—"

"This one's different," I interrupt quickly, before my track record sounds worse than it is. It's true that Charles Garnier, Jacques de Molay, and Emily were terrible choices, but since then, I've done dozens of smaller favours for the ghosts of the Panthéon. "This one's for Émile Zola."

"What does he want? To dictate you a new book?" Gaby asks hopefully. "You could become a celebrated writer, Zola's heiress or something like that. You're already Victor's."

I laugh out loud. "Their styles are completely different. I don't think I could pull that off. But no, he wants me to apologise for him, to none other than Paul Cézanne. We're going to the House of Winds tomorrow."

"Ooh, I love it when you talk museums."

Marie snorts, then quickly covers her mouth. "You guys are so weird. Is that really the first thing we're going to do in Provence? Find all the museums?"

"Not all of them. Just this one... to start with." I grin. There's no better way to get to know a region than by visiting the local museums. "And as much as I'm interested in Cézanne's old studio, this is about Zola's favour."

"What did he do?" Gaspar asks, still sounding a bit annoyed.

Since Émile asked, I've done my research. "Oh, this is quite juicy. You may not know this, but Zola and Cézanne were best friends. They grew up together in Provence, both dreaming of becoming artists. When Zola moved to Paris, he wrote long letters and spent the summer months back here.

"And then he found fame. He always tried to take Cézanne with him, introduce him to the scene and get him to stay in Paris, but Cézanne never cared for the city and ran back to Provence. They remained friends until Zola wrote L'Œuvre, his 'Masterpiece'." That's literally the name of the novel, talk about projection. "And this is where it gets juicy: the book is pretty autobiographical. The main character is a struggling artist who's best friends with a successful writer. And it ends with the artist committing *freaking suicide*. He hangs himself."

Gaby gasps accordingly. "Please don't tell me he based this character on his actual best friend, the struggling artist."

"He sure did." The third friend of the Inseparables also got a part, but as in life, it was a much smaller one. "Obviously, Cézanne took it badly. He immediately broke off all contact and never spoke to Zola again. Apparently, he still doesn't."

"Who would?" Gaspar asks, fascinated despite his dour mood. "His friend basically told him to kill himself."

"I wouldn't go that far. I'm sure that's where Zola deviated from reality and made it about the plot rather than his friend, but yeah, it still looks bad." No wonder he wants me to apologise.

Gaspar shakes his head. "Jerk."

"Why doesn't he apologise himself?" Marie asks. "If I were Cézanne, I wouldn't accept anything less."

"It's probably because ghosts are limited in their ability to travel," Gaby explains. "They have to be remembered in one place, right? I mean, that was the case with Josephine Baker."

"That's pretty much it, yes, but Zola shouldn't have any trouble travelling to Aix. He's well remembered there."

"So, he's a coward," Gaspar says, with such finality that it's almost encouraging.

I shrug, not ready to relent yet. "Maybe. Or maybe he's bound by what he experienced in life. He died before they could make up, and when Cézanne heard about it, he basically went into a depression. Even when they were feuding, they still meant the world to each other. Anyway, a ghostly existence is difficult. So many are stuck in the state they were in when they died. They wear the same clothes, have the same ideas—"

"If I could fall in love with you without ever having met you, Émile Zola can get off his high horse and grovel," Gaspar snaps.

"Aren't you a joy to be around?" Gaby mutters, causing Gaspar to growl.

Marie puts a hand on her leg as I sink back into my seat. I look out the window to hide the fact my eyes are burning. Ever since I met Gaspar, I wanted him to meet Gaby. She was so excited to meet him, too. Now that they finally have, they can't stand each other. Or at least Gaby thinks he's the worst person ever, while Gaspar makes no effort to win her over.

Hopefully this trip will help them overcome their problems.

As the landscape changes, my heart begins to ease. We pass barren fields of lavender, stretching to the horizon. We're three months too early to see them in their glorious purple, but just knowing they're there makes me smile again. The usual trees are replaced by olive groves, vast vineyards, and rows of pines. When I first see the sparkling blue of the Mediterranean peeking out from behind the hills, my heart's filled with hope.

This will be good for all of us, a place to come together and heal.

Chapter 10

After the drive down here, I dread our room arrangement, which has me with Gaspar. I was looking forward to some time alone with him, but given his recent mood swings, I'm not sure I can handle having him around me all the time.

As soon as I've stowed my luggage, I make up some excuse and step out of the small but quaint hotel near L'étang de Berre. The large body of water draws me closer, as if I didn't have enough traumatic wet experiences in my life. But there's something soothing about the waves lapping against the shore and the glistening surface.

While L'étang de Berre looks like a lake, it's actually a lagoon, connected to the Mediterranean Sea by a channel between the land masses. It's mostly salt water, but unlike the ocean, it's sheltered. In the summer, the place is overrun with bathing tourists and sailing boats. Now, only a few of the latter dot the surface.

A fresh breeze is blowing, and I hug myself for warmth as I stare at the horizon. I really hope this will be the kind of break we need, instead of fuel for more drama and heartbreak. A tear runs down my cheek, and I let it roll, gritting my teeth at the sharp bite of cold as the wind blows across it.

Just then, I hear footsteps behind me and then a shy, "Alix?"

Hastily, I wipe the tears from my cheeks and throw a quick glance over my shoulder. Gaspar stands there, hands tucked into his hoodie, looking utterly miserable. "Sorry," he says.

I don't want to forgive him so easily, but man, my heart goes out to him. It takes all my pride to give him only the slightest nod before I turn away again, new tears burning in my eyes.

He comes closer, his presence looming behind my shoulder, even though I can't see him. "I don't know why this is so hard for me. I'm happy," he says, "truly, I am. But... maybe it was too much. I don't think I'm handling this living thing very well."

"Don't say that!" I can't bear to hear him talk like that. Instead, I spin around and wrap my arms around him, burying my wet, cold face in his shoulder.

Gaspar stumbles slightly, but he extricates his hands and puts them around me. His cheek rests on my hair, and he seems to absorb the feel of me. "I'm sorry. It's just... There's this whole world, and it's so full of light and people and... and I don't belong to it."

I pull my face away to look at him. "You *do* belong. You're alive now."

"Not really. I mean, my body is, but as a person, I'm still dead. Why do you think I was living under the opera house?"

It's a good question and I narrow my eyes. "Why were you?"

He shrugs. "Honestly, I don't really know. I mean, the whole opera thing was weird. Maybe because I like music. But mostly, I lived there because nobody cares who you are in the catacombs. Being upstairs was too hard, too complicated. So, instead, I hid in my happy place. One where it's easy to exist. As a ghost, a human, or something in between."

Sad as it sounds, it makes sense. But there's still something I don't understand. "Why didn't you reach out?" I remember the invitation and the eerie music. "Like, properly."

Gaspar pulls a face. "I was going through a lot. The adjustment, the unanticipated difficulties. It's not like I didn't toy with the idea of simply turning up, but what if your family had been home? And I think I realised that even though I'm alive now, being together is just as complicated as it was before. Your family already struggles to accept you can talk to ghosts, much less love a ghost. And now you want to introduce them to your resurrected boyfriend?"

"Yes!" I say, with a certainty that scares even me. "Yes, Gaspar, I want to introduce you to them. I don't care what they think or whether Hélène throws another tantrum. Thing is, I thought I'd lost you before and it just about killed me. So, no, I'm not letting anything come between us again."

A smile begins to form on his face. It's that sweet, sweet smile I first fell in love with. When it finally breaks out in full, he leans in to kiss my forehead. "I love you so much, Alix."

I snuggle up against him again. "I love you, too."

Maybe this is a whole lot more complicated than I'd thought it'd be. Gaspar is suffering from some sort of PTSD and will need time to adjust, but we'll get through this. Together. I won't let anyone or anything come between me and my hedgehog boy.

CHAPTER 11

The next day I set off with Gaby and Marie for Aix-en-Provence at the foot of Sainte-Victoire, a distinctive limestone massif that inspired many of Cézanne's paintings. I can immediately see why he struggled so much to leave. Aix is a beautiful town with fountains on every other corner, olive trees, and the kind of provincial houses that make you feel like you've stepped back in time.

We start our visit at the Bastide du Jas de Bouffan, Cézanne's home for over forty years. His father, a wealthy banker, had bought it and Cézanne inherited it when he died, making him quite rich and funding his bohemian lifestyle. It's a beautiful two-storey villa with yellow walls and long windows at the end of a triangular alley. There is another fountain just outside the entrance.

Unfortunately, the house is closed for renovation. If we return in a year's time, there'll be a brand-new, immersive Cézanne experience, but the only thing that would make it truly immersive for me would be to meet his ghost. I toy with the idea of ignoring the closed signs and seeing if I can get in anyway, but it's the middle of the day and I don't really feel a strong presence. There are construction workers on site and Cézanne was a recluse. With such a reputation, I doubt he'd be hanging around where all this noise would disturb his peace, so we decide to go to the atelier instead.

The atelier is on the other side of town, closer to the mountain and the nature Cézanne craved so much. It was here he spent the last four years of his life, creating until his death.

My first impression of the house is how colourful it is. It has the same yellow walls but paired with bright red wooden shutters. It's similar in style to the old family home, but the colours pop, with even more trees around the house. There's a pond in the garden and another fountain. The air is full of birdsong and a fresh breeze is blowing, adding to the atmosphere. It's not hard to see why Cézanne chose to paint as much as he could in the garden. It's exactly where we find him.

I recognise him by his dark, voluminous hair and wild beard—and, of course, the easel.

"Monsieur Cézanne?"

His shoulders hunch, but that's about the only reaction I get from him. At first, I assume he hasn't heard me, but when I repeat the greeting, it becomes clear he's simply ignoring me.

I'm not so rude as to block his view of the garden. Nevertheless, I approach him. "You know I can see you?"

Cézanne grumbles. His dark, beady-eyed gaze falls on me. "I'm dead. I no longer receive visitors."

For all I know, he wasn't exactly welcoming to visitors in life either. "I'm really sorry to disturb your rest—"

"Good." He stands, picks up his easel, and enters the house through a narrow door in the wall—without opening it first.

I stare at the house, too stunned by his abrupt refusal.

"What's going on?" Gaby asks as she joins me.

"Um, he's not in the mood to talk…" I shake my head and approach the house to knock on the door. "Monsieur Cézanne, my name is Alix. I've just arrived from Paris."

"Terrible city," Cézanne shouts.

While I'd read, he wasn't much of a people person, I'd never expected him to be quite so rude. "I don't want to disturb you—"

"Then don't!"

"I have a message. From an old friend." A silence follows, which I take as a sign of slight interest. "You see, I work at the Panthéon with your old friend Émile. He—" The silence is a little too oppressive, no longer a good sign. "Monsieur Cézanne? Are you still there?"

I look through the windows into a room frozen in time, just like its former inhabitant. There's a long ladder for drying paper, brushes and paints, old coats and hats, and small arrangements I recognise from Cézanne's still life paintings. The only thing I don't see is the artist himself.

Perplexed, I step back. "He's gone."

Gaby snorts, but quickly covers her mouth. "Sorry. Is he ghosting you?" The amusement is still more than evident in her voice.

I roll my eyes. "Something like that."

"Can't you summon him back?" Marie asks, as she also steps up to the house.

"Maybe. But it's probably considered pretty rude. Besides, he's made it more than clear he doesn't want to talk to me."

Gaby shrugs. "Either that or he's not interested in hearing Zola's excuses."

I sigh. "That's probably it. I shouldn't be the one making excuses, anyway. Do you think I can convince Zola to come to Aix?"

"You're the one who's friends with him. I just live vicariously through you." Gaby grins. Then she hooks her arm into Marie's. "Shall we see if we can go in?"

Unfortunately, the atelier is also part of the renovation plan and just as closed to visitors. It's a shame, because just a glimpse of the room makes me itch to take a closer look at this blueprint from the early 1900s. No wonder Cézanne hangs out here, where everything is exactly as he left it.

We can't visit though, and there's little point in driving to the Carrières de Bibémus, an area of limestone caves on Sainte-Victoire where Cézanne built a hut to get even more in touch with nature. It's about an hour from here and I doubt he'd appreciate me turning up there. *If* he's even retired there. I'll just have to try another time or go with plan B and summon Zola to his hometown to deliver his own apology.

We decide to shelve the plan for now and spend the day wandering around Aix instead. It really is the city of a thousand fountains, each more picturesque than the last. It's delightful, just modern enough not to have fallen behind the times, but still retains the charm of a bygone century.

Eventually, we make it to the Cours Mirabeau in search of a café. This central street is three times as wide as a normal street and perfect for a stroll on a sunny day. There's a restaurant I'd read was frequented by both Zola and Cézanne, but unfortunately it's burnt down. The loss of history—it was the oldest café in Aix—is painful, especially as it happened so recently. There's no mourning ghost to be found near the blackened ruins.

Closed museums, burnt-out cafes. We're really out of luck today. But Gaby finds something for us to look at.

"Are those penises?" She looks up at the wrought-iron balconies. It's true, one of the balconies has a charming phallic pattern, surprisingly subtle for its subject.

Marie starts to giggle and I join in while Gaby takes pictures. "For art, you know."

I doubt Cézanne would appreciate the motif, but he's decided to keep to himself, so he doesn't get a say in how the other inhabitants of Aix express themselves.

Having had our fill of laughter, we find a modern café and brave the cold wind to bask in the early spring sunshine, while enjoying a coffee and a slice of cake.

"So," Gaby says, interrupting my sunbathing, "I take it Gaspar didn't want to join us today?"

"He wasn't interested."

Gaby raises an eyebrow. "He's not interested in spending time with you anymore?"

"What? No, he's just not into art or museums." I'd asked him this morning and he'd decided to stay with Malou. Not that she's good company during the day. Unlike me.

Annoyed, I push the thought out of my mind and force a smile on my face. My best friend shares a look with Marie that makes the coffee I just drank taste even more bitter than usual. "What's going on?"

They both turn to me. Marie bites her lip. "Don't you also think he's acting a bit strange?"

Judging by Gaby's huffing and puffing, strange doesn't even begin to cover what she thinks of him. "Strange how?"

"Well, he used to be with you every step of the way, following you around like a faithful puppy, and now..."

"Now he's alive." I tell myself I'm glad he's not with me all the time. We need boundaries. "Of course he followed me as a ghost. I was the only one who could see him."

"And who does he see now?" Gaby asks, surprisingly confrontational.

The words cut me to the quick. "No one..."

"Exactly!" Gaby shakes her head in annoyance. "Alix, I'm sure it's traumatic to die and then come back to life within four months, but according to Gaspar, he came back for you. And yet, he seems to have lost all interest. Besides, he's incredibly rude."

"That's not true!" Okay, the last part is kind of true lately, but that doesn't mean he doesn't love me. "Can we please not do this? He loves me and I love him. And yes, what he's been through was traumatic, but you're not exactly giving him a chance."

Gaby's mouth falls open. She takes a moment, then shakes her head as if she can't believe what I've just said. "I... No, I'm not gonna say it."

"Say what?"

Marie strokes her hand, wisely staying out of our argument.

Gaby and I don't fight often, and I'd hate to see that change. I just want her to get along with Gaspar. Or at least give him a chance to prove her wrong. "Tell me."

She looks so completely conflicted, but then she takes a deep breath and blurts out, "You sound like your sister."

For a moment, I'm too stunned to say anything intelligible. This isn't like Hélène and Cédric. Comparing Gaspar to *Officer* Cédric is an insult to his beautiful soul. He's just having a hard time. If only...

"Oh god, I'm sorry!" Gaby cries. Then she flies around the table and gives me a big hug. "You're nothing like Hélène. And Gaspar is a much better person. You're right, I haven't given him a real chance. I just... After all you've been through, having your heart torn out and mangled... Are you happy?"

She looks me in the eye, demanding the truth. As I return the hug, unable to keep up our fight any longer than she can, I can only shrug. "I will be. We just need some time to adjust."

Gaby smiles warmly. "Of course." She lets go but keeps smiling. "Let's go back to the hotel so you two can have some time alone before the sun goes down."

As incredibly thoughtful as that is, the moment she mentions time alone with Gaspar, an irrational feeling of dread settles in.

Chapter 12

When we get back to the hotel, I immediately notice Sébastien's motorbike in front of the hotel. Dix is prowling around it, stroking the silver paint, and running his hands over the handlebars. Remembering he always wanted a motorbike but never got one before he died, I go over to him.

"Figured out how to ride it yet?"

Dix startles, then grins and swings a leg over. "I'm not an idiot."

"Well, not wearing a helmet would make you one... if you still had a head to crack open."

"Low blow, History Girl," Dix says, but he's grinning wildly. A mischievous gleam enters his eyes, and a moment later, the engine howls and stutters. "Not bad, eh?"

I chuckle. "Spooky." For everyone else, the bike just roared to life on its own. But that's as far as his powers go. Dix can coax sounds out, but he can't actually drive it.

The noise is enough to call Sébastien to the window above the bike, though. "What are you—Alix." The initial annoyance quickly fades and is replaced by an open smile. "Gaspar told me you were out all day."

It's good to see his face, even though I only said goodbye to him two days ago. "Well, I'm back."

"Any luck with Cézanne? Did you fix a ghost friendship on your first day here?" he teases.

"Unfortunately, no. He took off the moment I mentioned Zola."

"Ouch." Sébastien makes a face and shrugs. "Hey, do you want to..." he hesitates, and a shadow passes over his face. "I thought my mother would be home by now."

I'm a little surprised that he's ready to see her, having just travelled south today. Maybe it has to be like a Band-Aid, ripped off as soon as possible. "Sure. Let me just check on Gaspar and freshen up a bit. See you in thirty?"

The smile comes back. "See you then." As I walk towards the entrance, I hear him scolding Dix. "Get off my bike. You don't have a licence."

"Relax! I'm not riding it!"

Their exchange brings a grin to my face. You wouldn't know it from their bickering, but Sébastien missed Dix a lot when he went rogue. It's good to see them together again.

I find Gaspar in our room, sleeping on his bed. Maybe he really is a hedgehog boy, not made for the day.

I cautiously crawl onto the bed on all fours and lean down to kiss his sleep-tousled hair and then his cheek. There's the softest little intake of breath, followed by a purr, as he turns and wraps an arm around my back, pulling me onto his chest. "You're back," he says sleepily.

I kiss him and for the next few minutes we do nothing else. I still can't get over how alive he feels. Gaby was wrong. Gaspar hasn't lost interest in me. If anything, he's even *more* interested. One of his hands is buried deep in my hair, while the other has moved from my back to my ass, then back up under my blouse. I shiver as his fingers dance up my spine.

In the back of my mind, I hold onto the fact I'm supposed to meet Sébastien in a little while.

"How was your day?" I whisper in his ear, not wanting to take this much further at the moment.

"It got better as soon as you walked in."

Giggling, I kiss him again. "Sébastien's waiting for me downstairs. But I can text him," I add quickly when I see him frown, "if you want to do something instead." I'm a little worried Sébastien might go alone. Sure, he's a big boy and all, but I have a feeling he'd appreciate another living soul.

"What are you doing with Sébastien?" Gaspar asks, not letting me off the hook so easily. His hand remains on my back, but his fingers are no longer dancing.

"You know what. He wants to go see his maman."

Gaspar's arms fall away, and he sighs.

Bereft of his touch, I lift my head. "You can come, too." We'd have to borrow Gaby's car, but that shouldn't be a problem.

"No, thanks." He snorts and folds his arm under his head, making it clear he won't be touching me again any time soon.

"Why not?"

"Because it's weird. Does he really want to show up at his mother's door with a whole group?"

I have to admit it would look a bit odd. "Are you sure, though?"

"Just go."

"I can also *not* go," I don't want Gaspar to feel like I'm putting Sébastien's needs before his, "if you'd rather go for a walk with me. Maybe watch the sun set over the bay or..."

Gaspar sighs. "Of course I want to, but I'm fine. You go with Séb. He needs you more than I do."

Even though I know what he means, his words hurt. As if Gaspar doesn't need me anymore now that he's no longer invisible to the rest of the world.

Slowly I push myself to my feet. "Okay. If you insist." I give him a quick peck before disappearing into the bathroom to use the toilet and freshen up.

As the water runs from the tap, I grab the sink and stare at myself, shakily taking breath after breath, trying not to cry. *Don't be ridiculous*, I tell myself. *Gaspar loves you. He's being his usual understanding, selfless, emphatic self. He knows all about Sébastien's story and how much it means to him. It has nothing to do with me, and it certainly doesn't mean he's lost interest in me.*

When I'm convinced no tears will fall, I wash my face and quickly run a brush through my hair until my long waves fall smoothly on my shoulders. Satisfied with what I see in the mirror, I leave the room.

Gaspar is still on his bed, but instead of watching me, his back is turned. Deliberately assuming he's asleep because I can't face the alternative, I grab my bag and head back downstairs.

"There she is," Dix calls. "Only five minutes late. That's got to be a record."

"Stop it." Sébastien elbows him in my defence, which immediately eases my heart. I can't stay sad for long with these two idiots around.

"Shall we?"

Sébastien's mother lives in a beautiful villa on the outskirts of Marseille, near the coast. Unlike Cézanne's 19th-century house, this one is modern, with lots of glass and angular corners. The roof gleams with photovoltaic panels. The sun is about to set, turning the house red. Margot Villeneuf is either extremely well paid or she took Charles Roubert to the bank for forcing her to leave her son behind.

The latter makes me smile grimly. I don't know her and yet I already feel a kinship between us.

I get off the bike, take off my helmet, and wait for Sébastien to do the same. But he sits frozen on his bike, looking anxiously up at the house. Where I see a woman's revenge, he appears to see a mother who's sold her child.

"Hey," I say quietly, stroking his arm. "Let's meet her."

He looks at me as if fighting the urge to leave instead.

Before he can say anything, Dix appears from inside the house and announces, "She's home. Just put coffee on." He notices Sébastien's condition and sighs. "Oh, come on. It's Maman. She'll be so happy to see us... *you*." Dix swallows. "Please."

He needs us. Without us, Dix can't introduce himself to her. I could offer to speak to her on his behalf, but I want Sébastien to meet her, too. I take his hand and massage it a little. "I'll be with you every step of the way. And if it's terrible, we'll just leave."

Sébastien takes a deep breath and nods. Then he squeezes my fingers as he gets off the bike and takes off his helmet. There's a question in his eyes as he looks at our hands.

"I don't mind," I say quietly. If I have to hold his hand through this, I'm happy to do so.

Together we walk down the driveway and ring the doorbell. Someone shouts that they're coming and we hear footsteps behind the door. Sébastien's grip tightens, and he swallows hard as the door opens.

Margot Villeneuf is a beautiful woman with a stylish shoulder-length bob of ash-coloured hair. She's wearing an expensive-looking jumpsuit with a deep-cut triangle between her breasts, looking effortlessly sensual. The similarities between her and Sébastien are more subtle. He got most of his looks from Charles, but the shape of his chin and curve of his lips are just like hers.

"Salut?" she asks, friendly but confused. "Do you need anything?"

Sébastien's jaw is so tight I'm not sure he can speak at all. Unlike Dix, who nudges him and hisses, "Say hello to Maman."

"Ma...man." The syllables come out of his mouth like crystallised honey, barely viscous and brittle. I don't think Margot even heard him.

Time for me to fulfil my support duties. "Salut, Madame, I'm Alix Dubois and this is Sébastien. *Your* Sébastien."

Her eyes widen and a hand flies to her mouth. I hear a short gasp, then her gaze sweeps up and down Sébastien's body, having already forgotten all about me.

While Sébastien stiffens even more, Margot recovers quickly. "Oh my... Come in. Please, come in." Her gaze finds me again and she smiles. "You, too."

"And me," says Dix, but no one acknowledges him.

Margot leads us into her spacious living room, where we are greeted by a view even more breathtaking than I'd imagined. The entire back wall is glass, leading onto a terrace. Ahead of us, the Mediterranean glistens in the setting sun. Steep cliffs jut into the sea, covered in wild olive and pine trees. If there's a beach, it's far below us, down some mountain paths. The view is a rugged beauty I could never tire of.

"Pretty great, huh?" Margot says, not without pride. "Sit down, I'll open a bottle of champagne."

She leads us to a white leather sofa that's almost too beautiful to sit on. The room is so wide and open I can easily imagine elegant dinner parties, served from the modern open-plan kitchen.

Sébastien is still so tense that I rub his arm and whisper, "Relax. She's happy to see you."

Someone else is certainly happy to see her. Dix has followed Margot into the kitchen and is talking to her non-stop. "How do you like Sébastien? He's a bit of a bore, so if he doesn't say much, just ignore him. Alix is cool, though. She'll make sure he behaves."

"Dix," I say, earning a wild look from Sébastien. I suppose he doesn't want to lead this visit with his trauma.

Fortunately, Dix relaxes and comes over to lean against the sofa behind us, his head poking out between Sébastien and me. "Do you think you'll talk to Maman eventually?"

The needling works and Sébastien relaxes, though he looks a little annoyed now. Not a good start.

Margot returns with three glasses of champagne. "I can't tell you how long I've waited for this day, Sébastien. You look good."

"You waited?" he asks, his voice torn between surprise and accusation.

"Of course. I was hoping you'd come see me one day."

"That would've been easier if I'd known where you were."

I put a hand on his knee to slow the train of accusations. Not that I blame him. "We only found out recently and happened to be in the area for my sister's wedding. I hope we're not imposing too much by surprising you like this."

Margot smiles at me. "Not at all. I'm glad you stopped by." She looks at her son. "*Really*. So, are you two a couple? Married?"

"She's a friend," Sébastien says, flustered, while I blush. "Alix is a friend, a good friend."

His mother laughs. "I see. Well, I'm pleased to make your acquaintance, Alix. It's nice of you to bring Sébastien to your sister's wedding and to encourage him to come here."

Now I'm nervous, too, and quickly remove my hand from his knee. "Sébastien isn't my date or anything like that. He... My sister is getting married to his cousin. Oh, your nephew, Cédric. She's becoming a Villeneuf."

"I heard he was getting married. In Rognac, right?"

"You know?" Sébastien asks, sounding like he has a stuffy nose.

"My sister keeps me up to date with family stuff. She even invited me, but I told her—"

Sébastien stands. "You've kept up with the family?"

Margot's smile fades and she looks at him with regret. "I had to. It was the only way to find out about you."

"You knew where I was all the time? Aunt Éveline could talk to you all the time?"

"Darling, your father and I had an agreement. It included a 'no contact' clause."

"Sit down and listen to her," Dix hisses. "You know who she was up against."

"Yes, and she was paid handsomely," Sébastien mutters, forgetting his own preference to keep Dix's presence a secret.

Margot notices immediately. "You're a ghost whisperer," she states, not without sadness. "When did he do it?"

She knows. I inhale sharply when I realise she knows immediately what Charles has done. That it would be too much of a coincidence if Sébastien also happened to have a near-death experience.

Sébastien falls back onto the sofa and sighs. "When I was seventeen."

"Didn't even wait until you were an adult." She snorts and shakes her head. "Typical."

Dix nudges Sébastien, but he's still too stunned to react. Once again, I step in. "His whisper ghost is here, too. We call him Dix and he's very excited to meet you."

Surprised, Margot's eyes land on me. "You can see ghosts, too? Is that how you two met? Through GoPol?"

"No, Alix is... an independent agent."

That's one way of putting it. "I've been a ghost whisperer all my life. I always thought I was the only one, the strange girl who was friends with the dead."

"You're friends with ghosts?"

I nod. "Yes. I work at the Panthéon. I know it sounds crazy, but I'm really good friends with Victor Hugo and some of the others. Émile Zola sent me here to try and get in touch with Cézanne so they can mend fences, but Cézanne doesn't seem keen. I'll have to try again some other day."

It's not that I'm babbling out of control. I'm just trying to lighten the atmosphere, to allow us to move onto safer ground than the deep trauma Sébastien suffered when his mother left him. There'll be time for that later.

"Fascinating! And you're not with GoPol?" Margot laughs, slightly puzzled. "I would've thought they'd pick you up right away."

So, she knows about that, too. "I... Well, I was lucky. Sébastien here fought for me to stay independent."

"And your father agreed?" she asks, looking back at him.

Sébastien shrugs. "Not at first."

Or at second, at third...

Margot shakes her head in disbelief. "That's incredible. You're a rarity, Alix."

Despite my earlier intentions, I can't help asking, "Is that why you left? My track record with Monsieur Roubert isn't great. He... Why did you leave?" It's not my question to ask, but Sébastien and Dix both stare at their mother, eager to hear the answer.

She sighs heavily and smiles sadly before turning to Sébastien. "Your father and I had our different opinions about... pretty much everything. I didn't want to leave you with him for... obvious reasons, but he wouldn't give you up. I told myself he loved you too much. You were his pride and joy. But I couldn't stay. It would've killed me to stay. I had to sign a lot of declarations when I left."

It seems Sébastien isn't the only one with trauma from that time.

Margot leans forward, her smile widening. "And that's why I'm so glad you came to see me on your own. Hey, do you want to come to my lab later this week? Both of you! Officially, I do marine biology research—and I do—but unofficially, I work on ghost research."

I gasp in surprise. "Really?"

She nods eagerly. "I can show you the lab. There are some surprises there, especially for... Was it Dix?"

He perks up immediately. "Me?"

"I've been working on a device to communicate with ghosts. It all started with a Ouija board and other tools that have been used by mediums for centuries. It's not quite like talking face to face, but you'd be surprised how versatile it is."

"Yes, yes, yes," says Dix, eager to get started.

I'm just as excited. Not because I need a device to talk to ghosts, but to learn more about this ghost research. I thought the only interface between my world of ghosts and the government was GoPol. Margot managed to get away from Charles. What if I could, too? What if I could do ghost research?

Sébastien is the only one who doesn't share our excitement, but he doesn't protest. "Sure. We can do that."

"Wonderful. Let me check my calendar." Margot takes out her mobile phone and looks at the schedule. "Ah, I can move that. How about Thursday morning? We could have lunch in downtown Marseille afterwards. I'll text you the address." She looks up, her gaze meeting Sébastien's. "Could I have your number?"

Reluctantly, he obliges. "Of course."

Margot smiles. "Now we can keep in touch."

Despite himself, the corners of Sébastien's mouth twitch. She's finally broken through the thick wall he's built around himself. "I'd like that," he admits.

"Let's make it happen, then. Come on, let's have a drink and you can tell me everything. You, too, Alix. I want to hear all about your friendship with Victor Hugo."

Sébastien takes his glass and settles a little deeper into the couch, more relaxed now.

Dix grins from ear to ear, adding his own commentary to everything we say. Some I—or Sébastien—translate. Others we just comment on with an eye roll. The alcohol loosens our tongues, and at some point, Margot invites us into her kitchen to cook dinner. If she had other plans for the evening, she never mentions them, paying as much attention to Sébastien as is humanly possible.

When we leave the house at half past nine, I couldn't be happier. There's still a world of trauma to overcome, but this has been a balm for Sébastien's soul. I'm glad we made the trip and reached out. We didn't get around to our plan to take down GoPol, but by the sounds of it, there'll be plenty of time for that later.

I jump as I see a lone figure standing at the end of the driveway, looking straight at me. In the light of the streetlamps, I see a man with a beard almost long enough to reach his navel and an old-fashioned black cap. He's wearing what looks like a robe, but it's too dark to see any details.

Sébastien puts a shoulder in front of me, ready to protect me. "Can I help you?" he asks firmly.

The stranger ignores Sébastien, his gaze still fixed on me, as if he knows all about me. "Alix Dubois. We meet at last."

A shiver runs down my spine as I hear my name on his lips.

"Your reputation precedes you." He gives me a sly smile. "Then again, the future always does. It's an honour to finally meet the one who'll raise the dead and bring chaos and destruction to the world."

CHAPTER 13

When my family arrives three days later, I still don't know anything about the ghost who gave me that chilling prophecy. He never introduced himself and vanished as soon as he'd said his piece. Sébastien told me not to pay any attention to him, but he doesn't believe in things like predicting the future, unlike Marie, who offers to read my hand or question her cards. After the confusing advice with my double love life last time, I politely decline and stick to Gaby's plan, which includes a day on the lake—she deems it necessary exposure therapy—and another of sightseeing and wine tasting. The boys join us, even Gaspar, and we have a surprising amount of fun. It's the perfect distraction.

But now my sister, a.k.a. Bridezilla, is here, and has dragged Odile and me to a sister spa day in Salon-de-Provence. She must've booked it before everything happened, because she's not exactly happy to see me and just snorts as I get into the car.

Neither is Odile, who's stuck in the back seat and won't even look at me.

Fortunately, the scenery in Provence is so beautiful it distracts me from my sisters' ire. That is until Hélène can't hold it in any longer. A few kilometres from Salon, she asks, "Have you enjoyed your stay so far?"

My first thought is how I've been told I'm going to bring chaos and destruction to the world—and somehow raise the dead. Then I think of the one dead person I definitely *didn't* raise, and who's the reason for this new quarrel with Hélène and Odile, plus the unspoken real subject of her question. My answer has nothing to do with either. "Yes, we hired a small boat yesterday and spent the day on the lake. Beautiful weather, much warmer than Paris. The day before we hired bikes and did a wine tasting tour, which I highly recommend."

And before that, we visited the mother who abandoned Sébastien to be murdered by his father, and met a ghost who prophesied nothing but darkness for me. All normal activities in Provence.

"How nice," says Hélène, in a voice that's far from nice, and Odile snorts.

I decide to turn the question to her. "Do you have any plans apart from the wedding?" We're here for two weeks, after all.

"Well, this spa, for example."

"Right." And with that, the conversation dies again.

We soon arrive in Salon-de-Provence, another picturesque town with beige buildings, shingle roofs, green trees, and fountains. We pass a pretty sand-coloured Gothic church with a bell tower in the middle of the nave. Long, narrow windows look down onto the street, and a few tourists are taking pictures in front of it. A man in a long robe with an impressive beard is standing on the steps.

My head whips around and the "Stop!" is out of my mouth before I think better of it.

The tyres screech as Hélène jumps. "What?"

The ghost I saw in Marseille is watching me from the steps of the church. In daylight, he's clearly from another time, perhaps one of the oldest ghosts I've ever seen. Late medieval, I'd say. He looks straight at me through the car window and makes an inviting gesture towards the church. His resting place.

"What church is this?"

Hélène groans. "Don't even start. You can't see ghosts, anyway."

"Yes, you *can't*," Odile says, so pointedly I'm almost convinced she's discovered my secret.

"But it's pretty," I say, in a voice I hope will convince her of my historical interest.

"We have an appointment," Hélène snaps and drives off.

When I look in the side mirror, the ghost is gone.

"Collégiale Saint-Laurent," Odile says, reading from her mobile. "It's the burial place of Nostradamus."

I don't dare meet her gaze for fear of giving myself away. "Cool."

Yeah, isn't that cool? *The* Nostradamus—astrologer, apothecary, physician, and famous seer—has prophesied I'll practically end the world. I mean, that's kind of his thing.

Nostradamus made a lot of prophecies about the end of the world, things like frogs falling from the sky and battles in the clouds. Experts aren't too convinced about the legitimacy of his prophecies because he simply made so many. If you search long enough, you can find evidence in his 'Les Prophéties' for every major catastrophe that's ever befallen us, even things like 9/11, when he lived during a time when the English had barely set foot on the American continent. It's ridiculous conjecture, not true fact.

And yet he knew my name. And where to find me.

The spa isn't far away. Hélène marches in, puts on her friendly, professional face, and signs us in. We're given plush robes and slippers before being led into a relaxation room. The lights are dimmed and soft music is playing. Someone offers us infused water and leaves us alone.

Under normal circumstances, I would've enjoyed this, maybe even relaxed, but my mind is racing, and no amount of infused water and relaxation music is going to change that. I don't want a spa. I want to go and visit the church, meet Nostradamus, and find out what he wants.

It doesn't help that Odile is watching me every time I check. When we go into the sauna, she asks Hélène, "Do you want to go straight home afterwards or do we have time to see the town?"

Hélène looks at her as if she's gone mad. "Can we please enjoy our spa day first?"

"It was just a question," says Odile, immediately offended. Then she glares at me, as if it's my fault she stuck her neck out.

I decide to smooth things over and ask Hélène, "Are you excited?"

The change in her is instantaneous. She immediately relaxes and smiles. "Of course."

"Nervous?" I say, trying to match her energy.

Hélène laughs. "A bit, but that's normal, right? I mean, I wouldn't know. I've never been married before."

Yeah, she's definitely nervous.

I put my hand on hers. "It'll be fine."

She sighs in relief. "I know. That's why I need this day. Not only will our skin look the best, I'm really looking forward to the massages."

We talk a little more about the wedding, which means not thinking about *who* she's marrying. I'm trying to be a good sister today and keep the focus on Hélène and Hélène alone. Odile is a little less enthusiastic, but she doesn't bring up the church again.

The massage is wonderful. There's a lot of tension in my muscles, not that I'm surprised, but it doesn't stop me from thinking. While the music lulls my sisters to sleep, my head spins over what Nostradamus said.

How am I supposed to *raise the dead*? More importantly, *why* would I do such a thing? The Chevalier would love for me to join him, but I can't see myself fiddling with bones and bringing to life what should be dead. As much as I appreciate having Gaspar back, the general idea still terrifies me as much as it does Hélène. I tell myself it's okay because he's only been dead a few months. Imagine the chaos that would ensue if I brought all the greats back to life. I don't think society is prepared for that.

In comes the chaos and destruction.

I sigh. Right now, I can't see myself ever willingly participating in anything that would lead to such an outcome, but lately I haven't always been able to do things willingly. If someone's going to force my hand, I need to know more. How can I prevent this?

"You look more tense now than you did before the treatments," Odile comments as we're ushered back into the relaxation room to enjoy a light meal, while Hélène receives a special bride-to-be package.

"It was nice." My body feels good. It's my head that's killing me.

Odile snorts. She looks at the big clock. "We have an hour and a half before Hélène comes back. We're supposed to have a peel, but I suddenly don't feel like it."

"What are you talking about?"

"The church is about twelve minutes away by foot..." Odile regards me with a challenging look. "Do you want to go visit Nostradamus or not?"

I gasp, surprised at my little sister's sound reasoning and ready plan of action. Twelve minutes there and back... that'll give us an hour in the church. "Let's go."

I don't like the grin on Odile's face, but I'm not going to turn down this golden opportunity. Together, we rush back to reception, tell them we're going for a walk, and change into our clothes. Following Odile's instructions, we race through the city until we're back at the Collégiale Saint-Laurent.

As we catch our breath, Odile asks, "Truth or dare?"

"What?"

"Pick."

Truth is clearly what she wants, so despite the dangers, I say, "Dare."

Odile laughs quietly. "Fine. I dare you to tell me to my face that you've lost your ability to talk to ghosts."

I want to keep my little sister safe from GoPol and all the other dangers I've encountered lately, so that should be easy. Except it's not at all. The moment our eyes meet, I feel the words slip from my head.

"I knew it!" Her eyes blaze. "We'll talk about it *later*. First, you've got a date with the prophet." And with that, she marches off, leading the way into the church.

Sighing, I follow.

Churches are a historian's dream. Especially big ones like this. They're often some of the oldest buildings in a town, full of local history and records of every person who was born, married, or died in the area—and in this case, famous graves.

The arcade is beautiful. Long arches rest on columns that merge at the top, creating the characteristic pointed shape of Gothic architecture. The interior is made of limestone, probably quarried locally, and light floods in from the tall, narrow windows, making the whole church bright and airy. On the sides are statues of the usual suspects, and at the front rises the altar.

The tomb of Nostradamus is off to the side, before the actual interior. It's a fairly simple arrangement: a picture of the seer, an old inscription, and two signs with information. It's not even clear exactly where the bones are laid to rest.

There aren't many visitors in the church at this time of day.

Someone is sitting far away from us in the front, and a couple of tourists are slowly making their way around, examining each statue and painting in detail.

And then there's the man himself. Nostradamus.

I still can't believe he's real. And I'm used to ghosts.

"Is he here?" Odile asks.

When I nod, she takes a deep breath.

"I'm going to pretend I don't know you when you start talking to yourself."

So kind.

My heart flutters as I approach the old man. Our last meeting happened so quickly, it could've been a dream, but he's here now. And apparently, he's been expecting me.

"I charted your arrival a little earlier, but I blame the modern calendars for making me inaccurate," he says. "Very well, Alix Dubois. What do you want to know?"

Not "what can I do for you" or "hey, sorry for spooking you the other night." Apparently, I was supposed to come here with an agenda, not as a result of a spur of the moment decision. "What you said three days ago..."

"Ah, yes. You're going to raise the dead and bring chaos and destruction to the world."

"Yes, about that. I don't intend to do anything like that, so..."

"The future cares little for your intentions. It simply will be."

Whee. Talk about a tough pill to swallow. "So, you're saying there's no way I can stop this?"

"Why would you want to stop it?" Nostradamus frowns.

"Chaos, destruction, the dead rising..." My summary makes Odile raise her eyebrows. "That doesn't really sound like something I would do."

"Haven't you already raised one?"

He's talking about Gaspar. "Technically, I didn't. I didn't even know he was planning to."

"And yet, he's yours." Nostradamus smiles. "And I believe you've caused a lot of chaos and a bit of destruction for the authorities."

"You mean GoPol?"

He nods. "As I said, my dear, your reputation precedes you."

"How?"

"The stars told me. They see everything."

I was expecting some kind of ghost whisper net to relay messages. Nostradamus' answer sounds a lot wackier. The stars don't know shit. They're just burning balls of gas. If that's where he gets his information, I'm safe. On the other hand, he knew about Gaspar and everything else, so maybe the stars are more knowledgeable than I thought.

I'm deeply conflicted and realise I simply don't *want* him to be right. Logic is my only defence, but it's crumbling under the evidence. "I don't want this."

This time he doesn't even bother to reply. The message is clear. The future doesn't care what I want. All he says is, "You are a catalyst for change, Alix Dubois. Even though change is not always a bad thing, it always involves the destruction of something old. What matters is not the chaos you create, but what you build out of it."

That sounds marginally better. At least it means whatever I'm meant to do, it's not necessarily the end of the world. This makes it one of the more positive of Nostradamus' prophecies. Unfortunately, it's not the only prophecy he has for me today.

"You're here for a wedding, aren't you?"

"Not in this church, but yes."

Nostradamus sighs heavily. "Then consider yourself warned. They'll be wed, but not everyone who came here will survive the night."

CHAPTER 14

"Alix!"

Odile runs after me and grabs my arm. A car whizzes past, so close I feel the wind in my face. My pulse is so loud in my ears it drowns out most of the world. I have no idea how I got here. My breath catches in my throat, my head still swimming.

"What happened in there?" Odile shouts, increasingly worried. "Sorry for the terrible pun, but you look like you've seen a ghost."

The pun is horrible enough to snap me out of my panic. "I did."

"Yes, I know. What did he say?"

"He..." I can't tell Odile. It's bad enough I'm scared shitless. I don't want to freak her out, too. Heck, she could be the one who dies. Maybe now she wants to become a ghost whisperer like me and does something stupid. Or Charles decides to kill her to teach me a lesson or... "Nothing. He said nothing."

Odile gasps in disbelief. "Do you honestly expect me to believe that? You ran out of the church and almost got run over because Nostradamus said nothing to you?"

Please, brain, give me an excuse, a lie, something to cover up what I can't say.

My brain refuses to cooperate, but someone else steps in. "You shouldn't talk to that old crook," a grumpy voice says. I look up and see a familiar face across the square. For some reason, Paul Cézanne is here, no canvas in sight. His hands are crossed behind his back and he looks up at the church with disdain. "Nothing he says is positive. It's all doom and gloom."

"What... what are you doing here?"

Odile groans. "Oh god, what is it now?"

I cross the square as Cézanne continues, more open with his information than three days ago. "But that's life, isn't it? It's all crap and then you die. Alone. Unloved." He snorts and turns away.

"Wait!" I run after him, and this time I put all my intention into making him stay.

Cézanne sighs, his shoulders slump, but he remains in place. "Please, I just want to be left alone."

He's definitely not a dead man who'll ever agree to rise. "Zola. He wants to talk to you."

"I have nothing to say to Émile."

"I don't believe that's true." When he frowns, I explain, "I read about your friendship. You were as close as brothers. I know what he did was wrong, but he wants to apologise." Technically, he asked *me* to apologise, but that'll never fly with Cézanne.

Sure enough, the painter snorts. "Émile never apologises. Not for his art. That's always unapologetically him. His novel revealed what he really thought of me."

"He was an idiot." This is probably the only time I'll ever call the great Émile Zola an idiot, but I still don't know what possessed him to do that to his dearest friend. "But it's been so long. He... he misses you."

Cézanne's lips curl slightly. Probably because I called his estranged friend an idiot to his face. "What do I have to do to get you to leave me alone?"

It may sound grumpy, but I get the feeling it's the only way he knows how to express himself. He misses his friend, too. "Can we meet? All three of us." That does *not* include my sister. "Maybe in a neutral place that means something to both of you. The College Bourbon, perhaps."

At the name of his old school, Cézanne perks up a little. It definitely means a lot to him. "They've renamed the place."

"What's it called now?"

"I don't know. I didn't keep up with people when I was alive, I'm certainly not interested in keeping up with them now I'm dead."

And yet, Cézanne knew the school had been renamed. Either it's a ghost thing, like a part of you getting lost when old memories are replaced, or he cares a lot more than he wants me to know.

"Well, I'll find out and meet you there tomorrow."

"Seven sharp."

That's a bit early for my holiday taste, especially considering I have to get myself to Aix first, but if that's what it takes to get those two boneheads talking to each other, I'm happy to sacrifice my sleep. "See you then."

Cézanne barely nods before disappearing.

I take my first real breath since storming out of the church, only to have Odile yank my arm and glare at me. "You want to explain what's going on? And don't you dare lie to me again."

"Odi..." I feel like a terrible sister and yet... "I'm just trying to protect you."

"Of what?" she asks, marginally more gently.

"All my mess. GoPol." It sounds so pathetic now.

Odile crosses her arms. "You don't get to decide what's good for me. I may be the youngest, but I'm not a child anymore. I was there for you!"

And she's right. "Things... things got out of control."

"Did you ever lose your ability?" When I shake my head, tears spring to her eyes and her lower lip quivers. "You lied. About the spirits, about Sébastien, and now about Gaspar. You lied just now when I asked you what Nostradamus said." Her voice cracks and she angrily wipes away a tear. "You don't trust me. Not *at all*!"

"I'm scared!"

Odile's eyes widen. "You... you're scared?"

Now I'm the one who blinks fast. "GoPol arrested my whisper ghost. They tried to eliminate her. They arrested me, too. And then Charles set his whisper ghost on me to kill me. And I know he's willing to do whatever it takes to protect his agency. He's more than happy to hurt me, he hurts... Charles is the reason Sébastien is a ghost whisperer." If that doesn't get the point across, I don't know what will.

Sure enough, Odile pales. "Are you saying what I think you are?"

I nod, finding some strength in the gesture. "He killed him and then brought him back to life. Sébastien thinks he consented to it, but it's all fucked up. He's *so* fucked up, and I'm on my way to fucked up." If I'm not already far beyond the point of return.

Odile throws her arms around me and hugs me. "I didn't know!"

"I didn't want you to," I remind her, eagerly returning the hug. "I'm afraid he'll go after my family. He hates me so much."

"Because you stole his little soldier son?"

"Soldier son?" I ask, perplexed.

"Isn't that what he did to Sébastien? He turned him into this perfect GoPol agent, trained him up, brainwashed him, and then decided which age his whisper ghost should be?" She tilts her head back to look at me. "And then you came along and took him away from all that."

I grimace. "I wish. He's still a GoPol agent and he's still reluctant to take a stand."

But he *has* taken a stand. Not only did he eliminate C-Trente, but he took the brunt of his father's wrath to negotiate a truce of sorts for me. He may not have completely turned his back on GoPol, but he's all mine.

Odile studies my face and seems to come to her own conclusion. "So, what's the deal with the two of you... and Gaspar?"

With a sigh, I tell her about the ruse we'd played to protect me from GoPol's prosecution. When I get to Gaspar's surprising resurrection, Odile gasps.

"He's really alive?"

I nod, unable to stop smiling. "Yes. He's back from the dead. I... I thought he was gone for good, but he's here, alive and well."

Odile smiles warmly. "That's wonderful. I'm happy for you."

Finally, someone is! "I'm sorry I kept you in the dark."

She hugs me again. "Honestly, I get it. But I'm glad you told me. You shouldn't have to go through this alone, Alix. I mean, I know you're not alone, you've got Gaspar, Sébastien, and Gaby... but I'm here, too. I'm your sister, after all."

"So is Hélène and she's—"

"Hélène!" Odile's eyes widen.

I immediately panic, too. A quick glance at my phone shows me we've been gone for two hours already. "Oh, she's going to be so mad."

"So, so mad!" Odile agrees.

One more look and we're both running, Nostradamus' shocking prophecy all but forgotten in the turmoil.

Chapter 15

Hélène almost refused to take us home she was so angry. Odile and I apologised profusely and offered to pay for the spa, but we still got the silent treatment. I don't really care because I got Odile back, but I feel guilty, nonetheless. Making it up to Hélène is just one of many things on my to-do list. The first is to reconcile Cézanne and Zola.

I wake up at half past five the next morning. Last night I'd asked Gaby for her car keys so I could be in Aix in half an hour. I try not to wake Gaspar, only to find he's already up. He's sitting next to his bed with Malou on his arm, stroking the little hedgehog as she begins to tire.

"Morning," he whispers. His smile is everything.

"Morning. When did you get up?"

"I don't sleep well," he admits. "Not since... you know."

Deciding I can spare a few minutes, I sit next to him. "Do you have nightmares?"

"I don't dream."

It sounds so weighty. "Never?"

Gaspar shakes his head. "And I sleep an hour or two at most."

"That's not enough." Maybe that's why I caught him napping during the day earlier this week.

He shrugs. "I know. It's not normal."

I quickly wrap my arm around his shoulders and hug him tight. "Normal is overrated." That elicits a chuckle from him. "We'll find out what's going on. Together." I kiss his cheek.

Gaspar turns and catches my lips in a real kiss. With a hand on my cheek, he says, "Whatever it is, it's a sacrifice I'm happy to make to be with you."

"I know. But maybe we can find a way to improve your condition, because it sure isn't fine." I nudge his nose and smile at him. "Hey, I'm going to Aix to meet with Paul Cézanne and Émile Zola to try and talk some sense into them and get them to reconcile. Do you want to come?" My heart almost overflows when he nods. I laugh and kiss him. "Alright, I'll get ready while you put Malou to bed." I quickly run my fingers over her spikes, entrusting her to Gaspar. Then I get up, pick out my clothes, and disappear into the bathroom.

Half an hour later, we're in the car on our way to Aix. On the way, I tell Gaspar about my previous meetings with Cézanne and his reluctance to meet with Zola.

"I get it," he says. "If it were me, he'd be so dead to me, too," he says as we roll into Aix.

I follow the navigation system to their old school—its new name is College Mignon. "It was a shitty move for sure, but they were so close before. I mean, they led different lives that seemed irreconcilable, but I firmly believe Cézanne still has a lot of love for Zola."

"It's possible to love someone and still feel betrayed by them."

I swallow. Is he talking about us? Cautiously, I look at him. His face seems neutral enough, so I dare ask, "Is that how you feel about what Sébastien and I did?"

Gaspar sighs heavily. "Honestly, I don't know what to think. I like Sébastien. He's actually not that bad and I know he cares about you. He protected you when I wasn't around. I was never able to protect you."

"You're here now. And you *did* protect me. Remember when you took a sword for me?"

"True," he says, with a little snort. "But it's not the same."

"It was more than enough. And you can protect me from now on. Not that I want to be in mortal danger again." If anything, I seem to be bringing the danger this time.

He smiles again, as sweet as I remember. "Yeah, let's hope it doesn't come to that. We could use a break. You know, time to sort things out. To just be... us."

I return his smile. "I'd like that."

As soon as we're done here, I'll take him out on a date, just the two of us. But for now, we've arrived at the old college.

Most of it has been replaced by more modern buildings, but there are a few old elements that have been allowed to remain. I'm standing next to an old brick wall, trying to invoke the spirit of Zola. There's a little time left to inform and convince my friend of the change of plan.

Fortunately, the presence of his old school is enough to summon him. Not that I recognise him at first, because the ghost that appears is so much younger: a blond teenage boy, a bit small for his age. He scowls at the school before turning to me. One look and he's rapidly ageing, leaving behind the awkwardness of his youth to become the confident artist and political activist of his later years.

Flustered, he straightens his jacket. "Pretend you didn't see that."

"Why? It's nice to see—" His almost frightened expression makes me reconsider my words. "You have bad memories of this place."

"The worst... and the best." Zola sighs, then nods at Gaspar. "I see you've found your friend again. He seems much more solid than last time. Almost—"

"Yes, he came back." I haven't told my Panthéon ghosts about Gaspar's resurrection yet. Part of me is afraid they'll judge me harshly, the other is afraid they'll start asking for their own resurrection. "Um, so, about Paul..."

The distraction works. Zola's shoulders slump and his eyes are full of misery. "He refused to accept my apology, didn't he?"

"He refused to hear it from me," I admit, "and he's right. I firmly believe he needs to hear it from you."

"Alix..."

"How would you feel if your best friend sent someone else to make amends? Would you respect that?"

Zola becomes even more deflated. "Of course not. It's just... he doesn't want to see me. He never comes to Paris, and when I'm in Aix, he's nowhere to be found. He's made it very clear he hasn't forgiven me and won't. That's why I sent you. He doesn't know you. I thought you could do your thing and slip in my apology before he realised we knew each other."

"Well, I've *done* my thing, and he'll meet with you. Here. In about five minutes."

Zola's eyes widen in panic, and for a moment it looks like he's going to bolt. "Five minutes? I'm not prepared for this. I don't know what to say to him or... Alix, what should I do?"

I take a step towards him and put my hands on his shoulders. "Relax. You've been preparing for this for over a hundred years.

Let your heart speak." I point to the school. "Be inspired by this! The good old days."

He snorts. "You mean the times when I was bullied and beaten up just because my father had died and we were dirt-poor? Those days?"

You'd think the greats were worshipped all their lives, but Zola reminds me his didn't exactly start out rosy and peachy. His family moved from Paris to Aix when he was very young so his father, an Italian engineer, could build a dam, but he died when Zola was seven, leaving the family with a meagre pension. Zola clawed his way up in the world, and a big part of how he survived his early years was Cézanne. "You had friends here."

Zola's face softens. His gaze turns inward, and I notice him becoming younger again. "I did. The best of friends. If it wasn't for Paul and Baptistin, I wouldn't have made it out of this place alive. The food was shit and the classmates were deplorable, but we were... glorious."

I can't help smiling. If I hadn't already known from my research, it would be clear now how much he loves the days when he was part of Les Trois Inséparables.

"School couldn't keep us down. We spent every hour in the countryside, taking long walks, bathing in the river, fooling around. We had dreams. Such big dreams, of words, of art, of a better world. The landscape was poetry, and we were blessed to exist in it. If I could... If there was the afterlife we'd all thought there was, I'd imagine it would be here. Just days of sunshine, long fields, rugged mountains, and poetry. Just me and... Paul." He looks past me as his voice takes on a strained tone.

I look and see Cézanne has joined us. Seven sharp. "Émile," he says, with such venom I'm not surprised to see Zola shrink. "Have you managed to leave your opulent residence in Paris to visit the province?"

Zola, his usual dignified self instead of the dreamy boy, sighs. "You know how I love Provence and Aix." There seems to be a third thing he loves, but it remains unspoken.

Cézanne snorts. "If you did, you wouldn't be hiding in that monstrous, cold city that chokes the life and heart out of everything."

"If you gave it a proper chance, you'd find Paris invigorating, thought-provoking, and wonderfully diverse. It's always evolving, whereas here... everything is stuck in the past."

"This is going well," Gaspar mutters, and I'm tempted to massage my temples.

Sure enough, Cézanne's face darkens. "Oh, I know you think I'm an incurable curmudgeon, too set in my ways. You want me to change, but I happen to like who I am."

"Do you?" Zola scoffs. "I thought you always hated everything and everyone, starting with yourself."

As Cézanne's nostrils flare, I decide to intervene. "Hold it!" I point at Zola. "You wanted to apologise, not aggravate the situation." Then I turn to Cézanne. "And you wanted to hear him out."

Cézanne crosses his arms and looks down his nose. "Come on, then. Let's hear it."

Zola wrestles with himself. There are probably a lot of choice words running through his head, but I managed to pull him back from the brink. "Fine. I'm sorry about how things turned out. The book had to be added to the cycle because it wouldn't have been a true representation without *our* experience. I thought you'd be proud. That's why I sent you a copy. You were always the first to read anything I wrote. And it's a masterpiece, well received, moving..."

"It's moving because you made me kill myself in it!" Cézanne spits.

"I took a few creative liberties. Claude isn't you—or Manet, for that matter. He's a character first and foremost, and as such, he transports a thought, an idea, a story."

That's not enough. I know it, and Zola knows it, but ghosts are notoriously set in their ways, and he really thought he was doing his friend a great honour when he sat down to write this book of his popular Rougon-Macquart cycle.

Cézanne shakes his head. "The idea that his creation is pointless, that he doesn't have what it takes to succeed, that there's no other way for him to exist without the recognition he craves. He's a despicable character. A loser, as they say nowadays, a failure."

"He is noble in his pursuit of art," Zola counters. "Claude Lantier is a paragon, uncompromising and steadfast. Though it grieves him to hear others think less of him, though he suffers the pain of rejection, he sticks to his vision. He's strong in a way only we true artists can understand. When our art becomes more important than life. When it transcends life. That is to be admired."

I'm beginning to feel we're not really talking about the character anymore.

"Does he pay the ultimate price? Yes, he does. But it's for art. I thought you of all people would understand that. That's all we ever talked about."

Cézanne's nostrils flare, as if he were absorbing each despicable word to feel it burning on his skin. There is so much hatred in his eyes, so much pain. "If that's what you think, why did the *painter* fail, while the writer, who is nothing but a thinly disguised, pitiful self-portrait, succeeds?" He snorts. "You talk about the pain of rejection, yet you never had to feel it."

From the pained look on Zola's face, he's definitely feeling it now.

"You thought you were better than me. You were the chameleon, the one who adapted, who fit in, while I remained rigid and true to myself. And so I paid the price." He shakes his head in disgust. "Look at yourself, Émile. Look how far you've come from that snotty boy with ill-fitting clothes and a black eye. You're resting in the Panthéon in your beloved Paris. You have everything you ever wanted. Now go home and leave me alone."

As soon as he's said his piece, Cézanne turns and shuffles away, his hands deep in his pockets. Zola's eyes are filled with desperate grief. A young Zola would've run after his friend, apologising profusely and promising sweet nothings, but the older man knows the damage he's done in the spirit of art.

"I'm sorry, it didn't work out the way you wanted."

Cézanne might claim the honour of the Panthéon is all Zola ever dreamed of, but the stricken look on his face says otherwise. There is one thing he values much more than his art, even if he only realised after he'd made the wrong choice.

Zola closes his eyes, lost in thought. When he opens them again, bitterness tugs at the corners of his mouth. "I never should've written that damn book."

CHAPTER 16

After the failed reconciliation between Cézanne and Zola, Gaspar and I drive back to the hotel and pick up the others to go to Marseille. Gaby and Marie want to do some sightseeing, while we're meeting up with Sébastien to visit his mother's lab.

As we drive down to the coast, I can't stop thinking about the two ghosts. I did what Zola asked. We tried and we failed. Maybe it's time to move on, but I'm not ready to give up yet. While they were hurling all those hurtful accusations at each other, it felt like they still cared deeply for each other. Maybe I'm reading too much between the lines, but there is love there. It's just buried under a century of guilt, pain, and shame.

I want to do more for them. Zola clearly can't be trusted to plead his case, and Cézanne is too stubborn to take the first step. What we need is a mediator. A buffer. And, fortunately, I know just who that might be. They were Les *Trois* Inséparables, after all.

But that will have to wait for another day, because the rest of the day belongs to Sébastien.

After saying goodbye to Gaby and Marie, Gaspar and I meet Dix and Sébastien in front of the university's Biology school. It's right next to the Mediterranean, which looks like a light blue carpet covered in millions of diamond splinters in the sun. I love the centuries-old buildings of the Sorbonne, but there's something to be said for studying with a view like this.

Margot's lab is in an adjacent building with the same modern, sleek angles as her home. Everything in here is probably state of the art. Not that I would know. I enjoyed science, depending on the topics, and got through school reasonably well, but I'd never set foot in a lab until I had to break into GoPol's.

"How was your meeting with Zola and Cézanne?" Sébastien asks as we greet each other. "Did you manage to reconcile them?" He didn't used to care about ghosts, but things have changed since I introduced him to my way of whispering. Now he soaks it all up, though he's happier to watch me do it than inspired to make his own connections.

"Don't ask."

Gaspar grins. "They met, they fought, and then Cézanne stormed off and Zola moped. It was... demystifying."

"Demystifying?" I ask, confused.

He shrugs. "When we read Zola in school or talked about Cézanne's paintings in art history, they always seemed so dignified in an inhuman way. I mean, you hear about their major life events and how that might have influenced their work, but rarely in the context of them being real people who loved and fought, did stupid things, and hurt the people they loved."

"Oh, I know what you mean." I feel the same way, having spent the last two years dealing with the Panthéon ghosts. Don't get me wrong. I'm still in awe of what they achieved, but they seem so much more real to me now. No longer just names in a history book. "Anyway. I'm not ready to give up on them just yet. I just need to come up with a new plan of attack."

"Speaking of a plan of attack..." For a moment I'm alarmed, but then I see Sébastien swallowing. "Should I text her we're here?"

It's kind of sweet to see him so nervous when he's usually so confident and professional. I give his arm a quick rub and smile at him. "Of course. Don't you want to see her in her element?"

"Please don't embarrass me by being a no-show," Dix says, less helpfully.

But it does help. Sébastien gives him an annoyed look and sends a quick text to his mother's newly acquired number. Moments later, there is the *click-clack* of heels on long corridors. The door slides open to reveal Margot in another effortlessly sexy outfit. I hope Charles is kicking himself for driving this woman away.

She waves us in with a big smile. "Come in, come in." Then she notices Gaspar. "Someone else today?"

"This is my boyfriend, Gaspar. He and Sébastien are currently living together."

The usual kisses are exchanged, and we follow Margot down the corridor as she explains the layout of her lab. "This is where we study ocean floor samples. Tons of organisms in there. And there is our salt-water lab." Through the doors, a few people are working on their experiments. There's also a number of offices and archives. "But, of course, the real action is behind these doors."

Margot holds her access card against a reader and pushes open a double-sided door. There's nothing on the door about ghosts, but I can make out a warning sign: 'Restricted Access. Classified Research' and a contact number for Margot.

My pulse quickens and I'm thrown back to the Chevalier's secret lab in the catacombs. I wasn't prepared for that, and I don't think I'm prepared for what's behind these doors either.

Fortunately, my fears are completely unfounded. At first look, the lab appears surprisingly normal. Instead of a collection of bones or reanimated animals in boxes, there's an array of complicated machines and computers. In the centre stands a long work table covered with smaller gadgets and research papers. Next to it is a vertical glass box that looks a bit like a sleeping pod for a futuristic space mission. I wonder what it's for.

Margot walks into the middle of the room and spreads her arms. "And here we are. My little realm." She grins awkwardly at Sébastien, gauging his reaction.

The normally confident GoPol agent seems uncomfortable and unimpressed.

His mother's smile falters, and she glances over her shoulder, where a blue light's flashing next to a running computer. "Oh, looks like we've got ghosts in our presence." The cheerful tone belies her disappointment. "I suppose that must be Dix, then."

Dix is a lot more excited about being in his mother's lab. He's been strolling past the machines and now quickly joins Margot. "This is me?"

Margot looks past him as she points to a wiggly line on the screen that reminds me of brain activity monitors or maybe a seismometer. "This is a spectrometer. I use it to measure spectral activity or, in other words, the presence of ghosts." She picks up two long needles connected to a small console that reminds me of a modern divining rod. "With this, I can usually pinpoint the location of the ghost." She laughs when she realises how close Dix is standing to her. "Well, hello there."

The blissful smile on Dix's face makes it all worthwhile. "Hi, Maman."

I nudge Sébastien with my elbow, urging him to join her. "Go on. Have a look."

If I'm reading the situation correctly, this is awkward for both of them. I'm not quite sure what Sébastien expected from his mother, and I doubt he would have appreciated her suddenly fawning over him. Instead, Margot's love language is inviting him into her world.

He makes his way over and asks in a voice that sounds like he's dragging a cart out of the mud: "How does it work?

Margot beams at him. "These are basically like a theremin." She laughs awkwardly when she realises none of us know what a theremin is. "It's a musical instrument made up of two needles that create an electromagnetic field between them, which allows you to play the instrument without actually touching it. Look it up online if you don't believe me. Now, mine is a bit modified, but it works on the same principle. I create an electromagnetic field large enough to cover most of the lab. Whenever there's a ghost on the premises, this field is disturbed and creates a pulse. Like how the hand of a theremist coming close to the theremin elicits a sound." She hands the needles to a stunned Sébastien. "Try it. Take one in each hand and wait a moment." She picks up the small console and wraps it around Sébastien's wrist, allowing him to move around. "Now, Dix, if you could please hide somewhere around the lab."

The ghost obeys immediately, eager to interact with his mother. When Sébastien's gaze automatically follow his steps, Margot puts a hand on his cheek and draws him back to the needles. "Don't use your eyes. Pretend you're like me." She laughs and points to the device. "Now hold them close, like this. Perfect. Try to keep them parallel as you move. You should feel the vibrations as you get closer to Dix."

Sébastien tries his best to follow his mother's instructions, though his hands look awkwardly cramped around the needles in his effort to keep them still. He turns slowly, not daring take his eyes off them.

Dix has found a place in the corner to the right of the door. I try not to look at him, lest I give away his position, as I watch Sébastien try to find his way around the room by the vibrations in his hands alone. I almost clap when he turns in our direction. His angle is a little off, but maybe that's because he's still quite far away from Dix.

Slowly, he comes closer. Gaspar and I step aside to let him pass, but instead of walking through us, Sébastien jerks the needles to the left, almost stabbing my boyfriend in the chest. He stops.

"Well, this is awkward," Gaspar says, slightly amused.

Sébastien's cheeks flush as he lifts his eyes from the needles. "They're vibrating."

Gaspar carefully wraps his hands around the needles, stilling them. "True."

I hold my breath. Not only is their exchange surprisingly intimate, but I immediately think of Gaspar's not-so-distant days as a ghost. What does it mean that the spectrometer has picked him up? He's alive now, isn't he?

"Oh my, is there a malfunction?" Margot approaches and Gaspar drops the needles as if he's been burnt. She takes them from

Sébastien, leaving the console strapped to his arm. "Let me have a look."

It takes her only a few moments to come to the frightening conclusion that there's no malfunction. Curiously, she looks at Gaspar. "Now, this is a bit awkward. But according to the spectrometer, you're half ghost." She laughs nervously, then notices the stony faces of the people around her.

Hastily, I take a step forward. "That's impossible, isn't it? You can't be half ghost. That's like being half dead." My voice falters at the end as the implications truly hit me. Gaspar has been revived. He's alive now. So why is he appearing as a half ghost?

"Oh, it's not nearly as clear-cut, my dear," Margot tells me. She leaves the needles with Sébastien, who quietly undoes the console on his arm to put them aside, while she walks over to a whiteboard. "You see, spectral energy isn't just two dots." She writes 'humans' and 'ghosts' with a blue marker on each side of the board. "It's a whole spectrum."

She draws a line between the two words and points to the left. "Humans have very little spectral energy. It's not zero, as you might think, but it's very negligible."

"Why is it not zero?" Sébastien asks, and I'm proud of him for engaging.

"I suppose because we're still bound to our mortality. We will die, after all." Margot points to the other side. "Now, ghosts are the other way around. They're almost all spectral energy. Again, almost, because so many of them are loosely connected to life. Here's where it gets interesting." She marks a spot about twenty-five per cent in. "This is where ghost whisperers like you two sit. Your brush with death has left you with enough spectral energy to see ghosts. In a way, you're part ghost yourself. The same goes for whisper ghosts." They go in at the seventy-five per cent mark.

"Guess, we're no longer finding me?" Dix says as he joins Sébastien, his disappointment tugging at my heartstrings.

"Now, as for your boyfriend..." Margot's eyes light up with excitement. She points the pen at Gaspar before taking it to the board and circling fifty per cent. "Smack down the middle."

I look at Gaspar to gauge his mood. My heart's racing like crazy, but his face is unreadable, almost as if the explanation has gone right over his head.

"What do you think it means?" Sébastien asks, surprisingly calmly.

I'm glad some of that special agent training is kicking in. Feigning ignorance is a good strategy. It's not that I don't trust Margot, but I hardly know her and there's a lot more at stake here than just Gaspar and me. After all, he didn't resurrect himself.

Margot touches her lips, thinks for a moment, and then bursts out laughing. "I don't know, but god, I want to investigate this further." She looks at Gaspar apologetically. "With your permission, of course."

As much as I want to know more about what happened at the resurrection and understand what kind of state he is in now, I feel too protective. "Let's not get distracted. Gaspar and I are only here to support Sébastien and Dix."

"Of course. Excuse me, dear. I'm afraid professional curiosity got the better of me." With a last look at Gaspar, Margot waves Sébastien over. "I'll show you my translator."

"Translator?"

While he and Dix accompany Margot to another machine, I take Gaspar's hand. "Everything okay?"

"I'm half ghost," he says quietly. There's a hint of desperation in his voice. "I'm not really alive."

I hug him tightly. "You are in every way that matters." Kissing his cheeks, I whisper, "I love you in whatever form you are. Ghost, human, half ghost. It doesn't matter to me."

"It matters to *me*."

I hug him again. "I know."

Meanwhile, Dix has entered the pod. As the glass muffles his voice, words appear on a computer screen.

Curious, Gaspar and I come closer. It turns out the translation has the quality of automatically generated subtitles. It omits certain words or replaces them with others that sound similar. Nevertheless, the gist of what he's saying is translated practically in real time.

"You can talk to ghosts?"

Margot nods at me. "Pretty cool, huh? Here's a little secret. I do get the occasional visitor in my lab. Word has got around about my work, and from time to time, a ghost strolls in and talks to me."

"About what?"

"Oh, everything. There's an old lady who just came in to talk about the weather, some cat in the street, and her grandchildren. If you ask me, she's lonely and longing for a connection with the living."

I'm completely enthralled. This is not the GoPol way of working with ghosts, but much more like my own. "Would you call her your friend?"

Margot shrugs. "I suppose you could say that. I don't have time to talk to her all the time, but I'm always happy to have her around. Just like the others. There's a little girl who loves to follow me around the lab, then demands to speak to me to give me some pointers. I call her my little scientist."

Worried about the effect on Sébastien of hearing her speak so fondly of a child that isn't him, I glance at him. To my surprise, Sébastien smiles warmly. "Alix is the same."

"How so?" Margot asks curiously.

"She has a way with ghosts that's simply astounding. I think she has more ghost friends than real friends"—gee, *thanks*—"not just famous people. And she helps them. She treats every ghost with respect and empathy, sensing what they need and doing her best to help them, sometimes to her own detriment."—again, *thanks*—"Like, right now, she's trying to reconcile Émile Zola and Paul Cézanne after they didn't speak for almost a hundred and fifty years. And I'm absolutely convinced she'll succeed."

Okay, now I'm really blushing. I didn't know he was so on board with my favours.

"It's something I... I wish I could do," Sébastien confesses. "I mean, I like my job. Not hunting down illegitimate ghost whisperers but uncovering political conspiracies and stuff like that. But my experience with ghosts seems so rudimentary compared to Alix's. To be honest, GoPol's training in that regard is sorely lacking."

Understatement of the year, but I'm glad he's showing a bit more of himself to his mother. It's a good sign.

"No surprise," Margot says with a snort. Then she smiles at me. "You became a ghost whisperer at a very young age, right?"

"At three."

"Oh, I'm sorry. For the unfortunate event that led to that," she clarifies. "As for the ghosts, I imagine it's quite different when you've been around them all your life. Much more natural." Clicking her tongue, she shakes her head. "Man, you three are so interesting."

"Four," Dix says, and the computer promptly translates.

Margot laughs. "Yes, four, of course. I'm sorry, I'm dying to ask, Alix. What are your plans after you graduate? Because I could definitely use a partner around here."

I stare at her, stunned. "You want me to work here?"

"Only if you want to, of course. Look, why don't we arrange something for this summer? An internship? You come to Marseille, bring Gaspar with you, and I'll come up with a little project. All paid, of course. I've got some funds I could use." She turns to Sébastien and puts a hand on his cheek. "And you're welcome to come any time. Dix included," she says, before the ghost can protest.

Sébastien and I share a look. He seems happy, even excited, which matches my own energy. Ever since I set foot in GoPol's ghost archive, I've longed for a career in ghost research. It seemed impossible with the way GoPol has treated me, but now there's a chance. An internship sounds like the perfect way to dip my toes in.

Giggling, I say, "Let's do it."

Sébastien and I are still buzzing when we get back to the hotel. Today was a good day. Sébastien and Margot got on beautifully, and I'm glad their relationship has a chance to recover after being so brutally severed. I'm under no illusions it'll always be this smooth. There's a lot to unpack, but Margot seems lovely and willing to put in the work, while Sébastien has also come out of his shell a bit.

He deserves it.

"Could you really leave Paris?" Gaspar asks as we gather in the lobby.

"That's a bridge I'll cross much later. Provence has made a few arguments, though." I see why Zola kept returning here, never quite forgetting the beauty of the countryside. "I love it here."

Gaspar snorts. "Yeah, a well-paid internship in your dream field can do that."

I laugh and loop my arm around his. "That's definitely an argument. Will you come with me?"

"As long as I'm not the little project."

"Never." I meant what I said in Margot's lab. It doesn't matter to me which form Gaspar takes. I loved him as a ghost, and I love him in this form. He's my hedgehog boy, and that's all I need to know. "Let's get changed and find something to eat. Gaby wants to go back to Marseille. She's found a cute little nightclub she can't wait to try tonight."

Gaspar holds up his hand. "Say no more. You know I'm always good for a party."

"Are you coming, too?" I ask Sébastien.

There's no answer. Instead, his gaze is fixed on the entrance. A sleek black car pulls away from the kerb after dropping off its passenger. The doors open, revealing a tall man in a suit.

The monster himself.

Charles Roubert.

Chapter 17

The first thing that comes to mind is how there's still a mark on Sébastien's face. The cut has healed well, but it's too soon to tell if it'll leave a scar. My stomach churns at Charles' intrusion into what was supposed to be our getaway holiday. I know it's incredibly selfish, but I'm convinced he's here for us and not for Cédric.

It's the first time I've seen Charles since the New Year's party. From then on, it's all been C-Trente. But C-Trente is no more, and I'm the reason for it.

Charles has nothing but contempt for me, a mutual hostility. His glare hits Sébastien. "You have something to say, boy?"

Sebastian squares his shoulders. He hasn't been a boy for a long time. Not since Dix's creation. "Yes. I found Maman."

My heart overflows with pride to hear him stand up to his father. "Did you now?" Charles sounds less than impressed.

Sébastien turns away from his father to look at me and Gaspar. "You go and get ready. I'll take care of this."

Grateful for the chance to escape Charles, I let out a sigh of relief. I lean over and kiss him on the cheek. "Don't let him get to you."

I don't care what his father thinks of me kissing him while holding hands with another man. The days when I cared what Charles Roubert thought of me were extremely short-lived and are long gone. All he needs to know is I stand by his son.

"He has the same punchable face as my father," Gaspar says through clenched teeth. It's a far cry from my sweet boy, but I can't complain, because I'm dying to punch Charles myself. "They even dress the same. All prim and proper to hide their black soul underneath."

My heart goes out to him. Gaspar's father may not have been a psychopath like Charles, but he doesn't exactly sound like Father of the Year, either. "Will you ever reach out to your parents?"

Gaspar snorts. "Why should I? Honestly, my death is the best thing that could've happened to them. Now they no longer have to worry about me sullying the family name. Instead, they can play the grieving parents and have all their rich friends pity them. My mother will have a field day with that. As for me? I'm no longer obliged to show my face. It's a win-win situation, really."

He may pretend that's the case, but I know him better. He's only telling himself that to protect his heart. "Well, you've got me now."

"Do I?"

Before I can answer, we bump into Hélène and Cédric. It's the first time I've seen Cédric here in Provence and he's already getting on my nerves with the way his eyes light up. "Alix."

"Cédric," I sigh.

"Fancy meeting you here," he says with a cheesy grin, and it's all I can do not to roll my eyes.

"Yeah, so surprising."

Cédric nods at Gaspar. "And who's this gentleman?" He holds out his hand. "I don't think we've met."

Gaspar looks at the hand as if it were a giant insect. "We've met."

"Have we?"

Are we really going to do this?

Apparently so. "Yeah, I had to listen to that rubbish you call music when you drove Alix to Père Lachaise. Oh, and then you ratted her out to your uncle. How's the traditional death upon recruitment going?"

For the first time since I've known him, I see Cédric lose his composure and go pale. He's completely speechless.

Not so my sister. She wraps her arm around her fiancé's, and glares at us both before turning on me. "Why would you bring *him* to my wedding?"

"He's my plus one." It's her fault for letting me bring one.

"He's an abomination." Hélène turns around to explain to Cédric, "That's Alix's *true* boyfriend, you know, the dead one. Gaspar or something." At least, she got his name right this time.

Cédric's eyes widen even more. "He doesn't look dead to me."

"Well, we can't *all* look like that."

As childish as it is, I can't help but giggle. Right now, Cédric looks more like a ghost than any I've ever met.

Hélène throws a withering look at me. "Whoever he is, he's not your Gaspar. People don't come back from the dead. That's just wrong." And with that, she turns on her heels and drags Cédric into the restaurant.

Here we go again. I lived through something and my sister doesn't believe me. She probably thinks I've hired an actor just to ruin her precious wedding.

"Hope you chose better music for the reception," Gaspar calls after them.

I'm beginning to like this new vicious side of Gaspar. Calling out Cédric and refusing to fall for his sleazy behaviour has made a bad experience strangely satisfying. He doesn't take shit from either of them. Instead, he's fiercely on my side.

Now he wraps his arms around me and pulls me close. "Don't listen to that hag. What we have is good."

But Hélène has a point. There is something terribly wrong with raising the dead. Only how can it be wrong when it feels so right?

To distract myself from the double-chance meetings, I throw myself into Marseille's nightclub scene with all the enthusiasm Gaby could ever ask of me. We're quite a big group, with Odile and the boys joining us, as we head into town for a bite—less chance to cross Hélène's path again—and then start at the little club Gaby's scouted out.

It's a club named after the Count of Monte Cristo, whom Dumas had imprisoned in the Château d'If, an island fortress off the coast of Marseille. I appreciate the nod to historical literature and the reminder of my ghostly writer friend, the third in the alcove with Victor and Zola. The club itself may have been loosely inspired by a prison aesthetic, but the flashing lights destroy most of the atmosphere and the pole dancers behind bars are certainly not what Dumas had in mind.

All in all, it's a bit tacky, and with Gaspar complaining about the music, we only stay long enough for a couple of drinks. My phone finds its way into Gaspar's hands, and he pulls up some message boards to find us a real party.

"Here we go. Come on."

We file out of the club and follow him through some questionable streets I would never have stepped foot in if we weren't in such a big group and had a literal secret agent with us. Gaby throws me a worried glance, still reserving final judgement on Gaspar.

Gaspar knocks on a nondescript metal door. A slit opens and he has a quick chat with whoever's behind it. A moment later, the door swings open to reveal a staircase. Gaspar shakes the door-man's hand as if they were old friends, before heading down the stairs.

Another doorman ID's us at the bottom and opens the doors to an underground club with a strong indie-rock vibe. It's surprisingly cosy, with lots of comfortable tables and seating around a semi-circular dance floor in front of a stage where a live band is playing. The bar at the side is busy but not crowded.

"How did you find this gem?" I ask Gaspar as we grab an empty table.

"The less you know the better," he says with a grin, before pulling me straight back up. "Let the others get drinks. We're dancing."

And with that, he pulls me onto the dance floor, where I immediately fall into the rhythm. I lose myself in the beat and the feel of his body pressed against mine as we rock out to the music. I've never been much of a dancer, but when I'm with Gaspar it's so easy to let go. We hop and shimmy, twirl and headbang, laugh and kiss in a wild dance that knows no rules. And the best part? Everyone can see my boyfriend.

When I finally return to the table, I'm drenched in sweat, grinning from ear to ear, my mouth parched. Sébastien hands me a glass of water, which I gulp down immediately, and then a cocktail, which Gaby ordered for me earlier. She and Marie are on the dance floor, dancing slowly and kissing in spite of the beat.

"Who are you and what have you done with my sister?" Odile shouts over the music.

I stick out my tongue and laugh as Gaspar falls onto the bench next to me. He immediately grabs my cocktail and takes a long swig. "Oh, good one."

I take my glass back. "Trust Gaby to know what's best for me."

"And me." He looks at the drink with puppy eyes.

Laughing, I slap his hand away. "Get your own."

"I don't have any money." He's barely said it before Sébastien hands over his credit card. Gaspar grabs it and gets to his feet again. He kisses me and says, "I love this guy."

"What about you?" I ask Sébastien, who snorts at the comment. "Did you dance?"

"No," Odile answers for him. "I tried to persuade him to join me, but he preferred to watch our table instead." She leans forward. "Although I don't think it was the table he was watching."

"Don't listen to her," says Sébastien. "She's already had two cocktails and a shot."

I size him up. "And you?"

"Sober friend."

"Seriously?" With so many people, we didn't take the car, but took public transport to Marseille, intending to take two taxis on the way back. We don't need a sober driver. "Come on."

Sébastien looks at me as if I've asked him to undress in front of everyone. "You just sat down."

"One song." I finish my cocktail, already feeling the beat calling me back to the dance floor.

"What about Gaspar?"

"He'll join us when he gets back." I grab Sébastien's hand.

There's no way I could drag Sébastien out from behind the table, but with Odile encouraging him and promising to send Gaspar our way, he lets me lead him to the dance floor.

"I can't dance," he confesses, his lips close to my ear so I can hear him.

"Neither can I," I laugh. "Just feel the music as it comes."

Sébastien is not half as bad as he says he is. Sure, he's holding back, resulting in stiff, awkward movements, but by the time Gaspar and Odile join us, he's loosening up. What he needs is confidence, not dance moves.

I sway back and forth between him and the force of nature Gaspar is when he has music. Odile dances as if no one's watching, jumping and throwing her arms around. When Gaby and Marie join us, I can't help but forget all about my troubles. We dance and we sing—loud and wrong—and we laugh just for the pure joy of it. As I lean backwards into Gaspar and he wraps his arms around me, holding me tight while I watch my friends having fun, I can't think of a better place to be.

Chapter 18

We partied so late Gaspar is still out cold when I get up in the morning. I check on Malou, who is curled up in her cage, write a note to Gaspar, and go downstairs to grab a bite. My parents are just finishing breakfast on the patio, so I go over, kiss them both on the head and help myself to their leftovers.

"Late night?" Papa asks.

"Try early morning." We didn't get back until almost four.

Maman laughs. "Oh dear. And you're already up?"

"Didn't sleep well." Truth is, I woke in a cold sweat after hearing Nostradamus repeat his cursed prophecy and seeing all my friends drop dead at the wedding. "Are you enjoying yourself?"

Papa orders me a cup of coffee, which I really appreciate, and says, "We were going to drive up to le Château des Baux-de-Provence. Want to come?"

He really knows how to win me over. The castle was my absolute highlight the last time we holidayed here. It's a small medieval village on a hill about an hour from here. If I had to choose a wedding location in Provence, it would be this charming place with its rich history.

"I'm afraid I can't. I've already made plans for today." My coffee arrives and I soak up the blessed caffeine.

"You're a busy lady," Papa jokes.

"Don't forget we've got the rehearsal tomorrow," Maman warns.

I roll my eyes at the prospect. "I'll be there." It's bad enough I have to sit through the wedding once. Thanks to little Miss Perfect, we have to do it twice.

"Be nice to your sister," Maman warns. "She may not look it, but I think she's a bit nervous."

I'd be nervous, too, if I had to marry Cédric.

"She's putting so much pressure on herself to make sure everything's perfect, I'm a bit afraid she'll forget to enjoy it." Maman shrugs with a silly little smile. "Maybe you could invite her next time you go out?"

"Did she complain?" I highly doubt Hélène wants to hang out with Gaspar and me but leave it to her to find fault anyway.

Maman shakes her head. "Not directly, but she noticed you all went together, and I think she felt a bit left out." She reaches out and rubs my hand. "You two used to be so close. I know the last few weeks have been hard for you, but I thought you'd made up."

We did. After meeting a woman at the opera whose whisper ghost had murdered her sister, I swore to myself I wouldn't give up on Hélène. We would survive her marriage to Cédric. So, I groveled and made concessions that hurt. To be honest, it cost me a lot more than it cost her, and yet she's not prepared to show me the slightest bit of grace. No, she went right back to being her judgmental self. And now she's even allowed Charles Roubert to attend her wedding. As if that wasn't bad enough, I have to put up with her future husband.

"If Hélène wants to come, all she has to do is say so." I drink the rest of my coffee. "But now I have to go." I grab a leftover mini croissant and pretend I'm late for something. Although my parents technically know about the ghosts, they haven't come to terms with it yet, and after what happened to my Papa, I'm not going to drag them into my world.

I make my way back upstairs, ready to knock on Gaby's door, when the door on the other side opens and Sébastien steps out.

"Good morning," he says, with a gentle smile. If I hadn't known he'd been with us last night, I wouldn't suspect a thing. There are no bleary eyes, no squinting into the light. "Where are you going?"

"To find Baptistin Baille. He's a ghost."

"Naturally."

"You know him?" I ask in surprise. In the grand scheme of history, Baptistin didn't leave much of a trace.

Sébastien laughs. "No, but I know you well enough to know you don't go out to meet random guys. Do you need a ride? I don't have any plans today."

"And you want to spend the whole day following me around as I try to unravel this tangled web of friendship and betrayal between people who are long dead?"

His smile widens. "When do we leave?"

I'm beginning to enjoy these rides on the back of Sébastien's bike. The wind whips the hair flowing from my helmet, while my arms are wrapped around Sébastien's torso as we speed along the country roads towards Aix. There's something about my body pressed against his that feels just right.

We go back to the school where I last met Zola and Cézanne.

I'd tried to find a street in Provence named after Baille, but while he deserved an entry in the history books, no one had thought to commemorate him that way. If I had a few weeks, I might be able to find out which house he grew up in—if it hasn't been demolished—but since I don't have that kind of time, the school will have to do.

"I don't see anyone," says Sébastien, taking off his helmet.

Dix, who's just appeared at our side, shushes him. "Let History Girl do her thing."

My thing is I can summon certain ghosts if I concentrate really hard. At least the ones I know, who are willing to come. I'm hoping that being in a place with a connection to Baille will help, even though we've never met. I start by thinking of everything I know about him, starting with the portrait I found online. He moved to Paris like Zola—I probably have a better chance of finding him there—became an astronomer at the Paris Observatory, then later a professor of optics and acoustics at the École de Physique-Chemistry Industrielle. There was something about binoculars and becoming a Knight of the Legion of Honour, but that's about it.

When that doesn't work, I try to imagine him hanging out here with his friends, the scientist among the artists. It eventually does the trick.

His hair is short and light. Instead of a full beard, he has a thick moustache and a strip of hair under his chin that looks surprisingly fashionable. He has the appearance of a soldier, tall, and with a straight, rigid posture, but his light eyes carry the soul of a former poet. Most importantly, he's slightly translucent in the morning sun, not as robust as other ghosts.

He's fading, I realise. Despite his Wikipedia page, not many remember him as a person.

"Who are you?" Baille asks, confused. He looks up at his old school and his face softens. "Haven't seen these walls for a long time."

"I'm a friend of Émile Zola's."

Baille frowns. "A living friend?"

"Well, as you can see, I'm a ghost whisperer. I work at the Panthéon."

"Ah, I heard he was transferred there. How is he? I haven't seen him much lately."

Oh my, it seems like Zola has been a bad friend all around. Or maybe it's just a ghost thing. The proximity of their resting places has a lot more impact than the relationships they formed while they were alive. Or maybe the friendships of their youth simply weren't as strong in their adult years. Living people move on, so why not ghosts?

"He's doing alright, I think." Talking too much about Zola won't help the flickering of Baille's ghostly form. "He actually sent me here to apologise to Paul Cézanne. They met yesterday, but it didn't go quite as planned. I was hoping that, as one of their close friends, you could help me smooth things over. You know, make Les Trois Insèperables three again."

The mention of his friendship group strengthens Baille's appearance. He's almost solid when he laughs. "I haven't heard that old moniker in ages." Scratching his ear, he says: "Truth is, I loved them both, but the real inseparables were Paul and Émile. I was just blessed to tag along."

"Oh. I thought all three of you were the best of friends."

"We were. I'm just saying the two of them had a much closer relationship. You see, Émile was the dreamer. He was the smallest of us, but his dreams were the biggest. He was always destined to be more than he was born as. And through him, Paul also began to dream. His father was a banker with little interest in art. He always expected Paul to follow in his footsteps. If it weren't for Émile, Paul would never have given painting a chance. Paul was the art in Émile's words, but Émile was the sun in his life. I know they had a big falling-out, but I can't believe that stubborn old painter let Émile go. And of course, it only got worse from there." Baille leans against the wall behind him and sighs. "Paul has always been a creature of melancholy. Before Émile came into his life, he was a loner. Nobody wanted to mess with him because his father was wealthy, and he was quite tall with a stern expression. Then he met Émile and the sun dawned on his face. Émile's dreams gave him life. When Émile had to move to Paris, he was heartbroken. He tried to follow him, but the city was too much for him. While Émile flourished, Paul struggled, and then came the book. I think Paul cut all ties because he thought it was what Émile wanted. He wasn't just offended, he was heartbroken. And he was convinced someone as glorious and bright as Émile would only be dragged down by him. He accepted the label of failure and embraced it with all his heart, becoming an even worse hermit." Baille shakes his head. "But he never stopped loving Émile. His death destroyed him. He was never truly happy after that and died only a few years later."

My suspicions about Cézanne and Zola only deepen. Hearing how close they were, I wonder if Baille might have been the third wheel of the inseparables.

"So, you agree they need to get over themselves and get back together? Will you help me?"

Baille laughs and shakes his head. "I would love nothing more than to see Émile and Paul reunited as they should be, but… I don't belong here anymore. The only reason I still exist is because of them and a few papers I published over a century ago." True to his words, he fades away again. "But you have my blessing. I don't know what you can do, but if you think there's a chance, please, help them. Help them both."

With one last longing look at his old school, Baille disappears.

"So, what now?" Sébastien asks, reminding me of his presence.

Dix takes Baille's place against the wall. His arms crossed, he leans back. "You see, that's the problem with good old normal ghosts. They're so lethargic."

I remember Sébastien once telling me about the difficulties of working with ghosts on his cases. Perhaps he's right about Baille. So little is known about his private life—not even how he became friends with Zola and Cézanne—that the things that used to motivate him have already been lost. Perhaps he has an afterlife in one of the cemeteries of Paris, but here he's just a footnote.

Unlike his friends, who are all over this city.

"No, we're going to meet Zola again and kick his butt. If I've learnt anything from Baille's account, it's that there's no chance in hell Cézanne will take action. He thinks Zola is better off without him, that he was right to look down on him. Zola was his sun, but he was never his. That's where he's wrong."

\#

I ask Sébastien to drive me to the dam at Lake Zola, which originally brought the Zola family to Provence. We leave the bike in a car park and take our time walking the trails. Spring has come early, as it often does in the south, and everything is in bloom. There's a sweet smell and a constant buzzing in the air. The views of the striking limestone mountain above the trees are divine.

As we take in the scenery, I ask Sébastien how his meeting with his father went last night.

"Don't worry about it. He's not here for you."

"That's a first," I can't help commenting.

Sébastien winces, making me feel guilty because he used to get on well with his father before I came along—well, as well as you can with the man who murdered you.

"Don't tell me he's here because of Cédric."

"That's what he claims." Sébastien sighs, almost as if he wishes his father was here for him. "He seemed to be surprisingly okay with me finding Maman. Honestly, he didn't care at all."

And it's grating on Sébastien. He's suffered from his mother's absence all his life, while his father filed the relationship away long ago, never once thinking about how it might have affected his son.

"Well, he'll care once Margot joins forces with us to bring him down."

"You think she'd do that?"

"She adores you! You're her everything."

He doesn't seem as convinced of it as I am. Like Cézanne, he thinks he deserves to be abandoned. "She adores *you*. Look how quickly she offered you a job. Not that I blame her. You would absolutely thrive in her lab. The two of you together... magic."

The idea amuses me. "Margot doesn't even know if I'd be any good in a lab. Besides, she invited you, too. She just didn't offer you a job because you already have one. And you're her son. Would you want to work with your mother?"

"I work with my father."

"Touché." There's that. "She probably thought it'd be too awkward if she tried to recruit you away from him. Believe me, your mother would love to have you back in her life."

Dix grins from ear to ear. "She does, doesn't she? I always knew she never really left us." Sometimes, it's easy to forget that Dix isn't his own entity, but his comment sounds more like boyish hope, while the older, traumatised version has learnt to expect the worst.

I decide to change the subject and nudge Sébastien. "So, how's life with Gaspar? You two seem to be getting on quite well."

Through the budding leaves on the trees, the water of the lake glistens. We're approaching the dam.

"I quite like him," Sébastien admits. "He's a bit erratic, one day this way, the next day that, but on his good days, he's incredibly kind and funny."

The words make me snort. "On his good days?"

Sébastien regards me carefully. "He's obviously been through a lot. Sometimes, he's... moody. A little aggressive."

"Gaspar? Aggressive?" Despite my indignation, I haven't forgotten how he flew off the handle when I tried to reunite him with Marie. Or the painful drive here. But as Sébastien says, he's been through so much. It's only natural he has good and bad days.

Sébastien shrugs. "I'm sure it's just a phase. He's still getting used to being alive and a lot of it is frustrating. I think he feels caught in the middle. And after what my mother said, maybe there's more to it than that."

"He's not half ghost."

"He feels half ghost," Dix says, without much tact.

"Well, what's that supposed to mean? He's alive but also dead?"

"Well, for one thing, he can see ghosts, which makes sense. He's practically a ghost whisperer." Suddenly Sébastien frowns.

"Which usually means that there's a whisper ghost. Did he mention anything?"

The thought chills me to the bone. "You mean another Gaspar?"

"You know how it works."

"No, I don't. He's the first person to be brought back to life. Like really dead, not almost dead. He doesn't have a whisper ghost." Surprisingly, I find myself longing for his ghostly self. We were so good.

It's a ridiculous idea, of course. Gaspar is better off alive. We just have to find our feet again and redefine our relationship.

Sébastien lets it drop as we step onto the dam. "I'm sure that's it." He nudges my chin forward. "Looks like you didn't even have to summon him."

Sure enough, Zola is standing in the middle of the dam, lost in thought, watching the steep rock face of Saint Victoire rise behind the lake.

"Salut, Zola," I greet him.

He doesn't turn to me, but the corners of his mouth curl upwards. "It's beautiful, isn't it?"

"Very." So far, we've been fortunate with the weather, allowing us to see Provence's nature in all its glory.

"Every time I come back it feels like coming home. My life—afterlife—is in Paris and I'd probably die again if I had to stay here indefinitely, but my heart belongs to this place. Can you smell the wind?"

I put my nose in the air, trying to smell the breeze. It carries the faint scent of salt.

"Between the sea and the mountains is where I created my fondest memories."

Although he speaks of beauty, his words are tinged with sadness, as if Provence were lost forever to him.

Before I can ask him about it, he pats the dam. "My father built it. Or rather, he did all the planning and oversaw the early construction. He died before it was finished. It's the only thing named after him and not me."

"Do you miss your father?"

"He's long since moved on, along with my mother. As a Panthéon ghost, you learn not to get too attached to anyone, living or dead. Most of my peers are gone now."

Even his friend Baille. "But not all of them."

Zola chuckles, then turns to me. He nods at Sébastien and Dix before explaining, "Paul may not be a ghost of the Panthéon, but he's earned his right to immortality. He's had a huge influence. Have you heard about that Picasso guy? He called Paul the father of his painting style, his greatest influence. He even moved here to follow in his footsteps." He nods towards the other side of the mountain. "Bought a house somewhere over there."

From what I've heard about Picasso the man, he's not someone I'd want to meet, groundbreaking painter or not.

"Émile, why did you ask me to help you with Paul?" I ask quietly.

He sighs. "Because I miss him." Shaking his head, he looks back out at the mountain his friend painted so often. "He's not just my oldest friend, he's so much more than that. He's the shadow to my light, the lows to my heights, the depth to my prose, the ground beneath my feet. Without Paul, I'd never have broken free and learned to soar. I would've had my wings clipped and lived a short life of misery, but Paul... I'd be nothing without him believing in me. I *am* nothing without him."

"You love him." I'd suspected it ever since I heard them arguing and admiring each other at the same time.

Zola smiles sadly. "And don't we always hurt the ones we love the most?"

"Do we?" Dix asks Sébastien, clearly inexperienced when it comes to love.

Sébastien doesn't bother to answer, his entire attention on me.

Somehow, I'm supposed to fix this mess. Zola thinks I've got a chance, and Sébastien believes in me, too. But how can I repair something that was broken so long ago?

An idea strikes me. "Émile, how did you two become friends in the first place?" I now know they're more than friends, but the love they feel for each other is rooted in the boyhood friendship they both cherished so much.

"It was one of the worst days of my life," says Zola. "I had just started this new school, and everyone was horrible to me. I was smaller than most of my classmates and my clothes were often torn. My family was poor and everybody knew it. I was also the child with the dead father. So, one day at lunchtime, they cornered me and beat me up. And then this giant appeared." Suddenly he's smiling. "I was on the ground, bleeding from the nose, crying—embarrassing, I know. He could have just walked by, but no, he sent everyone running. At first, I thought he just wanted me for himself, but instead, he helped me up, brushed the dust off my clothes, and gave me his handkerchief. Then, hands in pockets, he shuffled off, never once saying a word."

I can see him now. The little middle schooler in his tattered clothes, looking a little worse for wear, and the dark, gentle giant, a loner himself, but feared by his peers.

"So, how did you become friends?"

"Well, of course I had to thank him. So, the next day I brought him a basket of apples. He didn't want them at first, but I refused to leave until he'd had one." Zola grins at the memory of his stubborn self. "And then I just kept refusing as he tried to chase me away."

And there it is. *Cézanne's 'Basket of Apples'.*

"I have an idea. Meet me tomorrow..." I shake my head, remembering Hélène's rehearsal. "Meet me in three days' time at Cézanne's atelier in town."

Chapter 19

"Hey. Us girls are hanging out in Gaby's room. We've got some cheap wine, and Marie says she's going to read tarot. Would you like to join us?"

Look at me, reaching out to Hélène like a good little sister. I deserve a gold star.

Hélène looks over her shoulder, which promptly calls her fiancé to her side. He leans against the door frame and smiles. "Salut, Alix. What can we do for you?"

"Apparently, they're having a girls' night. I don't want to be hungover for the rehearsal, though."

Please kill me now. If she doesn't want to drink, she can stick to water. I don't know why Cédric has to be involved. Last time I checked, he was not a girl.

"Oh, come on," he laughs. "It's just the rehearsal. And it's in the afternoon. Have fun with your sisters. I might even go out and see if the guys want to have a beer at the bar."

Yeah, good luck with that, buddy. I hope he's brought his own guys, because my two can't stand him and would rather gouge their eyes out than spend an evening with Officer Cédric.

Hélène leans over and kisses him, making *me* want to gouge my eyes out. Giggling, she says, "Okay."

"Have fun," he tells her, before giving her a playful slap on the backside as she leaves the room. I'm beginning to regret all my life choices.

"Don't make that face," Hélène admonishes. "Have you never been a little naughty in your relationships?"

I squeeze my eyes shut, exacerbating whatever face I'm making. "I won't talk about my relationship, and you won't talk about yours. Deal?"

Hélène rolls her eyes. "Fine." She's agreed, but the tone of her voice suggests I'm being childish. And maybe I am, but there are things I'd rather not imagine about my sister and Cédric.

I lead her into Gaby's room, where she, Marie, and Odile have already gathered. The beds have been pushed together and covered with a large blanket to protect them from all the snacks and possible wine spills. Malou is also there, currently enjoying a belly rub from Gaby, while Odile lays out a small number of outfits.

"This one's pretty," Marie exclaims, picking up a blue polka-dot dress and holding it up to the hedgehog.

"Hi, Hélène," Gaby calls. "So glad you could join us. I'm sorry we had to bail on your hen party. I just can't cope with small spaces."

My sister waves it off. "You didn't miss much." She sits on the edge of the bed, then comments on the dress Marie liked. "This isn't for the wedding, is it?"

"Of course not," Odile says. "You won't get to see the dress. It's bad luck."

Hélène laughs. "Isn't that for the bride, not the ring-bearing hedgehog?"

Odile clicks her tongue. "Well, do you want to risk it?"

The atmosphere's threatening to sour, so I grab the nearest bottle of wine. "Would you like a glass, Léni?"

"Yes, please." So much for her feared hangover.

I pour a glass for her and myself and join the others on the bed. It's not intentional, but as I cuddle up to Gaby, I realise I've put as much distance as possible between myself and my sister.

Hélène looks completely out of place on the edge of the bed and barely says a word as the four of us chat nonsense, like what films we were waiting for or which celebrity Odile thinks she saw at the Château des Baux-de-Provence. Malou is let down to get her steps in and we laugh about her trying to climb onto the bedside table.

After a while, Marie gets out her tarot deck and starts shuffling. She offers to Hélène first. "Would you like a reading for your wedding? It's just a hobby, so bear with me."

At first, it seems as if Hélène will say no. She probably believes in tarot as little as she does in ghosts. "What kind of reading?"

"Just a simple three-card spread that tells you about your past, present, and future. Nothing serious." I know Marie is playing down the cards to Hélène because she's already picked up on her scepticism. The last time Marie did a reading for me, she was quite serious.

Hélène finally relents. "Okay, sure." She laughs nervously and pulls her legs up on the bed. "I've always wanted to try," she admits. "What do I have to do?"

"Shuffle the cards again and think of the man you want to marry."

I'm glad it's not me, because the outcome wouldn't be pretty.

Hélène takes the cards and shuffles them a bit awkwardly before handing them back to Marie, who takes the top three cards and lays them out. "What now?"

"The card on the left is your past." Marie turns the card over. "Two of Wands. Not surprising after everything I've heard. It means a lot of planning and long-term goals. So, it's basically saying that you've thought about this for a long time and done all the work, and now you're ready to make a new commitment."

So far, so good. Hélène smiles, clearly proud of her achievement.

Gaby hands me the bowl of crisps as Marie turns over the next card. A major arcana that even I know.

"The Lovers," she laughs. "If that doesn't fit perfectly. It shows the trust you have in each other and in your relationship, and the harmony. You have a strong bond and fit well together."

I stuff my mouth with crisps, so I don't say the wrong thing.

Hélène looks happy with her spread so far. "Have you rigged this?" she jokes.

Marie laughs. "No. You shuffled. I'm just here to help you interpret. Shall we see what the future holds?"

Curious, Hélène leans over the cards as Marie turns over the last. While everyone looks at the card, I see Marie's smile falter. She swallows.

The card itself doesn't look too bad. It's the Five of Cups, and it shows a man bent over three fallen cups, while the other two remain standing. "What does it mean?" I ask quietly.

"Um..." Marie licks her lip. "Well, it can mean disappointment is coming your way."

I get the feeling disappointment is the mildest way to describe what this card means.

"Disappointment?" Hélène asks, offended. "What does that mean?"

"Well, it can"—again with the "can"—"mean a loss or grief, but you know, this could be about the loss of your old life. Maybe things aren't working out the way you planned." Marie is clearly struggling to interpret this in the best possible way. "Look, you had the Two of Wands, which suggests you're a planner. Maybe the future isn't quite as easy to plan as you might hope. Maybe there's a change you're not expecting."

"Like an unplanned pregnancy?" Hélène asks in horror.

Oh, please, no little Cédrics.

Marie nods eagerly. "For example. So, you might feel disappointed—*initially*—because it doesn't happen when you planned it. Or something else. Maybe a job change that forces you to make some big decisions about your relationship. It doesn't have to be a bad thing, just a little challenge."

I take out my phone and look up the card myself. The first result lists the Five of Cups as one of the most ominous cards to get in a reading. And it definitely stands for grief, sorrow, and missed opportunities. If it's about a job offer or an unexpected child, this would be one of Hélène's most extreme reactions.

Gaby leans over to glance at my screen, then shares a worried look with me. I'm no expert, but what I can tell from this card is that my sister is in for a rude awakening when Cédric inevitably disappoints her. If I were superstitious, I'd call off the wedding. But I don't need tarot cards to come to that conclusion.

"This calls for more wine," says Gaby. She stands and gives Marie a reassuring shoulder squeeze.

Hélène doesn't seem so happy about her reading now. She had such a positive start—Cédric really is her dream match by the sounds of it—only to be disappointed in the end. Pardon the pun.

"Do me!" Odile says excitedly, breaking through the clouds that seem to have settled. "I want to know if I should take a gap year or study in Paris."

"You have to pass your bac first," Hélène says with a snort. A good sign that she's back in top form.

Odile rolls her eyes and picks up the cards to shuffle them.

Her reading is much more positive than Hélène's, but still rather vague. I'm getting the feeling the cards can basically say anything if you push them hard enough. We go through Gaby's reading with a lot of laughter, and then Odile grabs Malou to get her a reading.

Since the hedgehog can't shuffle the cards, Marie does it for her. She fans them out and Odile puts Malou in front of them. We howl with laughter as she scrambles around for five minutes before actually touching a card.

"The Ace of Cups," Marie declares. "You're going to fall in love, madame."

I almost spit out my drink. "With a snail, right?"

Marie giggles and finishes her reading. "The aces are a sign of a new beginning. You have to let go of your emotional baggage, Malou, and live life to the full. And there could be a new love on the horizon for you."

"We could put out a dating call on her Instagram," Odile laughs. "Let them send us their hedgehog proposals."

"I'm telling you, she'll discover a new food group!" I pick Malou up and give her a quick cuddle before reaching into my bag to give her a treat. She gobbles it up like there's no tomorrow. "Ha!"

"Okay, Alix's turn," Gaby calls. She pushes the cards into my hand, a clear ploy to take Malou away from me and give her more belly rubs.

Cautiously, I touch the cards and shuffle them. I don't know what question to ask. Maybe something about Gaspar? Or about my lingering feelings for Sébastien? But I don't want to talk about that in front of Hélène. And besides... another question comes to mind as I shuffle the cards.

"Do I have to tell you what I want to ask?" I'm not sure I want to know the answer, let alone explain it to everyone else.

Marie shakes her head. "I mean, it would be easier for me to explain the cards, but I can just give you an overview and you can see how it fits into your question. Just think about it while you shuffle."

It's impossible *not* to think about now that I've remembered.

"What is it?" Odile asks.

"Yeah, stop being so mysterious," Hélène complains.

Gaby puts her arm around me and shoos them both away. "It's personal. Let her do it her way." She probably thinks I'm questioning the cards about the two guys I like.

But what fills my mind is much darker. It's something I don't want to share with anyone.

I hand the cards to Marie and fight the urge to abandon the whole thing. As much as I'm dreading the outcome, I need to know more.

It only takes the first card to tell me I've made a mistake. The card shows a person being stabbed to death by no less than ten swords. As with the Five of Cups, Marie's face falls. "So, this is the Ten of Swords. It's…" She's clearly struggling for a positive meaning, but there isn't one.

"Just give it to me straight."

The look she gives me seems to ask if I'm sure. When I nod, she sighs. "Okay, so the Ten of Swords usually means disaster, something out of control. There's a sense of betrayal associated with it. For example, if your question is about love, you may have been betrayed or suffered a terrible heartbreak."

"It's not about love. Move on to the next one." I'm anxious to get through this as quickly as possible.

The hanged man appears. Only he's turned upside down, so to Marie he's not actually hanging. "Alright, that's not a bad card. The Hanged Man usually just means a sacrifice has to be made in order to move forward in your love life or work or whatever it is you're curious about."

"Why is it upside down?"

She sighs. "It's reversed. That means the sacrifice... it'll be in vain. Usually, it means a period of giving and giving that comes to nothing."

Like my relationship with Hélène, then. Not that that was what I had in mind.

As Marie turns the last card, she gasps. In front of her is an ominous tower, struck by lightning. The good news is that it seems to be the right way up. Or at least, I hope that's a good thing. The right way up didn't really help with Hélène's cups or my swords.

Next to me, Gaby's growing quiet. She's obviously had a bit more experience with the cards and knows what this means.

"I know it looks bad. The Tower is a sign of great disaster, great loss, but it can also be a frightening change. Something really life changing." Marie's shoulders slump. "It means something old is going to die, and you're going to have to readjust your values and principles to forge a new path."

Something will die. I know it's not meant literally, but in my line of work...

"What the hell did you ask?" Hélène asks, looking horrified.

I must have set a record for getting three bad cards in a row. Betrayal, needless sacrifice, and complete disaster. Yeah, I'm done for.

"Alix?" Gaby asks, sounding worried.

My throat tightens and I feel my eyes burning. This was a mistake. This was a huge mistake.

"I need to catch up on sleep." Sleep where I can have more nightmares, now fuelled by this undeniable reading.

I don't realise I've fled the party until the door to my room closes behind me. The room is empty. As much as I want to throw myself into Gaspar's arms, I'm glad for the solitude. Just me and my thoughts. I slide down the door as tears begin to fall.

Something will die.

Not everyone who came here will survive the night.

It must be coincidence. Marie's cards can't really tell the future. Nostradamus can't either. It's not hard to see the conflicts in my present life. Nothing has been easy lately, and it seems to be just getting worse. And now—

Someone knocks on the door. "Alix?" Gaby's muffled voice. "Can I come in? Please."

Part of me wants to pretend I'm not here. The other wants to see my best friend.

Please don't let it be Gaby.

I push myself to my feet and open the door. Gaby's standing there, Malou in her hands, looking at me with worry in her eyes.

Without a word, she comes in, closes the door behind her, and puts an arm around me. "Tell me."

I don't want to, but I let her drag me to my bed, where she puts Malou in my hands and hugs me tightly.

"Was it Gaspar you were thinking of? His resurrection?"

I shake my head, then lean it against hers and sigh. "It had nothing to do with him or Sébastien."

"Oh, we're still thinking about Sébastien?" When I give her a look, she quickly relents, "Not the subject at hand. Come on, ma puce, tell me what's going on in that beautiful head of yours."

Another sigh. I haven't told anyone because I refuse to accept it. I don't want to cause a mass panic. But this is Gaby, and I'll explode if I keep this to myself any longer. "A few days ago..." I have to stop and take a shaky breath. New tears streamed down my face. "We went to Salon-de-Provence. That's where... that's where Nostradamus is buried."

"*The* Nostradamus?"

I nod. "He came to see me before to deliver a prophecy and I went to him for clarification, but it didn't really make things any better."

Gaby seems to understand why I ran from the room now. "Okay, hit me. What did he say?" There's no questioning the legitimacy or telling me there's no such thing as prophecies. Perhaps Marie's rubbing off on her.

"He said I'd raise the dead and bring chaos and destruction to the world."

Whatever Gaby was expecting, this wasn't it. I can see the disbelief in her eyes, the urge to call utter bullshit on Nostradamus. But it's not just him anymore. The cards have spoken, too. And damn it if the Tower doesn't portend chaos and destruction.

"Alright, let me try this. The first part obviously refers to Gaspar."

"I didn't raise him."

"I know that. Just bear with me…" Her eyes widen and her voice becomes more excited. "The Ten of Swords was in your past, wasn't it? So, big betrayal. That's Cédric and GoPol. Now you tried to make some concessions and make it work. You sacrificed a lot, but it'll be in vain, because GoPol is shit and Charles Roubert won't rest until he has control over you."

None of this makes me feel any better.

"And then you have the Tower. Normally you'd think something terrible would happen to you, but Nostradamus says the opposite. You're the Tower. *You're* the terrible thing that will happen to GoPol. You'll bring chaos and destruction to the agency and knock it down, forcing the world to take a different path." Gaby grabs my arms and holds me with her gaze. "This is good. Painful and scary, yes, but you're going to change the world."

You're a catalyst for change.

"What about raising the dead?"

"You can't bring down GoPol alone, of course. But you're not alone. You've got dozens—if not hundreds—of ghosts on your side. Maybe it's not a literal raising of the dead, like what happened to Gaspar, but a metaphorical one. The ghosts don't usually care about the living, right? But they'll rise for you. You, us, and your ghosts, we'll bring GoPol down." Satisfied with her interpretation, Gaby sits next to me again. "It's a good thing."

The way she says it reminds me of how Marie tried to read the cards favourably. Still, what she said makes a lot of sense. The prophecy still frightens me, but not as much as before. I'm not bringing the end of the world; I'm bringing change. And I don't mind if GoPol suffers chaos and destruction. They deserve it.

I've almost calmed down when I remember the second prophecy.

Gaby is good.

She gave me a great explanation to allay my fears, but she can't change this. And it was all I could think of. "He gave me a second prophecy. A warning."

"Another?"

"Someone will die. Someone will die at Hélène's wedding." I gasp as tears stream down my face again. "A betrayal's already taking place. There'll be an unnecessary sacrifice. What if Sébastien—or Gaspar—throws himself in front of me when Charles tries to kill me. What if I lose them?"

It would certainly be something Sébastien would do. As for Gaspar, he's already died once, I can't bear to see him lose his life again. Even if it's one of my sisters or Gaby, it'll be a disaster. Nothing will ever be the same again.

Gaby holds me so tight I almost drop Malou. "That's nonsense," she says. "Nobody's going to die at the wedding. Absolutely nobody." Apparently, this is as far as she trusts prophecies.

"Nostradamus said so."

"Nostradamus also said frogs would fall from the sky, and I've never heard of that happening anywhere," Gaby says, almost angrily. "He was a fraud. A great physician—well, he probably didn't do much more than prescribe bloodletting for everything—but absolute rubbish as an astrologer. Even his colleagues said he didn't really understand astrology and was cherry-picking the meanings. Believe me, I've seen a documentary about him and it's all rubbish. His prophecies? If you predict disaster every other day, you're bound to strike gold now and again. Shall we see how many of his prophecies *didn't* come true?"

I absorb every sensible word as if it's the gospel truth. "But what about Marie's cards?"

Gaby sighs. "They're just cards. Every card has so many meanings and interpretations. You could draw the next three cards and still find some great revelation in them. The cards are meant to make you think, to help you organise your thoughts. Like a reminder to Hélène that not everything can be planned, and that if she insists on doing so, she's setting herself up for disappointment. A therapist could've told her the same thing."

Even *I* could've told her that. Not that she'd listen to me.

"Perhaps, for you, the Tower is just a reminder that instead of holding on to something you want to preserve, it's time to let go and accept its loss."

"Like Hélène."

"Like Hélène."

She's getting married to a man who betrayed me in the past. My parents are desperate for us to get along and I want that, too. But maybe it's not the healthiest way for us. Maybe I *do* need to let go at some point. That doesn't mean I'm going to poison her wedding dress.

I put Malou down and put my arms around Gaby. "Thank you. You're the best."

Gaby smiles as she hugs me back. "I'm always here for you."

Chapter 20

I'd thought last night was terrible. This rehearsal is teaching me better. We're all crammed into the town hall where the main ceremony will take place, and Hélène is in full Bridezilla mode. My responsibility for the wedding is to keep Malou on a leash while she carries a little pillow with the rings on it.

What must have sounded really cute in Hélène's head is far from practical in the real world. First of all, Malou is a hedgehog, not a well-trained dog. Second, she's very small, so the pillow is likely to be dislodged. And third, the wedding won't be at night, which means we're trying to put all that responsibility on an overtired little hedgehog.

"Did you practise this at all?" Hélène yells when Malou starts exploring the benches instead of walking down the aisle, losing the pillow halfway. We haven't even tried it with real rings yet.

I pick Malou up and rock her, giving her some much-needed rest after working on this for the last half hour. "I don't exactly have an aisle at home."

"But a hallway."

"Hélène, dear." Maman comes over and puts her hand on Hélène's shoulder. "Alix is doing her best." She throws me a pleading glance, as if I'm a hedgehog whisperer and not a ghost one.

"Maybe if we put pellets in the aisle, she'll walk straight. Odile could drop them on her way up."

Odile nods eagerly. "And I could sew the pillow to her dress so it won't fall. Maybe tie the rings to it, too."

"And then I'll try to undo the knots while everyone's watching?" Hélène looks from Odile to me. "Don't you dare put pellets on the aisle. I don't want squashed cat food on my high heels. Again!"

"Darling," Maman says in a warning tone. "There's no need to be snippy."

Hélène huffs and points at me. "We've already wasted half an hour. How are we ever going to get through it?"

I now know why not everyone will make it out of the wedding alive. Come Sunday, I'll be behind bars for killing my sister.

I take a deep breath and look down at Malou. The poor girl is fast asleep. "She's sleeping."

"Then wake her up." Hélène seems to be at the end of her rope.

"I know you want the perfect wedding, and you have this cute idea in your head, but Malou is nocturnal. She's tired." Before Hélène can shout at me, I quickly add, "Look, how about this? I'll carry Malou. She'll still look cute, but if she falls asleep, no one will notice. I'm more than capable of walking in a straight line in a reasonable amount of time, and you won't have to worry about crawling under the benches to retrieve the rings."

Hélène breathes in and out of her nose like a horse. She hates this compromise, not because it's an unreasonable suggestion, but because it's not what she's planned. Common sense finally prevails, and she nods sharply. "Guess it can't be helped. Everyone back to their positions. We'll go through this again."

Maman silently thanks me and returns to her spot on the front bench. The rehearsal includes a small wedding party. There's my family and some members of his family—his mother is practically crying non-stop in the front row. I brought Gaby, Marie, and Gaspar. The rest include the witnesses—Hélène's high school friend took over my role—her unofficial bridesmaids, and a few friends for support. Sébastien and Dix are happily skipping the rehearsal. Lucky them.

Odile walks beside me as we return to the entrance. "Is Malou alright?"

"I think so. She's just exhausted."

"Poor baby."

We fall silent as we join Papa, Hélène, and her friends in the room near the entrance. While her friends try to cheer up Hélène, Papa looks almost as tired as Malou. Odile helps put the pillow for the rings on Malou while I hold her. Then we wait for the music and our cues.

I'm last before Hélène and Papa, and this time it all works perfectly. Not that I'm surprised.

Walking down the aisle with Cédric smiling at me, I feel like I'm attending my own funeral. I take my position next to Odile and look down the aisle, where I catch Gaspar watching me. He's crossed his arms and is rolling his eyes, making me chuckle.

I quickly reassume a neutral face when Papa leads Hélène down the aisle. She beams at Cédric, although it looks extremely fake after her previous outburst. And then it happens. Instead of focusing on her beloved fiancé, she looks over at the rest of us.

"Why aren't you smiling?"

"Because I'm tired?"

"What? You're nocturnal, too?"

I am, but that's not the point. "It's just the rehearsal."

"*Just* the rehearsal?" she shrieks.

"Hélène," Papa says in a strained voice. "Let's just get through this. Alix will be smiling at your wedding."

Tears fill her eyes. "No, she won't. She hates Cédric and she hates me. She'll do everything to ruin it for me."

If Malou wasn't a beloved living creature, I would've thrown her in Hélène's face by now. "I'm *trying*."

"No, you're not. You can't even *pretend* to be happy for me." Tears are streaming down her face, and her two friends are giving me dirty looks.

"I'm here. By your side. I woke up Malou for this and I've tried your way. I made peace with Cédric, despite..." I swallow, not wanting to get into this in front of his family and friends. "What more do you want from me?" As the Hanged Man pointed out, I've given and given, and it's never enough for her.

"I want you to be happy for me. Hélène still doesn't get it. "You used to be my best friend, and now you've all but cut me out of your life."

We're in deep trouble. I feel sorry for the town official and all the guests who have to listen to this. I'm about to swallow whatever she throws at me and bury my own feelings in the pit of my stomach, when Gaspar appears at my side.

"And you wonder why?" he addresses Hélène. "You've been treating her like shit all day. Never mind the last few months, when Alix could've really used her big sister. You never take her side, you never listen to her, and you're constantly berating her for things she has no control over. And yet she's here, trying to make this sham of a wedding work for you. And instead of being grateful she's able to put all these grievances behind her for you, you're being a grade-A bitch to her and everyone else."

Hélène gasps, her eyes wide with shock.

"You'll be lucky if she even shows up to your wedding after today."

"Hey!" Cédric steps in. "You can't talk to my future wife like that."

This must be the first time Cédric has shown a spine.

Gaspar's face promises murder as he turns on Cédric. "Don't even get me started, asshole. What you did to Alix is beyond despicable. I'm not buying your act. You almost got her *killed* just to get ahead. You used her, betrayed her trust, and never showed a shred of remorse." Before I can stop him, he spits on Cédric. "You and Hélène deserve each other. What you don't deserve is Alix's smile."

As mortified as I am by this public display, I'm also swooning hard.

"Get him out of here," Hélène says, seething, "or I swear he'll wish he was dead again."

"I'll show you dead." Gaspar's eyes blaze and he swings at my sister.

I barely manage to grab his arm without dropping Malou. Odile quickly takes her from me, so I can put all my weight into this. Papa and Cédric jump forward to shield Hélène, and for a moment, I'm afraid there'll be a fight right here on the steps of the altar.

But Gaspar restricts himself to a wicked glare and allows me to drag him out of the town hall. Hélène will probably throw another tantrum because I'm not available for the next run-through, but for all I care, she can carry the rings herself. I won't skip the wedding, but I'm more than done with this rehearsal.

Leaving the town hall, we run into none other than Charles Roubert. He sneers at me before nodding to Gaspar. "Ah, Monsieur du Charbonneau, is it?" he says with a disgusting smile. "Glad to see you alive and well after your fatal accident."

He knows. He knows about Gaspar.

"You." Gaspar lunges forward, and it takes all my strength to wrap my arms around his hips and try to hold him back.

Charles raises an eyebrow. "Boy, we've got quite the temper, don't we?"

"Just leave us alone," I plead as Gaspar struggles against my grip and growls.

Fortunately, Charles is in no mood for bloodshed and just snorts at me, "Keep your monster on a short leash." He walks into the town hall before I can even think of a response.

"Why didn't you let me kill him? Or at least remodel his face?" Gaspar rages, his burning gaze nearly scorching the door of the town hall.

As much as I love him for standing up to me, I can't let him loose on everyone that hurts me. "Please, just take me home. We'll go to the bar and get drunk and forget all this."

I trust Odile to take care of Malou for me because I really need a drink. Trying to appease my sister was more tiring than I thought.

The alternative to drinking is crying, which is the last thing I want to do. Not over her.

Gaspar grunts one last time before letting me lead him back to the hotel.

I manage to hold on to my anger to avoid tears until we're at the hotel bar. There, I let the alcohol take over as I rant about my sister, saying all the things I held in at the town hall.

"She's so self-centered and obsessed. It's like she has this perfect little plan in her head, and if even the slightest thing is out of place, it all falls apart. You know what? I know why she got the Five of Cups last night. She's practically setting herself up for disappointment."

"She's marrying Cédric, so that's a given," Gaspar comments, no less drunk. "Why did she have five cups yesterday?"

"The Five of Cups. It's a tarot card. And it basically said this wedding is doomed, but Marie made it sound nicer than that."

Gaspar lifts his tequila shot. "To Marie."

"To Marie." We put our glasses down and order a refill.

"Alix? Gaspar?" Sébastien enters the bar. It only takes one glance at us to ask, "How bad was the rehearsal?"

I snort, then giggle. "The worst. The absolute worst."

"Yeah. Hélène turned into Bridezilla and tore Alix a new one for not *smiling* at the right moment," Gaspar explains.

"Don't forget dragging Malou out in broad daylight, then throwing a tantrum because she wouldn't perform like a circus animal."

Sébastien looks at us as if we've both lost our minds. Instead of chastising us, he simply takes the seat on my other side and orders a tequila. "I had another fight with my father."

Immediately, I spin in my chair and grab his face while Gaspar steadies my hips to keep me from falling off. I scan Sébastien's face for injuries.

"I'm okay," he says with that soft broken smile of his I love so much. "He didn't touch me this time."

Relieved, I let him go. "Good, because Gaspar's in a killer mood."

"Alix wouldn't let me hit him," Gaspar complains. "I would've smeared his blood on the town hall steps. You know, laying a red carpet for Princess Hélène."

I make a face at the crude image. Fortunately, our glasses have been refilled and I can wash down the sour taste.

"Gaspar decided to be my knight in..." I look at him and can't help but laugh. "Not-so-shining armour. More like a dark knight."

He takes my hand and plants a kiss on it. "I'll be whatever you need me to be. Whether it's your knight or your monster."

I wrap my arms around him and kiss him as Sébastien takes a second shot. Right now, the memory of him defending me in front of my raging sister and her despicable fiancé is extremely hot. Sometimes you need a cute hedgehog boy, and sometimes you need a monster on your side.

Not that I really think he's a monster. A bit out of line and not a conflict resolution kind of guy, but nothing he said was wrong. In fact, he said everything I was too polite to. It was cathartic. Just like this kiss.

"I'd better go," says Sébastien.

Before he can leave, I grab his hand. "Stay."

"I don't want to come between you."

"You're with us," I explain. "We're in this shit together."

A flicker of surprise crosses his face, but he takes his seat again. I order more shots, knowing I'm setting myself up for a massive headache. But that's tomorrow. Tonight, I have to forget. Forget Hélène and Officer Cédric, Charles Roubert, and Nostradamus' stupid prophecy.

And I'll do it with my two favourite guys.

"I love you," I confess, the alcohol loosening my tongue.

"Who?" Gaspar asks, amused.

Spreading both hands, I tell them the obvious, "Both of you." I lean over to Gaspar and stare into his soft brown eyes. "I love you for always having my back, for your sense of adventure, and for your addictive smile."

The smile curls his lips, making my knees weak. He pulls me closer, and we kiss again. I almost slip out of my chair as I melt into him. He tastes like the tequila I've had way too much of already, and he makes me just as intoxicated.

I swivel back around and point at Sébastien. "And I love you for your steadfastness and loyalty. You make me feel safe. And your eyes." With a sigh, I lose myself in his ice-blue gaze.

Not as drunk as the two of us, Sébastien swallows. "Alix..."

My gaze falls on his lips and I find myself wondering if they taste of tequila too.

Suddenly I'm kissing him, too.

The last time our lips met, it was with adrenaline coursing through our veins. It was a kiss of desperation and pure elation at being alive. Now it's a slower, more lingering kiss, like a sensual exploration of each other. He's so gentle with me.

Gaspar wraps an arm around me and presses his body against my back. His hot breath blows over my neck just before his lips sear my skin, eliciting a soft moan straight into Sébastien's mouth, who shudders and presses his lips against mine. Caught between their kisses, I fall apart, only to be rebuilt stronger.

An extremely small voice in the back of my mind is appalled at what's happening, trying to tell me this is a really bad idea. I shut it out, because after what's happened today, I deserve this indulgence. I'm in love with Gaspar and I have feelings for Sébastien. It doesn't make any sense, and my sister will probably have a stroke, but man, it feels good.

Chapter 21

I wake up in Gaby and Marie's bed with a massive headache and no memory of how I got there.

"Good morning," Gaby whistles, "or should I say good day?"

Groggily, I rub my bleary eyes. "What... why am I in your bed?"

Gaby laughs and pats my hair. "Because you texted me you were going to elope with Gaspar, and when Marie and I ran home to stop you, you were trying to drag Sebastien into your room, with Gaspar already inside."

My eyes widen in shock. "Did I sleep with them?"

"No, you threw up on Sébastien's pants, and I decided it'd be better if you waited until you could enjoy that particular adventure." She giggles again, very amused.

Mortified, I pull up the blanket. My memories of last night are hazy. I clearly remember all the drama at the town hall, and that I started drinking with Gaspar. Sébastien joined us at some point, but I can't remember when I started kissing both of them. I did do that, didn't I?

"You should definitely embark on that adventure when you're sober, though," Marie exclaims, as amused as Gaby about my drunken shenanigans. "Gaspar was so hot yesterday when he came through for you. Chief boyfriend material. And Sébastien... well, he's always hot and looks at you like you're the sun, moon, and stars."

"I can't believe that half a year ago, I was trying to get you to date, and now you're in a full-blown ménage à trois," Gaby laughs.

"I'm not!" My cheeks are burning and my head is pounding. This is terrible. This is a disaster. Not a Tower disaster, but a disaster, nonetheless. I'm happy with Gaspar, and then I kissed Sébastien. In *front* of him.

"Does he hate me?" I ask in a whiny voice.

Gaby chuckles. "Which one?"

Oh, gosh, what if they both hate me? What if I've ruined this good thing I have with Gaspar? "My boyfriend."

"So, Gaspar's the boyfriend and Sébastien's the lover?" Gaby asks. When I look at her in pure horror, she laughs again. "Oh, ma puce! No one hates you. Well, maybe Hélène, but she doesn't count. Sébastien wasn't as drunk as you two, so he changed and took care of Gaspar. When we left, Gaspar asked if he wanted to continue alone."

"Gaspar and Sébastien?"

"I don't think Sébastien took him up on it. Like I said, you two were very drunk. Which, frankly, go you. After your sister's tantrum, I was ready to punch her myself." Gaby smiles at me. "You know what? I was wrong about Gaspar. He clearly loves you. I may not always agree with how he expresses it, but he's yours. They both are. And if he—or both—make you happy, I'm on board." She leans forward to hug me.

Marie hands me a glass filled with an indescribable liquid. "Here. I asked the kitchen to make this for you. There's also water and aspirin."

I start with the latter before braving the disgusting looking hangover remedy. It's just as bad as it looks, but I feel my headache diminish a bit afterwards.

After a shower and fresh clothes, I check my messages. Hélène wrote me a couple last night.

Hey. I tried your room, but you were asleep.

I'm sorry.

I know I've been a real bitch today. I'm just so nervous that something's gonna go wrong. It's silly, I know. I think the cards messed me up or something.

I shouldn't have lashed out at you. And Malou. Please tell her I'm sorry, too.

Anyway, call me when you're awake. XXX

I will do no such thing. As nice as it is for Hélène to apologise, there's no way I can face my sister with a huge headache.

All I type back is: *It's okay.*

Nothing is okay. It's not just the way she acted yesterday. I thought I could ignore everything else, but Gaspar's defence brought it all back. Hélène has been a terrible sister to me. And her fiancé is even worse. She was absolutely right. I'm not happy for her, and I doubt I'll ever be. I'm not going to fight it, and I'm not going to cause a huge scene by skipping my sister's wedding, but when the deed is done, I'm out of her life. If that means moving out and into Gaspar and Sébastien's apartment, then so be it. I'll bide my time until the Five of Cups rears its ugly head, and then we can revisit this decision. It's useless as long as she's so far up Cédric's ass.

By the afternoon, my headache has subsided enough that I almost feel human again. I slip out of Gaby and Marie's room, which they've graciously allowed me to stay in, and make my way to mine. Just as I'm about to swipe my card, the door opens and Sébastien steps out.

Stunned, I stare at him.

I kissed him last night, and according to Gaby, I even tried to convince him to sleep with me.

We're not together and I'm afraid I've ruined our friendship. He probably thinks I'm toying with his feelings or worse.

Gently, he closes the door behind him. "How are you feeling? Gaspar's still asleep."

"Terrible."

"Do you need an aspirin?"

Why's he so nice to me? "No, I've already had one. I just mean last night..."

Sébastien smiles. "Don't worry about it. We both had a shitty day and there was a lot of tequila involved." He laughs softly. "Look, I was going to head over to my maman's. Do you want to come along or do you want to get some more rest?"

"Some fresh air will probably be nice." I can't believe how easy he's making this for us. No drama, no awkwardness. It feels so mature. Just two adults who had a little too much to drink. Well, three adults. "Let me just get my jacket."

I enter my room and grab what I need, then plant a kiss on Gaspar's cheek. "Love you."

He doesn't even stir, and I try not to make any noise as I leave and join Sébastien and Dix outside.

Together, we ride to Marseille and enter the lab. Margot has given Sébastien and me a temporary access card so we can let ourselves in. We're just about to use it, when I hear voices coming from the lab.

"No way," Sébastien mutters, suddenly as pale as a sheet.

I stop to listen, and my eyes widen when I hear the same thing he does.

Margot has a visitor.

Charles Roubert.

CHAPTER 22

"Seventeen is just wrong," Margot exclaims. While her words fill me with hope, the tone of her voice is all wrong.

Sébastien and I sit outside the doors to avoid being seen through the small windows as we listen to his parents argue. He looks terribly pale, and his eyes are wide. I know he's questioning everything he thought he knew, and I reach out to squeeze his hand.

"What's wrong with seventeen?" Charles asks, annoyed.

"It's too young to create a mature whisper ghost and too old to be trauma-free."

Too old? I mouth at Sébastien. They're obviously talking about the day Charles turned him into a ghost whisperer, but instead of cursing him and threatening legal repercussions, his mother argues that the point of turning their son was suboptimal.

"I know you wanted him to be younger, but that would've been a waste of a whisper ghost. Not that Dix-Sept has proved particularly useful, but at least he's not a squalling toddler like that Dubois girl's."

Margot wanted Sébastien to be younger. She was in favour *of killing him.*

Tears run down my cheeks, and I have to stifle a gasp as Sébastien takes a shuddering breath. I hold onto his hand so tightly I might break a bone.

Dix isn't unaffected either. He stands in front of us, not bothering to hide, but his face is a stony mask.

"Don't knock her, she's probably the most competent ghost whisperer I've ever seen."

Yeah, me.

"Maybe," Charles admits to my surprise, "but her loyalties are all over the place. We didn't get to her early enough, and now she's nothing but a nuisance. There's no place for her in GoPol."

Margot scoffs. "Well, I've got a place for her here. Not everyone is cut out to be an agent. I kept telling you that, but you wouldn't listen."

"I did a good job with the boy. You wanted to turn him into a research project."

Sébastien squeezes his eyes shut. His jaw quivers. Apparently, his mother didn't leave because Charles drove her away, it was because they had *creative differences*.

I can't believe this is happening. Dix was so happy he'd found their mother, and our first meetings were great. She was lovely. Except she's not.

"Do you want to leave?" I whisper.

Sébastien opens his eyes. He stands as if he's eighty years old and his bones ache. He looks into Dix's eyes and nods. But instead of marching out of the building and never looking back, he turns, scans his card, and pushes the doors open. "Salut, Maman. Papa. Good to see you're still getting along."

I scramble up in shock, my heart racing at the thought of the confrontation. "What are you doing?"

"Ah, Sébastien and Alix," Margot greets us happily, as if she hadn't just defended the position of killing her son at a younger age. "You made it."

"You were expecting them and didn't warn me?" Charles asks. As usual, he glares at me.

"Warn you?" Margot snorts. "Are you scared to meet your son and his dear friend?" She winks at me. "Looks like you've made the great Charles Roubert tremble." She cocks her head. "No Gaspar today? I was hoping to run some tests."

As Charles snorts, my stomach turns. We never should've brought Gaspar here. Charles already knows his secrets, and if Margot doesn't, she's itching to find out.

It's too much. The betrayal, the casualness, the terrible implications. I don't know how Sébastien does it, but my knees are about to give out and I'm breathing too hard. Afraid of what will happen if I stay, I turn on my heels and all but run out of the building.

Sébastien calls after me, but I can't stop. As soon as I'm outside, I scream, unable to contain all the pain inside me. Two passers-by look at me strangely before continuing on their way.

I stumble into the parking lot and sink to the boardwalk before crying my heart out. How can two parents care so little for their only child? Was his birth an accident? Or worse, did they plan it, thinking of all the great ways they could shape him? His father wanted Sébastien to be the perfect GoPol agent, and his mother only saw his research potential. Did they split up because they couldn't agree on *when* to kill him?

I'm sick to my stomach. My thoughts are getting worse and worse, and suddenly I'm throwing up, emptying my stomach for the second time in twenty-four hours.

This is all so messed up.

"I never should've found her." Dix appears next to me, sitting on the boardwalk with his hands between his legs and a thousand-yard stare. His usual cheerful demeanour is gone. He looks as broken as Sébastien.

Urgent footsteps sound behind us. Relief washes over me when I see Sébastien coming towards us. "I'm sorry," he says before he's even reached us. "I'm sorry for having the worst parents in the world. I should've never brought you here."

"You're worried about *me*?" I ask him.

"She wants you," he says, his mouth a line of bitterness. "She doesn't really care about me, because I belong to my father now, and I can't offer her much."

Every word out of his mouth is like a dagger in my heart.

"But she desperately wants you to work for her. And she wants to study Gaspar. And..." He almost doubles over, panting heavily. "I'm sorry."

"Nah, it's my fault," Dix says sullenly. "You wouldn't even be here if it wasn't for me."

My heart goes out to him. I reach out and pull him close. At first, he tries to resist, like a teenage boy would, but then he clings to me as if there's no tomorrow. With one parent already an asshole, he'd pinned all his hopes on his mother, whom he didn't really know. She was supposed to be the good one. The loving one.

Sébastien looks down at us, a million emotions in his face. When he notices my gaze, he sniffs. "Want to get drunk again?"

I can't help but smile. "No, but I'm willing to sit there and take care of you while you get blindingly drunk."

Dix sniffles a little as he pulls back. "Too bad *I* can't get drunk."

I rub his elbow and nod toward the bike. "Let's go home."

The ride home is a silent one. It's not like you can talk much on a motorcycle anyway, but there's a stifling heaviness that not even the wind can carry away. I can't help thinking about how terrible it must be for Sébastien. How alone and abandoned he must feel.

Unloved by the two people who should love him more than life itself.

All I can do is hold him and remind him he's not alone.

CHAPTER 23

When we get back to the hotel, Gaspar's waiting for us. He is sitting on the bench by the entrance with a face like thunder. One look at me and he gets up, turns his back on us, and disappears into the hotel.

My heart sinks as I realise he's mad for some reason.

"Is it because of yesterday?" Sébastien asks.

While he'd quickly chalked it up to a drunken accident, Gaspar's awakening seems to have led to regrets. "I don't know."

I have to make a decision here. Sébastien needs me by his side as he begins to process the horrific truth of his upbringing. But Gaspar is clearly upset, too, and it's all because of my lapse in judgement.

"Go," Sébastien urges me.

"But I told you I'd look after you."

He snorts. "I'm a grown man. I can look after myself. Besides, I don't feel like drinking anyway."

"You don't?" They aren't even my parents and I feel like I need a drink.

"No, alcohol just numbs the pain until it comes back with a vengeance. I'd rather go for a run, get a bit of exercise."

So healthy and mature. I'm more of an ice cream and wine girl, but whatever works for him. "Well, let me know if there's anything I can do for you."

"Just go and take care of Gaspar."

It feels wrong to leave Sébastien alone after what's just happened, but my soul longs for Gaspar. I have to find out how much damage I've done. My heart grows heavy when I think of yesterday's kisses. I don't remember him protesting then, but my memory of last night is fuzzy at best. And according to Gaby, it's Sébastien I tried to drag into my room, not Gaspar.

I feel sick again when I carefully open the door to my room.

"Took you long enough." The words hit me like a train.

"Sorry. We've just been to see Sébastien's mother and found out she's also a psycho—"

"Do I look like I care?" Gaspar comes forward, not a trace of his characteristic smile on his face. There's only anger and pain. "It's always something with Sébastien. He cries out and you come running."

While I expected him to be angry about my wayward kisses yesterday, this is on a whole other level. "You're mad I'm being a good friend?" It's not like Sébastien has anyone else.

Gaspar sneers at me. "Are you a good friend or are you in love with him?"

Another train slams into me. My guilty conscience almost makes me throw up again. "I love you."

"That's not what you said yesterday."

The guilt washes over me and eats away at my resilience. Although I love Gaspar with all my heart, I can't deny that I'm attracted to Sébastien. It's as if we'd been through something terrible together. Or rather, we're still going through it and it's only getting worse.

Once again, Gaspar snorts. "If you really loved me, you wouldn't keep running away from me."

"What?"

"You're running from me. This was supposed to be a reset, some time off, so we could work on our relationship. Instead, you're running around playing matchmaker for ghosts and holding Sébastien's hand every time he wants to go see his maman."

"You don't know what you're talking about." I understand how it looks, but after today, Sébastien deserves all the hand-holding he needs. The strange thing is, the Gaspar I love would agree. "You came, too."

He rolls his eyes. "Because it's the only way I can see you."

"I thought you cared about him," I cry. It's all getting too much again, and my head feels like it's going to explode. "You can't be on board one day and hate it the next. This up and down is driving me crazy."

I cover my mouth, shocked to have said it. But it's true. One day, he's my sweet hedgehog boy, the next, he's a raging asshole.

"Oh, is it now?" Gaspar glares at me and raises his voice, "Am I *inconveniencing* you? I'm sorry I made things difficult by clawing my way back to life for you."

Stunned by his hostility, I take a step back. "That's not what I said."

"Do you know what it's like to be resurrected?" Spittle hits my face. "What it's like to be trapped in a body that's being rebuilt from the ground up? To have your bones exposed to the harsh air, then suffocated by flesh? Mending them is as painful as breaking them in the first place. Only you're dead. You can't faint or slip away. No, you have to hold onto the pain or it won't work. You have to remember it, breathe it in, and make it your own, so that your body keeps growing back to what it was before."

He's right in my face as he paints this horrible picture. It's so much worse than I'd thought. Things are always so much worse. I desperately try to hold the pieces together, but disaster keeps following me.

"And then, before the skin grows, you're raw. You're a lump of exposed flesh and a conscience," Gaspar spits. "You want to run away, but it's too late. You're tied to it now. And you think you'll just have to get over it, but it drags on for hours and hours until it turns into days. Have you ever felt on fire for a whole week?"

I taste the bitter bile in my mouth. There's nothing left in my stomach. "Please, stop."

His eyes are wide with madness. "It doesn't stop. That's the problem. It just goes on and on. Day and night." Suddenly he slams his hands against the door, making me jump. His arms cage my head, offering no escape from his wrath. "I went to hell for you. So, excuse me if I'm a bit pissed when I find out you've moved on to someone new."

Tears are streaming down my face and my whole body is shaking from the physicality of this fight. I've never had anyone yell at me like this. "I didn't move on. It was a fake relationship."

"Nothing about that kiss in the catacombs was fake," Gaspar shouts in my face, making me squint. "Or the kisses yesterday."

"I'm sorry!" I cry. "I was drunk, I didn't know what I was doing." Desperately, I cradle his face. "You're the only one I want, Gaspar."

When I try to kiss him, he jerks his head away. "Actions speak louder than words, Alix."

His words, however, are completely pulverising me.

"I'm sorry," I whisper, not knowing what else to say.

All in all, he's right. I'm the absolute worst. While I was pretending to go out with Sébastien, I grew fond of him and developed feelings. I'd thought I'd lost Gaspar and was slowly coming to terms with it. But as soon as I saw him again, all those feelings for him came back. It turned out they were just locked away where they wouldn't hurt me with every breath I took without him.

"Please," I try again, wanting nothing more than to fix this. "If you want me to stay away from Sébastien…"

Just saying the words feels like a betrayal. Sébastien needs me now. Can I really turn my back on him, like his parents did, just to save what I had with Gaspar? It's not even a question of who I love or don't love. A friend needs me. And maybe that makes me a shitty girlfriend, but the old Gaspar would've understood. On *his good days*, the new Gaspar also understands.

There is bitterness and guilt in these thoughts. I know it's impossible to go back to the way things were, but these glimpses of his old self keep me hooked. The constant changing of his tune, however, messes with my head. Loving him hurts, and yet I can't imagine doing anything else.

"If this is about last night, I promise you it won't happen again. Sébastien and I are just friends, but he needs me right now—" I begin slowly, trying to find a compromise.

"I need you, too!" Gaspar shouts, spittle flying again.

The abrupt change makes me jump and miss a heartbeat.

"I came back for you, Alix! I went through hell for you! I'm here for you. No one else. Just you, you, you!"

My heart is racing too much for my mouth to form words. I know I should say something, but my mind is filled with guilt, regret, and self-hatred.

Disgusted by my silence, Gaspar pushes away from the door and huffs. After a brief moment, he glares at me. "Get out of the way."

"What?" I squeak.

Instead of explaining, he grabs my arm and yanks me into the middle of the room. Then he throws the door open. "Don't wait for me."

"Where are you going?" I scream, terrified to my bones.

But Gaspar doesn't regale me with an answer. He's out the door in seconds, slamming it shut with such force I feel the shock from head to toe.

Is this the disaster that will befall me? Have I betrayed Gaspar? Has he realised his great sacrifice was for nothing?

My stomach turns, but there's nothing in it to make me vomit. Instead, my head spins and darkness invades my vision. I hear my own breathing, unnaturally loud. Stumbling, I try to follow him, needing him more than anything, but the floor tilts beneath me and my knees give way. I brace myself for the impact when someone catches me.

Gaspar!

But it's not him. The distorted voice at my ear is more sullen than angry. "He's an idiot."

"Dix?"

We sink to the floor, where he holds me, just as I held him an hour ago. I wish he had a heartbeat I could measure my breathing against, but just having his arms around me helps me through the wave of nausea.

When it passes, the tears flow. "Gaspar…"

"Is an idiot," Dix repeats.

Sighing, I lay my head on his chest. "How much did you hear?"

"More than enough to know Gaspar's full of bullshit."

I snort. "No, he's not. I let him down. I didn't appreciate what he did for me, and I was always distracted. And now he's gone. It's all my fault. I'm the worst."

Dix shakes his head angrily and glares at me. "Oh, please. If anyone's been to hell and back, it's you. No one's coming after *him*. So he died? Boohoo, poor baby. Accidents happen all the time. Every day, there are thousands of new ghosts. But you know what they don't have? A caring ghost whisperer, who treats them as if they're still alive. Who respects their wishes and their dreams. Doesn't he know how lucky he is to have you by his side? Someone as kind and caring as you to make the transition to the afterlife a piece of cake?" He huffs again. "He was afterliving the dream. He even got himself a living girlfriend. I've never had a single girlfriend—or boyfriend."

"Dix…"

"I don't care. It is what it is. I'm just saying how lucky he is. You didn't ask him to come back to life. You were happy with him being a ghost."

And it fills me with guilty dread when I remember how much *happier* I was when he was just a ghost.

"Instead of staying and helping you fight GoPol, he goes off and gets himself resurrected. And now he wants to blame you?"

"He did it because he thought he'd lose me."

"But he wouldn't have," Dix exclaims loudly. "If he'd just stuck around long enough to see what was really going to happen, he wouldn't have had to throw a tantrum now."

I refuse to accept the easy way out. Gaspar isn't in the wrong. I am. "What he did was good, Dix. He did it for me. *For us.* I should've appreciated it more. He went through so much to be with me, and I took him for granted. Instead of listening to him and helping him adjust, I've been running all over Provence since I got here. There's so much else going on, I forgot he needed me, too."

"Everyone needs you," Dix insists. "And maybe I'm just a kid, but I can see how it's tearing you apart. You didn't ignore Gaspar. You were there for him. You've made sure he has a roof over his head, and you've made him feel included. But your heart is bigger than that. It cares for more than one person. More than just the living. And that's what makes you so bloody awesome. Seeing you help others should make him love you even more. You've done nothing wrong."

Biting my lip, I say, "I kissed Sébastien. Twice now."

"Oh, it was a lot more than once yesterday." Dix shudders. "This will be the only time I talk about it. To you or Séb! But from what I saw—and I certainly didn't sign up for this when I did—Gaspar had no complaints last night." He pulls a face but manages to carry on. "I wasn't there when you kissed Séb the first time. It probably wasn't what Gaspar had in mind when he decided to resurrect himself for you—I'll give him that—but last night? He was absolutely into it."

"Gaspar was drunk."

"And so were you. So, he gets a pass but you don't?" Dix rolls his eyes. "I didn't die so young I don't know what it's like to get drunk."

The stark reminder of Dix's death pulls me out of my own misery and refocuses me on him. "About your death... I'm so sorry about what happened today."

Dix groans and throws his head back. "It's alright."

"No, it's not." I shift in his embrace so I can kneel and look into his face, searching for the telltale signs of how much this has really hurt him. "You were hoping your maman was different. That she was a poor woman who fled when she could, too weak to save you."

Sullenly, he looks at me. "Sometimes, I thought he'd killed her. That she'd never left, that she was dead. That was bullshit, of

course. If she were dead, we'd have found her as a ghost. Instead..."
His voice breaks and his gaze loses focus.

I wrap my arms around his head and pull him against my chest.
"It's okay to cry."

"No, no, it's not," he protests. "Men don't cry." But his hands
are clawing at my back, holding me as if he'll never let go.

"Yes, they do," I say softly. "They do it all the time and there's
nothing wrong with it. It's okay, Dix. It's okay to feel this much."

"But I'm dead." His muffled voice breaks my heart. "I have no
more feelings."

Just for that lie, I want to burn down GoPol and raze it to the
ground.

"Rubbish. You lost your life, not your soul."

Dix looks up and blinks. He's clearly hanging on my every word
now.

"You're still you, Dix," I say, as gently as I can. "With all the
feelings, the pain, the memories, the hopes and the dreams. None
of that died with you. And no one... Do you hear me? No one, not
even your stupid parents, can take that away from you."

He buries his face in my shoulder again. His arms crush me, his
fingers digging into my back as his shoulders heave when he finally
cries.

My body aches and my shirt is soaked with tears that aren't
real, but my discomfort is nothing. It means nothing if there's

the slightest chance I can heal some of this hurt in this eternally seventeen-year-old boy.

Chapter 24

Gaspar truly hasn't been back all night. I wish he was still a ghost so I could summon him. Instead, I cried into my pillow until the early hours of the morning, blaming myself too much to find comfort in anyone else.

Now, in the morning, my eyes are bleary, and my heart is heavy. Gaspar's unmade bed makes me cry again. For a moment, I contemplate staying in bed and hoping the world will forget me. Instead, I drag myself up, take a shower and get dressed.

Despite the object of our quarrel, I have a promise to keep. I love him, but I won't let everyone down. His struggle with Sébastien I get, but the ghosts are innocent. I can't disappoint Zola, just because my boyfriend has suddenly decided he wants me all to himself.

To my surprise, Sébastien and Odile are waiting for me at the car.

"What's this?" I ask, fearing the next big disaster.

"Dix told me you shouldn't be alone today," says Sébastien, with a smile that belies the horrors of yesterday.

"And I met Sébastien at breakfast," Odile says cheerfully. "We chatted a bit about ghosts and what you're currently working on. So, I decided to come along." She opens the car door and points at me. "And don't try to talk me out of it. You owe me a good ghost story."

Confused, I get behind the wheel. "Why do I owe you?"

"Because you lied to me, and because I looked after Malou for you the last two nights."

"You love looking after Malou. You steal her every time I'm not looking."

"Not true."

Sébastien chuckles in the back seat.

Odile's eyes widen. "Oh, sorry, did you want to sit up front?"

"I'm good," he tells her, despite having to fold his long legs behind me.

I watch him in the rearview mirror and can't help but notice how relaxed he looks. Maybe exercise really does do the trick. Or maybe it's Odile. Just this little exchange has lifted my spirits already.

She makes herself comfortable in the front, which she so rarely gets to occupy, and connects her phone to the car so we can all listen to her musical hits. "So, what's on our to-do list?" she asks interrupting her sing-along.

"First we have to find a supermarket and buy some apples."

"Apples?" Odile interrupts her singing. "Is that important or are you just hungry?"

Now that she's mentioned it, my stomach growls, reminding me I haven't eaten dinner or breakfast, and threw up everything I ate before. "That's the most important thing. Ideally, we can also find a basket."

Odile stares at me as if I've told her we're going cancan dancing. "She's gone mad, hasn't she?" she asks Sébastien.

I catch his grin in the rearview mirror. "I get it."

"You do?" I ask in surprise.

"Do you want me to tell her or wait until she sees it for herself?"

"Hey, we can't all see ghosts here." Her voice may be a bit snippy, but I see the light in her eyes. She wants the gossip. "Alix never tells me anything, so you have to."

I concentrate on driving while Sébastien tells her about Zola's apples. I'm impressed he remembers the little detail and understands its importance. Perhaps we'll make a good ghost whisperer out of him, after all.

An hour later, the three of us pull up at Cézanne's atelier. The supermarket was a success, and we got a medium-sized basket, which I filled with small red apples, the kind Zola might've had access to nearly two hundred years ago.

"It's pretty," Odile exclaims when she sees the house, "but closed."

"We just have to go in the garden."

Sébastien hands me the apples and I lead the way to the back of the house.

As before, I find Cézanne painting again. This time, he notices me immediately. "What now?" he grumbles.

I notice Sébastien is explaining what he sees and hears to Odile in a hushed whisper. Ignoring them, I raise my basket. "I come in peace. With a gift from Émile."

At first, Cézanne stares stubbornly ahead, but the redness of the apples catches his eye anyway. I see the moment he realises what I'm holding in my hand. To my relief, his face immediately softens.

"A basket of apples," he says, a soft smile transforming his grim face. "Oh, Émile."

Zola doesn't know about my apple plan, since he can't be trusted not to spoil everything before I've had a chance to break down Cézanne's walls a little. "He misses you."

Cézanne sighs and his canvas vanishes. "I miss him, too. More than life itself." He shakes his head in dismay. "Do you know the worst?"

"No."

"I let my pride come between me and my best friend. With one letter, I destroyed decades of love and friendship. I was so embarrassed and afraid of what he'd really thought of me that I cut all ties. And then he died. He died before I could…" Cézanne's voice falters. "He died before I could put things right. Before I could forgive him and tell him why it mattered so much to me. And he was so young, too. Only sixty-two. He still had so much to give. They said he was assassinated."

"There's a good chance of that," I admit. The reason Zola is in the Panthéon is, like Victor Hugo, he was not only one of the greatest writers but also a political activist, famous for his public defence of Alfred Dreyfus. The Jewish artillery officer was framed for passing on military secrets to the Germans. It was the scandal of its time, with huge implications of racism and corruption. Zola was instrumental in getting Dreyfus reinstated, but he made some enemies in the process.

It's not proven, but the prevailing theory is someone bribed the chimney sweep to block Zola's chimney, and he died of carbon monoxide poisoning.

It's all very sad, but I doubt the details matter much anymore. They certainly didn't matter to Cézanne, who was never interested in the rest of society. Or as he once famously said: "I don't understand the world, and the world doesn't understand me."

"When I heard…" He's still struggling to speak. "When I heard he'd died before I could put things right… We never have as much time as we think we do."

He closes his eyes for a moment, working through the emotions that seem to be building in him. I would hug him if I didn't know that, historically, he hates being touched. Especially by women.

"My whole world broke down," Cézanne finally admits. "And it was all my fault. I'd let him get away. I couldn't hold him. I never could." The pain in his eyes tugs at my heartstrings. He'd tried so hard to follow Zola as he'd soared, but life in Paris had never been for him. "He died thinking I hated him, and I'll never forgive myself for that."

He's about to turn and flee where I can't follow, but I feel we're on the right track at last. The walls are finally down, and I can't let him put them up again. "He's still here. You can tell him how much he means to you, how much you want him here. You *do* want him here, don't you?"

Cézanne pauses, his back still to me. "He doesn't want to be here."

Instead of arguing, I ask. "But you do?"

He turns, pure despair in his eyes. "Yes."

I open my mouth when I catch a flicker in the corner of my eye and smile. It's time for me to take a step back.

Zola has arrived.

Chapter 25

"Paul."

"Émile."

The two men size each other up. A million emotions pass between them without a single word being spoken. This is different from when they met at the school. Instead of trying to explain their pain, they just let each other feel.

"What's going on?" asks Odile impatiently.

Like me, Sébastien is enthralled by the ghosts.

Finally, Zola breaks down. "I'm so sorry."

"So am I."

And that's all it takes to put aside a quarrel that's lasted centuries but meant so little in the grand context of their love. One more look, a huge sigh, and then the two are in each other's arms, telling each other everything that has happened since.

Next to me, Sébastien lets out a breath he must've been holding. Maybe I shouldn't be surprised he's moved by the display of genuine affection, but it's so rare for him to show any real emotion, I can't help but marvel.

Since he seems to struggle to form words, I put my arm around Odile and begin to lead her away, giving Zola and Cézanne all the time they need to catch up. "They've reconciled and are hugging it out."

"So, are they a couple?" Odile asks. She's probably never really learnt much about either ghost.

"They're much more than that," I answer with a smile. "They're soul mates. Bonded beyond life and death."

Odile pulls a face. "Look at you, getting all sappy."

"There's nothing wrong with being sappy." Sébastien joins us, his voice a little hoarse. "I'd prefer the world to be a little sappier than... what it is."

Sounds like Sébastien has something on Dix in that regard. Not that I've ever seen him cry, either.

"Ugh, don't you dare get sappy with Alix now. It's bad enough one sister is getting married. I don't need the other running off with a guy—or two."

Although I could've done without her addition, I put my arms around Odile, much to her disgust. "You'd better believe I'll never turn my back on you again, whether I get married or not."

"Too sappy!" Odile shouts to the sky, but she clasps my arms and smiles.

Sébastien laughs. "Honestly, what you just did was amazing."

"All I did was bring Cézanne a basket of apples." I wonder what the caretakers will think of this little gift when they find it in the garden tomorrow.

"No, you did much more than that. You healed them." He smiles, then turns around to throw another look back at the two ghosts.

As Odile and I get into the car, my sister leans over and nods at Sébastien. "Don't take this the wrong way, but I like him a lot better than Gaspar."

Odile's comment stays in my head the whole drive back. It's not that I'm contemplating ditching my boyfriend for Sébastien now—I might have feelings for the GoPol agent, but they're confusing at best, because I still love Gaspar. What I can't ignore, though, is how little anyone else likes him now that they've actually met him. Sure, Gaby says she's on board, but when I eventually tell her about our fight yesterday, she'll be back on the Gaspar hate train in no time.

And therein lies the problem. I needed my best friend last night, and yet I didn't go to her for fear of having to hear her rant about

Gaspar. I simply can't think of a way to talk to her about my struggles without making him sound like a total asshole. And maybe that's because he *is* a bit of an asshole. And that's a thought that scares the shit out of me, because it makes no sense. The boy I fell in love with wasn't an asshole.

"Are you okay?" Odile asks as we park the car in front of the hotel.

Startled, I look at her. "What?"

"You haven't said a word since we left Aix."

"Sorry, I tuned out. I didn't get much sleep last night."

Odile makes a show of holding on to her seat. "And you're telling me this now?"

"And here I thought I heard you complain about not being able to see ghosts. Well, you're home now, alive and well," I joke. "Thanks for coming today."

Checking in the rearview mirror, I catch Sébastien looking at me thoughtfully. I have no idea how much Dix told him or if he kept it vague. He clearly has thoughts, but as usual, he doesn't push me. Something I appreciate very much.

"So, what do we do now?" Odile says as we get out of the car. "There's still so much day left."

"Well, I'm going to take a nap, but maybe Gaby has some plans."

"Oh yeah, I've always wanted to be the third wheel," Odile mutters.

Not finding it in me to entertain her right now, I give her a non-committal shrug and make my way to my room. Maybe Sébastien can keep her company, since she likes him so much.

The truth is, I like him, too. I just can't let these feelings develop into anything more. Not when I already have Gaspar. *If* I still have Gaspar.

To my surprise, I find him sitting on the floor of our room with a sleeping Malou on his arm. He lifts his head when I open the door and looks at me with his big brown eyes, as if he's afraid of me. He even has to swallow.

Unsure of what to make of his return, I close the door and lean against it. "You're back." The words are almost too soft to traverse the suddenly massive distance between us.

Gaspar squeezes his eyes shut, as if I hit him. When he opens them again, his face is full of misery. "I'm so sorry, Alix. I don't know what got into me last night."

His voice is so thick with regret I want to forgive him immediately, but I can't get Odile's words out of my head. "You got jealous, I guess." And whose fault is that? "Look, about Sébastien..." I pause, waiting for his reaction. It's more instinct than calculation

But instead of flying off the handle, Gaspar hangs his head. "I'd totally understand if you'd rather be with him. You know, I always said you deserve someone like Sébastien. And after last night... I don't think I can say the same for me."

This is so different from yesterday's tune my curiosity gets the better of me. I push away from the door and make my way over. "You think I don't deserve you?" Unable to bear his rejection, I sit on the bed near him instead of joining him and Malou on the floor.

Gaspar's eyes widen. "It's the other way around. I don't deserve *you*. The things I said yesterday… I can't even believe they came out of my mouth, you know. I'm not jealous of Sébastien. Well, maybe a little bit, because he's alive and doesn't have a million problems like me."

I can't help but laugh. "Are you sure we're talking about the same guy? He's got a truckload of problems." My heart aches as I remember the disappointment that was Sebastien's mother.

"True, but when it comes to being with you, he's a socially acceptable choice. I thought that would change if I were alive, but I'm just as dead as before."

"We *are* going to sort this out." Whatever happens between us, I won't abandon Gaspar.

"Maybe." He lowers his head to take a deep breath before looking up at me again. "I'm afraid I'm losing you," he whispers.

My heart goes out to him. All the doubts I had on the drive back are blown away as he opens his heart to me, and I drop from the bed to my knees before him. "You're not going to lose me. Look, I know I haven't paid as much attention to you as I should have. So many other things were happening that I took you for granted."

"Just like you should have," Gaspar says vehemently. "I want to be your rock. I want you to be able to lean on me as you deal with all the craziness in your life. Instead, I've added to it and chipped away at your foundation." He leans over to put Malou back in her cage, then drops to his knees to mirror my pose and cradle my face.

When I flinch at his first touch, his face falls. "I'm so sorry, Alix. Please, I wasn't in my right mind. I don't know what came over me. I never meant to hurt you."

"I didn't mean to hurt you, either."

We look into each other's eyes, and I see him asking for permission. When I give him the slightest nod, Gaspar leans over and kisses me softly on the lips. Like Zola and Cézanne, so much more passes between us when we don't speak. There's a lot of love between us. We may have only known each other for a short time, but we've been through hell together I don't know what I am without him. He risked it all to be with me.

The memory of what he's endured makes me break the kiss. Guilt gnaws at me that he had to suffer for my sake. With a hand on his cheek, I tell him, "You should've told me about the resurrection."

"Beforehand?" Gaspar asks. "I wasn't sure if it would work, and I didn't want you to worry if it didn't. You know, if I just ceased to exist."

"You think I wouldn't have been worried if that had happened either way?"

"Not if GoPol had taken away your powers. Then it wouldn't have mattered."

My heart aches for him, but it wasn't the before I meant. Shaking my head, I clarify, "What I meant is afterwards. The whole process... you should've told me about all that. You shouldn't have had to keep it all to yourself."

"You didn't want the details and I wanted to keep them from you," Gaspar insists. "You weren't supposed to know how horrible it was, because I knew you'd feel bad about it. And then I went and made sure you suffered for it."

He moves his thumb to wipe a tear from my cheek. I didn't even know I was crying. "I'm so sorry, Alix. You're everything to me, and I'd do it again and again for you. If there's even the slightest chance that you still love me—"

I press my lips back against his with an urgency that sets my heart racing. I need him. In whatever shape or form, I need my hedgehog boy like I need air to breathe.

Suddenly we can't be close enough. One hand on the back of my head, the other in the small of my back, he pulls me to him. His body crashes against mine like the waves on the cliffs, and like the waves, his love for me eats away at the wall of doubt I've built around myself.

My hands roam over his body, fingers sinking into his soft curly hair or digging into his hoodie. Then they're under his clothes, brushing skin that's hot to the touch—not a ghost, but a living breathing boyfriend.

"I love you," I say, gasping for breath. "I could never *not* love you. I—"

Gaspar steals my words and my breath with another passionate kiss. Then he lifts me up and lays me on the bed before kissing my neck. "I love you, too."

Panting, I throw my head back and wrap my legs around his, holding him close. When he was just a ghost, this would've been impossible. But he's not dead anymore. And neither am I. I've never felt more alive than in this moment, so full of pain and fear, but also longing and love.

Living hurts. But it's the best kind of pain, the kind I can never get enough of. Just like I can never get enough of him.

My sweet, sweet hedgehog boy.

CHAPTER 26

Yesterday was magical. First, I got to witness Zola and Cézanne reunite and find peace and happiness after such a long time, and then Gaspar and I made up and came together for the first time. I didn't get much sleep during the day, but I slept really well in Gaspar's arms at night, and I feel like we're finally back on track.

I'm in full bliss mode during breakfast, which takes Gaspar and me over an hour to finish because we can't keep our hands off each other. We have one day left until the wedding and I know exactly how I want to spend it.

Giggling, I pull Gaspar up and drag him with me through the foyer. As we wait for the elevator, Gaspar leans over and kisses my neck.

The elevator pings and he reluctantly pulls back a little. My good mood is shattered when Charles Roubert steps out of the elevator.

To my surprise, Sébastien is leaning against the wall behind him, looking as if something has died inside him.

"Ah, if it isn't the freelance ghost whisperer and her zombie boyfriend." Charles gives me a toothy grin. "I can't wait to see what they do to him when this story breaks."

"Papa," Sébastien says in a warning tone.

Charles snorts before pointing at Gaspar. "This is what she'd rather make out with. Too bad you already threw your career away for her."

Gaspar sticks two fingers in his mouth and makes a few dry-retching noises behind Charles' back as he leaves.

Concerned, I check on Sébastien as he steps out of the elevator. "What did he mean?"

"Don't worry about it."

"Séb..." I don't want him to keep it all inside and bottle it up. If he's going to suffer consequences for my actions, I want to know.

Gaspar looks back and forth between us. "Hey, why don't you two get out of here and talk while I hold down the fort?"

Just two days ago we'd had a huge fight because I was spending too much time with Sébastien. Now he's okay with it? I have that whiplash feeling again. Hopefully it's just his way of making up for what he said, but I can't help but wonder if I trust him. What if he changes his mind tomorrow? "Are you sure about this?"

"If you two already had plans—"

"You want to talk to Alix?" Gaspar asks him. "Because you look like you desperately need someone to talk to."

Sébastien blushes slightly. "Only if you don't mind."

Gaspar pulls me to him and gives me a quick peck on the cheek. "Everyone deserves a little Alix in their life. Besides, I have to do something."

That only makes me worry more. "What is it?"

"You'll see after the wedding." He lets go of me and pushes the elevator button. "Have fun, you two."

I look at Sébastien, wondering if he knows what this is about, and he shrugs. "Do you want to go for a walk, perhaps?"

"Anywhere where the chance of running into your father is practically zero."

He cracks a smile. "I know just the place."

Sébastien takes me out into the countryside. Away from the hustle and bustle of the cities, we take a long walk along the Arc River. It doesn't take long for the serenity of the surroundings to relax my shoulders. The leaves rustle in the wind or when a bird takes flight. The paths are covered in dappled sunlight, which isn't quite strong enough to lose our jackets. The play of light and shadow continues on the river next to us, the murmur of water a constant companion. For the first ten minutes, we just walk and soak in the tranquility.

But that's not why we're here.

"So, what did he mean about your career?"

Sébastien shrugs, as if he doesn't really care. "You know I'm on probation, right?

"Yes?"

"Well, he offered me an out."

"An out?" That doesn't sound like Charles.

Sébastien nods. "Apparently he and my mother had a long talk and made up or something."

"Ugh."

That gets a small smile from him. "When we were there, she showed us the nice things she's working on. She told my father about the other stuff."

A stone settles in my stomach, and I'm reminded of how interested Margot was in Gaspar. And now Charles makes a threat in the same vein. "What other stuff?" I force myself to ask.

"He wouldn't tell me any details since I can't be trusted, but remember how he scheduled me for a second whisper ghost creation?"

"You're not going to let him do that again, are you?"

The fact that Sébastien doesn't openly protest makes my anxiety rise. Not even the beautiful river scenery can distract me.

"He made me an offer." Sébastien takes a deep breath. "My mother's been advancing the creation of whisper ghosts in the last twenty years. She's made great progress—"

"Meaning she's killed how many?"

That question earns me a pained look. "Not a detail he divulged."

I feel like I'm in a horror movie. "So, what's the plan?"

"Apparently, she's made it to the point where she *doesn't* have to kill someone to create a whisper ghost." Another troubled breath. "The reason my father is so excited is, if it works, it will provide him with an unlimited resource."

The thought sends a shiver down my spine that not even the sun can dispel. "Do you want unlimited whisper ghosts?"

"Hell, no. Having Dix is bad enough."

"You love Dix."

"Well, here's the thing. He'd let me keep Dix if I do this for him."

I remember now that GoPol had scheduled Dix's destruction for helping me. Apparently, Margot told Charles more than just about her experiments.

"This process doesn't just create whisper ghosts, but it creates them independently from you. They wouldn't be like Dix. They'd be..." He struggles with the words, which tells me this is going to be bad. "They wouldn't be attached to me, they'd be freely distributed to other people. Like my father and other more... worthy prospects."

My head is spinning as it tries to grasp the concept. "Wait a minute. So, he's going to let you leave GoPol if you provide him with a certain number of whisper ghosts, pieces of you he gets to distribute freely?" It sounds fantastical. Fantastical and frightening.

Instead of having to hire among those who've had near-death experiences, GoPol could train up their own super-soldiers, then give them a whisper ghost who they don't give a shit about because they mean nothing to them. Is it more ethical than killing people? Not really. Not when the whole thing hinges on slicing up Sébastien's soul.

"Why doesn't he do it himself?" I ask angrily. "If he's so keen to try this, he should create his own whisper ghosts. Wouldn't they all be more pliable anyway?" Despite my suggestion, the thought of endless C-Trentes makes my heart race.

Sébastien must be thinking the same thing, because he shudders. "He wants mine because they're younger and fitter."

And that's why he made his first creation when Sébastien was seventeen. He put his son through training after training, molding and shaping him until he was the perfect little soldier. And then he killed him in his prime. Not a screaming toddler like mine, or an older, less pliable ghost. Now, he sees Sébastien as a lost cause, but he won't let his resource go, not after all the time he's wasted raising and training him.

"How many ghosts does he want of you?"

"Well, starting with one. If it works… a dozen."

"A dozen?" I shout so loudly I disturb a pair of birds in the branches above him. "You told him no, of course, didn't you?"

Sébastien stops and turns to me with a heavy sigh. "I said I'd think about it."

"What? Think about what? Why would you do such a thing?" My breaths come hard and fast as my fear for him surges.

"Because he'd let me go."

"Your father will never let you go."

And that's the truth. If this scheme works, Charles won't stop until he's wrung every last bit of his son.

Time seems to stand still. The river keeps flowing, the leaves keep rustling, and the birds keep singing, but the two of us are frozen, gazes locked, holding our breath. After all we've been through and all we've uncovered, I can't believe Sébastien is seriously considering this.

After a moment, he inhales sharply. "It's either that or…" He looks to the side.

"Or what?" I know he wouldn't be stupid enough to trust his father's word. I'm missing a piece of the puzzle. A piece he desperately wants to keep for me. Dread fills me. "He's going to eliminate me."

"Nothing as crude as that, but you can bet he's threatened to ruin you and your whole family, starting with taking Gaspar away from you."

I can't help the tears shooting into my eyes. They're fuelled by anger and impotence. It feels like Charles has all the power and I have none. And to take Gaspar away from me so he can give him to Margot to cut up and study? I can't breathe.

Sébastien takes a step forward and wraps me in his arms just as my knees are about to buckle. "I won't let that happen."

"By letting him kill you a dozen times over!" I slam my hands into his chest and push him away, stumbling back. "You won't survive this."

"I told you, it's a new process. No killing."

My lips curl into an insane smile. It's all horribly clear to me now. Nostradamus' prophecy... I'm not going to lose Gaspar. It's Sébastien who will take the proverbial bullet for me.

As soon as the thought takes hold, the words rush out of me. I tell him about my day in Salon-de-Provence, about how I found out it was Nostradamus who'd given me the prophecy, and how he'd given me a second, much more terrible one. "It's going to be you! I'm going to lose you."

"Alix..." he reaches out, cautious, as if I were a wild animal.

"No, no, you don't understand. Someone's going to die. That someone is you. You're going to *die*." The dam breaks and tears are streaming down my face.

Slowly, Sébastien closes the distance. When I don't flee, he pulls me back into an embrace. For a few precious moments, he does nothing but hold me close, stroking my hair and making soothing sounds.

"It's going to be okay," he whispers.

"How?" My body aches just thinking about tomorrow.

"There are no such things as prophecies. I'm sure you met the real Nostradamus, but he's not and never was a seer who could accurately predict the future. That's all in people's heads. Besides, I wasn't planning on doing this tomorrow. We have a wedding to get through, don't we?"

He sounds so reasonable and calm, I almost believe him. "So, Nostradamus got the date wrong, big deal. You still thinking about it?"

His silence says it all.

"What about taking down GoPol? We had a plan."

"A plan that relied on my mother incriminating him," Sébastien points out bitterly. "She's not on our side."

And she's hurt him. We haven't had a chance to talk about it, and now it's messed with his brain and reopened every wound he'd thought closed long ago. "You don't think we can do it without her?"

He sighed heavily. "I think *you* can do anything. But you need time. My father is after you now. I won't allow it."

"Shouldn't that be my decision?" I ask petulantly.

Sébastien winces, and for the first time his cool, calm demeanour cracks. "Do you really think I could stand by and let something happen to you?"

"So, you'd rather risk death or mutilation?"

"I would risk everything for you."

Stunned, I look up at him, straight into his ice-blue eyes. The cold, mature mask is gone, and he looks at me with such fear my knees almost buckle again.

"I love you, Alix. I know I shouldn't, but I do. Before I met you, I had no one. Nobody but Dix. And I accepted that. I wasn't sad or angry or anything, I just was. I had a purpose, and that purpose was all there was to me. You pulled me out of that stupor. You made me see the world with new eyes. See *myself* with new eyes. With you, I'm wondering what else could be out there for me."

"Then why throw it all away?" I ask, my heart splitting in two. One half belongs to him, the other is Gaspar's. My mouth longs to say the words back, but my head keeps it together. If only just.

He shrugs, helpless. "I don't see it as throwing anything away. I see it as giving you a chance. Maybe us." I can almost hear the question in that last statement.

It tears me apart to say what I have to say. "Sébastien." To soften the words, I place a hand on his cheeks. "I... I like you a lot. And you have my word that I will always fight for you. I want so much for you. I want you to live a full life, to find love, and to heal."

Struggling to continue, I wet my lips. I can already see the pain in his clear eyes. "You know I'm with Gaspar."

He steps back almost immediately. "Of course." The mask slips back. The feelings are swept under the rug. And he pulls back, always the mature one.

I manage to grab one of his arms and clasp his hand with both of mine. "That doesn't mean you're not important to me." *I love you, too.* "It's just—"

"You're with Gaspar. He loves you, you love him, and now you're both alive and can be together." It freaks me out how easily Sébastien manages to smile. "You deserve this and so much more. I will do everything to protect your happiness."

Not what I wanted to hear.

I shake my head vehemently. "Don't do this, please. We'll find another way. We'll figure it all out. Together."

But he pulls his hand away and gives me another dull smile. "I'm sure you will." He even manages to laugh softly. "You ended a century-long dispute between two stubborn men. You talked down a manic whisper ghost murderer, and you defeated the last Grand Master of the Knights Templar. This will be a piece of cake for you. All you need is some time."

Time. Time he wants to buy me by giving himself up to his horrible parents.

"Séb..."

"It's going to be okay, Alix. No deaths tomorrow. I promise."

And the day after tomorrow? And the day after that?

The words catch in my throat, and I feel even more helpless than before. If I can't even protect Sébastien from himself, how can I hope to protect anyone?

Chapter 27

It's the day of the wedding and it looks like we've used up all the good weather with our extended stay. It's grey and stormy outside, with rain threatening to come down at any minute. Appropriate for a day that could end in disaster.

Gaby, Marie, Gaspar, and I arrive at the town hall together, and I take some time to greet my living grandparents, my uncle, and a few cousins I haven't seen for a while. More than half the people present are strangers to me. They must be Cédric's family or his and Hélène's colleagues.

I watch anxiously as they enter the town hall. It's almost a relief when I see Charles Roubert talking to a surprisingly serious Cédric. I should be worried that they're talking, but all I can think of is that if Charles is here, he can't hurt Sébastien.

Now if only there was a sign from my favourite agent.

"Alix!" Odile comes running. Like me, she's wearing a floor-length blue dress and a matching headband in her hair.

She immediately makes for the cage Gaspar is carrying. "There's my date," she exclaims, taking the cage from him. "I'll get Malou ready. You should go to the back. Hélène is freaking out."

The last thing I want to do right now is look after my sister. But it can't be helped. This is her big day.

I lean over to Gaspar and kiss him on the cheek. "Let me know when you see him."

He sighs but nods. "Will do. Don't let Hélène walk all over you."

I roll my eyes and walk briskly towards the small room at the back reserved for the bride. Cédric spots me on the way and has the audacity to wave. Ignoring him, I text Sébastien instead.

No reply. Please, just let him skip the wedding he never wanted to attend.

Not everyone will survive the wedding night.

"Ugh." How am I supposed to enjoy and support this wedding if I can't get that damn prophecy out of my head?

I find my parents in front of a closed room. Maman has her ear to the door and seems to be talking to Hélène. "Sweetie, it's going to be okay."

"What's going on?" I ask Papa.

He smiles at me. "You look beautiful, my dear." With a sigh, he nods at the door. "I think your sister has the usual wedding jitters."

"Léni, please open the door. It's almost time," Maman pleads.

"I'm not doing it!"

All this drama and *now* she decides to back out? With no time for this shit, I approach the door and loudly rap my knuckles against the aged wood. "Open the door, Léni!"

"Go away, Alix."

Maman looks at me scandalised. "She's just nervous. Most brides are."

I'd be nervous too if I had to marry Cédric, but my sister chose him. "You can't be serious," I say through the door. "After all the backstabbing, you're backing out of marrying Officer Cédric?"

The door unlocks and is torn open. "Don't call him that!" She gives me a long look. "And I didn't stab you in the back." Without warning, she grabs my arm and drags me into the room, locking the door behind her. "This is all your fault."

"What?"

"You made me do that tarot reading!" Hélène cries. Despite her despair, she looks absolutely beautiful. The dress is an elegant off-the-shoulder mermaid gown, paired with long white gloves. Her long brown hair is twisted into a knot at the back, with a few tight curls framing her face. A medium-length veil tucked into the knot completes the look.

"Wait, this is about the tarot cards?"

She nods eagerly and begins to pace—as well as she can in a dress that restricts her leg movement. "I can't stop thinking about them.

Everything goes well and then bam, disappointment. And now look." She points to the window. "It's raining."

The wind has shifted and long streaks of water are running down the window.

"You're disappointed it's raining?" I ask, amused. This is so typical of Hélène. The biggest disappointment in her life is when the weather doesn't play ball.

"Stop laughing!" She shouts, then raises her hands to her face.

I quickly step in and grab her hands before she can ruin the make-up. "You're spiralling. There's nothing wrong with rain."

"It'll ruin the wedding photos."

"Or it will make it a wedding to remember." I take her hands in mine and give her a warm smile. "Look, I know you want every-thing to be perfect. And I get it, this is your big day. But life isn't all perfect and tidy. It's messy as hell. Now, you can either complain that things aren't going your way or you can enjoy the ride. Just think of the fun we'll have posing in the pouring rain and laughing about the weather."

The anxiety fades from her features, and I get a small smile. "Those would be pretty unique pictures."

"Oh, yes. And you'll get lots of pretty ones here in the town hall too. It's the best of both worlds."

She sniffles slightly, but the smile remains. "It's not a bad omen?"

I've been asking myself the same question, but I'm not letting that show on my face. "I'm sure there's a saying that rainy wedding days are a blessing."

Hélène rolls her eyes at my superstition. "I'm doing the right thing, aren't I?" The smile turns to a frown. "Marrying Cédric? I know you don't like him and that you think he's done you dirty, but you don't know him. Not really. He's so funny and caring. He does so many good things in the world. Like, how he always helps our neighbour with her shopping or offers to babysit the twins downstairs. If anyone needs help, he's always the first to jump in. And he loves me. He loves and supports me so much. He's my biggest cheerleader and a true romantic."

I suppose all those things could be true, while he was still throwing me under the bus to further his own career, desperate for his dream job and the approval of his revered uncle. If I say the right things now, I could probably break them up and rid myself of him, but would that make my sister happy in the long run?

"Do *you* love him?"

Her whole face softens. "Very, very much."

My heart aches a little, but I force a smile on my lips. "Then go out there and marry your man."

Hélène throws her arms around me and hugs me tightly. "I will. Thank you, Alix. I'm sorry I've been such a bitch to you."

"Maybe you need more spa days."

She throws her head back and bursts out laughing. "Maybe. We should make it a regular thing. My treat."

I don't know about that, but if she's paying, it probably wouldn't be the worst thing in the world. "I'd like that. Now go. Your special someone is waiting for you to start the rest of his life with you."

With a last hug and a happy giggle, Hélène unlocks the door to find my parents jumping aside. "I'm ready."

As she steps out, my mother mouths her thanks at me. Papa offers his arm to Hélène, while I join Odile, who presents me with my bridal hedgehog. I don't know how she got the pretty blue veil to stick to Malou's spikes, but it fits her perfectly. Instead of a pillow, she's got a little bag under her belly, just big enough to hold the rings. To top it all off, she seems to be awake, settling into the crook of my arm as soon as I give her a belly rub.

"I'll tell them we're ready." Maman gives Hélène one last hug before she gets things started inside the town hall.

Hélène's two friends join us at the entrance, exclaiming how beautiful Hélène is and taking selfies with her. Then the music starts to play, and our procession begins.

When it's finally my time to walk in, just before Papa and Hélène, I let my gaze roam across the benches. The town hall is decorated with baby blue and white flowers and there are so many guests that almost all the pews are filled. I see Gaspar sitting next to

Gaby and Marie, smiling at me. I return the smile before scanning the benches again.

He's still not here.

The ceremony goes off as planned. Hélène and Cédric exchange their vows, Malou elicits a lot of oohs and aahs from the guests when she presents the rings, and the happy couple share a long kiss. The guests stand and applaud as they walk out into the foyer. Odile and I follow in their wake, and I can't help but look for Sébastien again.

Instead—two rows from the end—I see Nostradamus.

Dressed in his dark medieval garb and with his dour mood, he sticks out like a sore thumb. As I pass him, he utters the words that have been stuck in my head all day, "Not everyone who came here will survive the night. Beware the hanged man."

Chapter 28

The wedding party is being held in a restaurant near the lagoon. It would have been a beautiful sight if the clouds weren't hanging low and the water wasn't more grey than blue. As much as the weather bothered Hélène before, she couldn't care less now. She and Cédric have cut the cake and opened the dancefloor. And now she's dancing with all her friends as if it were a catacombs rave.

Everyone's having a good time. Everyone except me. I sit at the family table, biting my nails and sending messages to Sébastien that go unread, while Nostradamus' words continue to swirl in my head. *Beware the hanged man.* My tarot card. *An unnecessary sacrifice.* If that doesn't scream Sébastien, I don't know what does.

"Still nothing?" Gaspar sits down next to me, slightly sweaty from dancing with Odile.

I shake my head and press the call button. The phone rings and rings, but no one answers. "What if he's already dead?" I saw

Sébastien lying paralysed on the floor of the catacombs, eyes wide open, his mind in a haze of horror. Why would he let them do this to him again? Or maybe he didn't? Maybe he went for a ride on his bike, unable to make it through his cousin's wedding, and now he's lying in a ditch with the rain pouring down on him. A road accident like Gaspar's.

"If he was dead, he'd be here as a ghost." Gaspar takes my hands and pulls at them. "Alix, he's fine. It's not going to happen today. Now come and dance at your sister's wedding."

I put the phone down, but when I look up at the dance floor, I see Nostradamus standing in the middle of it. People are swirling and laughing around him as he stands there in his dark robe, still as a statue, his eyes fixed on me.

Gaspar glances over his shoulder. "Let me handle this."

"What do you mean, handle it?" I jump up as Gaspar marches off, pushing people aside to get to Nostradamus. But by the time he's reached him, the seer is gone.

"Someone just died," the words are whispered in my ear, but they strike like a blow to my head.

The music is distorted, and the room spins faster and faster, matching the rhythm of my heart as it nearly bursts from my chest.

"Alix?" Maman appears in front of me, looking slightly worried. "You don't look so good. Is everything okay?"

No, I want to scream. *Nothing's okay.* But I just look at the guests again, hoping against hope to see those ice-blue eyes.

If he was dead, he'd be here as a ghost.

Hélène is laughing with her friends. Gaby and Marie are kissing at the back of the room. Odile is dancing with Papa. But I don't see Sébastien. And I don't see Charles.

"I have to go."

I tear myself away from my mother and run towards the exit. Belatedly, I realise I don't have Gaby's car keys. I'm about to turn back when Cédric comes down the corridor. "Alix."

"Not now."

"I need you."

Surprised, I actually pay attention to him. His eyes are wide open and he's breathing hard, as if he's run here. I thought he'd just come back from the toilet, but he looks as if he's seen something he shouldn't have, and my mind darts ahead to Sébastien. "Where?"

Cédric takes my hand and pulls me along. "Come quickly. You've got to help me."

My pulse is pounding in my ears, my heart is racing as we run down the corridor and out into the rain. At first, I think we're going to get a car, but Cédric pulls me towards a small shed at the back of the restaurant.

And then he runs through the door. The *closed* door.

The truth hits me and my stomach drops. My hand hovers over the handle, not wanting to be anywhere near it. Whatever is behind that door... I don't want to see it.

But I can't stop myself. I feel like a stranger in my own body as I watch my fingers close around the handle and press down. The door opens and light streams into the shed. The frame creates a rectangle of light, broken only by the shadow of two legs hanging off the floor.

"What have you done?"

Beware the hanged man.

CHAPTER 29

"You have to help me!"

Cédric is all over me, sweat pouring from his face. He seemed so agitated, so alive. But in reality he's hanging from the ceiling, his body still swaying slightly.

"Why?" I ask him, horror clawing at my chest. "Why, Cédric?" I want to push him, slap his stupid face until he cries out, and scream.

"It was a test," he confesses. "Of my loyalty. If I wanted it, I'd have to do it here. He said he needed me. He still does, doesn't he?"

I just stare at him, incredulous. "Charles did that?"

"I texted him," Cédric continues. "I told him where I was and that he could trust me, but it's been a few minutes and..."

"Tonight? Tonight of all nights?" I shout and then I push him anyway. "You're such an idiot!"

Cédric stumbles backwards and falls through a chair onto the floor. My breath comes hard and fast, but I can't let him get the better of me now. I grab the chair and push it back upright so I can climb up and reach the knot around Cédric's neck. It's too tight with his weight hanging off it. I try to lift him, but even with the adrenaline coursing through my veins, he's too heavy for me.

"Alix?" a new voice calls from the door. Gaspar.

"Help me, please."

Without hesitation, Gaspar leaps forward and wraps his arms around Cédric's legs to lift him up. I dig my fingers into the rope and, after a few agonising seconds, I manage to loosen the knot so I can slip the rope over his head and Gaspar goes down with the body.

As I jump from the chair, Gaspar sets Cédric down and checks his vital signs. "He's dead." He looks up at the ghost of Cédric and shrugs his shoulders. "Congratulations on your new ghost life. Hope you like it."

The crude words turn my stomach. Cédric shakes his head. "No, no, no. I'm supposed to be a ghost whisperer. You need to do CPR."

"Please," I say when Gaspar hesitates, clearly convinced it's too late for that.

With a sigh, Gaspar complies. Meanwhile, I take out my phone and call the emergency services. If I count from the moment Nostradamus told me someone had just died to now, Cédric's brain has been without air for at least ten minutes. That's if he didn't break his neck in the first place. Gaspar is right. My brother-in-law is dead.

The ambulance and the police arrive and take over. Once again, I feel like a stranger in my own body as I calmly explain how Gaspar and I were looking for someone else and found Cédric instead. The first responders check on Cédric, but quickly pronounce him dead and put him in a body bag instead.

"No, no, no," Cédric cries as they close the bag. "My uncle will revive me. I'll be a ghost whisperer. You can't let them take me."

"I have to tell my sister."

A police officer accompanies me as I walk back to the restaurant, dazed. The flashing lights have already attracted people's attention and a small crowd is gathering near the entrance. Cédric keeps whining in my ear about his deal with Charles, refusing to accept what he's just done to himself.

"Alix?" Hélène meets me in the middle of the crowd, my family not far behind. "What's going on out there?"

"You," Cédric says with renewed fervour. "You brought Gaspar back. You can bring me back. Right, Alix? You can bring me back, right?"

It's impossible to tune him out, and for the first time I curse my ability to see ghosts. Still, I have to ignore him to break the news to my sister. She deserves to hear it from me, not a police officer. "It's Cédric, Léni. He... he hanged himself."

The Hanged Man. An unnecessary sacrifice. Hélène's Five of Cups. Not just disappointment, but grief and mourning.

The truth is staring me in the face now, and I can't help thinking I should've stopped the wedding when I could. I don't know if it would've changed things for Cédric, but at least my sister wouldn't have been widowed five hours into her marriage.

My mouth is moving, explaining what I found, but I can't hear my own words. Hélène screams, then collapses. My parents and Odile rush towards her, while I just stand there, the harbinger of her sorrow. Cédric finally leaves me alone to apologise to Hélène, but she can't hear him.

The police officer takes over, allowing me to distance myself from the tragedy that's befallen my family. The crowd disperses around me, as if they know how entangled I am in all this.

Suddenly, someone throws their arms around my neck and pulls me into an embrace. Gaby. "I'm so sorry, Alix!" The news of Cédric's death has spread quickly.

Gaby pulls me to the side where she, Marie, and Gaspar form a protective ring around me, shielding me from curious looks. Gaspar explains what happened in the shed, while Gaby holds me and strokes my head.

"I feel terrible now," Marie says, looking pale. "The cards..."

"The cards didn't kill him," Gaspar snaps. "He did it."

"Charles did it," I whisper. Sure, Cédric is an idiot and led himself to the gallows, but his uncle promised to bring him back from the brink. He didn't do it to kill himself, but to fulfil his lifelong dream. It's another death at the hands of Charles Roubert.

Just then, Dix appears. "There you are! Quick, you... you need to come."

Not again.

"She's doing something to him, and I..." Dix's voice trails off as he flickers like a hologram with bad reception.

"Car keys," I say to Gaby.

Nostradamus never said there'd only be one death. If Dix ceases to exist, it can only mean one thing.

"Please, Gaby, I don't want to lose Sébastien, too."

I know she must be confused, but there's no time to lose. We lock gazes and she huffs. She pulls the car key out of her purse, but before I can grab it, she wraps her fingers around it. "I'm driving."

"Gaby, this could be dangerous."

"And you think I'm going to let you go alone? I'm coming. No discussion."

I don't have time to argue with Gaby, so I hurry to get my handbag off the table. If Sébastien is where I think he is, I'll need the access card Margot gave me.

On my way out, I see Gaspar standing there, arms folded, face dark. "It's always going to be him, isn't it? He needs you and you come running."

I stare at him, stunned he would bring this up now. Well, too bad. I don't have time for his shit anymore. "Bye, Gaspar."

Chapter 30

"Gaspar's not coming?" Gaby asks as she drives as fast as the speed limit allows.

I wish she would go faster. Dix is still with us, but he's glitching so badly my heart's in my throat all the time. "I don't know what his problem is, but no. He's not coming."

Gaby glances at me, but keeps her mouth shut. This isn't the time for that discussion. In the back of the car, Marie repeatedly shuffles her cards and spreads them out, which tells me she doesn't like what she sees, adding to my anxiety.

I drum my fingers on the dashboard, probably getting on Gaby's nerves.

"Is Dix still here?" she asks.

A glance in the rearview mirror confirms it. He's in one of his more stable periods. "Barely."

The fear of losing Sébastien is overwhelming, but it's not just his life that's at stake. If Sébastien dies, he'll become a ghost and Dix will cease to exist, no longer a part separate from Sébastien. In a way, it's even crueler than death. It'll be as if he never existed. There was never a Dix-Sept in this world, no one to remember him except me and his older self. He's like a little brother to me and I can't bear the thought of losing him.

At last, we arrive at Margot's lab. I jump out of the car and run to the door, Gaby and Marie behind me. Frantically, I slam the access card against the reader and am relieved when the door opens.

All the labs except the one at the back are dark. It's the weekend and late at night, so there's no one here to witness the horrors being unleashed. I'm not surprised to find Nostradamus waiting for me.

"I wouldn't go in there if I were you."

"Shut up."

"Alix, should we—"

Impatiently, I tap my card against the reader. The minimal delay has me worried that Margot's blocked the card, but there's a hum and I push the doors open. "Whatever you're doing, stop it!"

Three people are in the room. Margot is standing in front of her machines, adjusting settings. Charles is watching her from a safe distance, arms folded. As for Sébastien, he is stuck in that strange machine Margot uses to communicate with ghosts. His chest, legs, and arms are strapped in, and a multitude of cables and tubes are attached to his body. There's a bead of sweat on his forehead and his face is contorted, as if he's having a heart attack.

"That's your son!" I shout, barging into the lab. "You're supposed to love and take care of him. Keep him safe!"

"Not now, Alix," Margot says irritatingly gently. "We're almost there."

She cranks up a setting and Sébastien screams in pain. Worse, Dix flickers violently.

"Stop!" I scream.

But just as I reach for Margot, Charles steps forward and puts a gun to my temple. "Easy now, Mademoiselle Dubois."

I freeze, the threat of the weapon a shock to my system.

"Phones on the table over there," Charles shouts at Gaby and Marie, who must have been trying to call the police. "This is a government-sanctioned situation. If you interfere, I have every right to arrest you. Now go over there and be quiet." As soon as the two shuffle into a corner, Charles taunts Margot. "I told you that girl was nothing but trouble."

"I find her quite commendable," says Margot, the calmest of all.

Tears of anger and helplessness fill my eyes. "You have to stop this, please." I turn to Charles, only to stare down the barrel of his gun. My heart jumps into my throat. "You already killed Cédric today. On his wedding day."

"He went through with it?" he asks, sounding amused of all things.

"He trusted you. He trusted you to be there and bring him back."

"I had more important things to do." He couldn't be more bored if he tried.

"Your nephew is dead!"

Charles snorts. "It's not much of a loss, is it? He'd never have made it as a GoPol agent. He's nothing more than a sycophantic gendarme. He doesn't have the drive or heart to do what needs to be done."

"He betrayed me and killed himself for you." How is that not ambitious enough?

"So? That just proves he's an idiot. Can you really imagine someone like him dealing with ghosts? Crawling through the catacombs, hunting down terrorists? No, Cédric has always been inferior to Sébastien. Even when they were children, my son beat him every time. It wasn't even close."

His callousness takes my breath away and I realise he was using Cédric. He toyed with his admiration and willingness to prove himself to get to me, and only entertained his ambitions when he was about to lose the super-soldier he'd had his heart set on.

"Alix?" Sébastien's voice is broken by pain and muffled by the glass. "What are you doing here?"

"You promised!" I tell him. "You promised not to do this."

"Oh, that's my fault," Margot says. "I had an opening today and forgot all about the wedding. You see, he came to see me to talk about you."

"Me?"

Margot nods. "Yes, we had a good chat about how much you mean to him and what you've been through with my ex-husband. He loves you." She smiles, as if that makes her genuinely happy. "Anyway, we came to an agreement. He'll let me try this new technique and I'll protect you from GoPol."

Charles snorts, making it clear how well that protection is working for me.

The Hanged Man. An unnecessary sacrifice. It's both Cédric and Sébastien. Two young men caught in a web of abuse and brainwashing, betrayed by those who should have looked out for them.

"I told him it could be dangerous and painful, possibly even fatal, despite my best intentions," Margot confesses, "but he was so heartbroken he was willing to do it anyway. For you. He loves you so much, Alix. It's quite remarkable."

My gaze goes to Sébastien. While she's fascinated at her son's capability of caring deeply for another human, I'm mortified. He's hanging in the restraints, breathing hard through the pain Margot is making him endure. I can't help thinking I drove him to this. By rejecting him, I drove him into the arms of a woman with no scruples.

"I hope you're proud of yourself for destroying all my hard work," Charles says. "He was perfect, top of his class, a dedicated and highly capable agent. Now look at him, bargaining his life away to keep your sorry little ass safe." He presses the gun harder against my forehead. "But I've had enough of you and your intrusions."

He glances at Margot. "Sorry, Margot, but she has to go. You've caused enough trouble, Mademoiselle."

"No!" Sébastien shouts from his prison. "Don't! I beg you! I'll do anything. I'll go back to work. I'll be yours. You can use me however you want. You can kill me as often as you like, punish me, torture me. Please, leave Alix out of it. Please."

While Sébastien begs for my life, Dix lunges at his father, but it's no use. He's no longer a ghost whisperer and can't be stopped by a ghost.

Charles rolls his eyes. "That's all nice and well, boy, but unfortunately your little friend doesn't know what's good for her. She'll never be able to keep her nose out of my business. Can you guarantee her silence? I don't think so."

"Well, I can," says Margot. "Look at her. She came running here from her sister's wedding, still wearing that pretty dress, to save him, knowing full well what was waiting for her in this room. Alix is clever, brave, and so full of potential. She may not be in a relationship with Sébastien, but she obviously loves him almost as much as he loves her." She smiles. "As much as I'd like to see if my soul splicing works, I'll be happy to drop it if you come and work for me. Starting immediately."

What's going on here? Margot wants me to work for her so much she'd consider letting Sébastien go?

"You can have our son. I'll take her."

"No." Charles shakes his head and meets my eyes. "It's too great a risk. She dies tonight."

Gaby screams, "No!"

"Papa, please!" Sébastien cries.

My heart stops and my breath catches in my throat. Nostradamus warned me not to come in here. The other person who's going to die tonight is me.

Just then Charles crumples at my feet, blood seeping into his hair. Margot's behind him, a heavy apparatus in her hands. She sighs. "You always lacked imagination, Charles."

CHAPTER 31

I have no idea what's happened, but I'm on my knees on the floor, Gaby and Marie hanging onto my shoulders, crying. Charles is lying on the floor, motionless. Since no ghost rises from his form, I assume he's still alive. Unimpressed, Margot produces a pair of handcuffs and ties him to a table. Then she tapes his mouth shut. "We'll decide what to do with him later. Maybe he'll be my test object for soul splicing. That would please you, wouldn't it?"

Horrified, I look up at her. I appreciate her saving my life, but I don't trust her at all. Especially if she still has Sébastien trapped in her machine.

But before I can collect my thoughts, Nostradamus comes in. "I told you it'd be a mess."

"Sometimes you have to get your hands dirty."

My mouth falls open. At first I think I've misheard, that Margot has accidentally spoken as if in response, but she looks straight at

Nostradamus. "He's always been a nuisance. Why do you think I left him?"

"Wait a minute. You can see ghosts?"

Margot sighs and rubs her nose before smiling at me. "I'm the same as you. Well, almost. I was born not breathing, so I've been a ghost whisperer all my life. Luckily, my mother used to work for the Ministry of Defence and already knew about ghost whisperers, so they let me keep my ghost."

My brain can't comprehend this. She never responded to Dix. She made a great show of communicating with ghosts in her lab. She left GoPol.

"Oh, sweetie. I'm sorry I had to deceive you a bit there. You see, when Nostradamus told me you'd be coming, I just had to make sure we'd meet."

My gaze whips from her to the ghost. "You did this?"

He raises his hands. "Don't blame the prophet. I only see what happens, I don't do anything."

"Alix, what's going on?" Gaby asks anxiously. "Who else is here?"

"See, that's exactly why we need more ghost research," Margot points out. "I assume you're good friends with Alix and know about her unique abilities. Currently, we have two ghosts in the lab. My son's seventeen-year-old whisper ghost and my esteemed colleague, Nostradamus."

"No way," Gaby mutters.

Dix comes closer, his face full of pain. "You saw me?"

I think of all the times Dix watched her, longing to talk to her while she pretended not to see or hear him, and my heart goes out to him.

Margot tries to put a hand on his cheek, but Dix pulls away. "Of course, I saw and *recognised* you. I've been a GoPol-trained ghost whisperer for over fifty years. I know my ghosts."

Unlike me, who still fails to recognise them at first glance.

"But you weren't important," she tells Dix. "I knew that if I continued to ignore you, you'd bring me my true son. And with him, the girl who'll raise the dead."

Hate burns alive in me. The way she shuns Dix and only calls Sébastien her son drives me mad. She may have been a ghost whisperer all her life, but she's nothing like me.

"So, you told her that, too?" It now makes sense why I saw Nostradamus in front of her house the first time.

"It's all I have left. I tell people what's coming. But few listen." He raises an eyebrow at me, reminding me he warned me against entering the lab.

"Well, I listen. And I'm excited. Alix, I meant what I said. I want to work with you."

I'm glad Gaby and Marie are with me, because I would've ripped the bitch's head off. "Why? Because of some stupid prophecy? I'm not going to raise the dead. I have no interest in it."

"Oh, it's going to happen," Nostradamus says, raining on my parade. "Chaos and destruction. Mark my words."

"You raised that boy. Gaspar du Charbonneau," Margot points out.

"That wasn't me."

Margot looks a little surprised. "If it wasn't you, then it must have been my old friend."

"Friend?" I'm not ready to hear the next part. This next disappointment.

Sure enough, Margot mentions the Chevalier. "Romain Coullier. He used to work for GoPol. He was my ex-husband's partner, but he was absolutely wasted as an agent. Brilliant in the lab, though. We worked together a lot, had a little affair, too." She says it so casually, as if that's what people do. "That's why my marriage fell apart, you know? Charles was so ridiculously jealous. He let it cloud his judgement and refused to hear any reason when it came to Sébastien's whispering career." She snorts at Charles, who softly moans as he comes to, only to find himself tied up.

"That you wanted to kill him earlier?" The words are full of acid.

"It's more natural this way, wouldn't you agree?"

The fact she doesn't even deny it makes me sick. Slowly, I pull myself out of my friends' embrace and stand up. "Let him go."

"What, Charles?"

"Sébastien."

Margot relaxes and laughs. "Does that mean you've made up your mind? To be honest, I couldn't care less if you keep your mouth shut. Go and bring down Charles Roubert. I'll even hand you the tools. Or we can put him in the machine and see how many times we can splice his rotten soul. All I want is for the two of us is to work together. You may not have been the one to resurrect that boy of yours, but your involvement alone tells me you're the key to this."

"Key?"

"To solving the greatest questions of the universe. The mystery between life and death."

Her eyes glow with the fire of passion and she sounds genuinely excited. And here I am, feeling nothing. I'm not interested in the mysteries of the universe. I'm not wooed by this promise of greatness, this life-changing opportunity. All I want is for this horror to stop.

"Let Sébastien go."

"You're such a sweet girl," Margot says with a gentle smile. "So caring and innocent."

"And that's a damn good thing," Gaby hollers.

Margot chuckles. "Very well, I'll give you Sébastien. As promised," she reminds. She turns to her machine and quickly types in a few commands.

The cabin opens and the bonds are released. Sébastien groans and I see his legs give way. Fortunately, Marie takes the initiative and steadies him, before slowly removing the tubes and cables from his body.

"Now, it's your turn," Margot says. "I've already prepared the contract. You will all have to sign an NDA, of course."

As she rummages through her desk for the contracts, Gaby approaches me. "Alix, you can't do this. She's just using you."

"To get to the ghosts, I know." That's why the Chevalier was so interested in me. It's not me these researchers are so interested in, but my connections. Connections they could easily have made themselves if they'd seen ghosts as more than just tools. The Chevalier may have reconsidered after being torn apart and spat out by GoPol, but Margot will definitely enjoy the chaos and destruction I'm supposed to bring.

"Exactly," Margot exclaims. "When Nostradamus told me you were well acquainted with all those important ghosts in Paris, I knew I had to work with you. I mean, you're in the presence of the great Marie Curie and so many other great minds. Imagine what we could achieve if we put them all together."

It would sound great if I didn't know for a fact that there are few limits to her research. She willingly tortured her son and may have killed others as she explored the science behind it. I know Marie Curie took a lot of risks to advance her field of science—heck, she died for it—but she never forced others to join her or knowingly hurt them. We may not have the closest relationship, but I'd vouch for any Panthéon ghost that they'd never agree to that.

"What if I don't want to join you?"

Margot freezes, the cheerfulness draining from her face. "Do I really have to threaten your two friends? Or maybe kill Sébastien after all?" She cocks her head and snorts. "Look, Alix, I'm a big fan of collaborations, so let's not spoil this one before we've even gotten started."

"Maman," Sébastien starts. He's still struggling to stand on his own two feet, blinking as if he's about to faint.

"Stay out of this, boy. Alix is a smart girl." Her cold stare hits me again. "I don't think you realise how much I'm offering you. You don't have a scientific background, but I'll teach you. I'll pay you, too. Handsomely. And your friends can get out of here unscathed. You won't get a better offer."

I have no idea how Margot plans to take on all five of us, but she sounds so confident I believe her, even if she isn't pointing a gun at my face.

"I wouldn't do it without a security of course. I'll keep Dix for myself. He's still connected to Sébastien, so if you give me any reason to doubt you, the man you care so much about will suffer for it."

As if she hasn't already brought enough suffering to Sébastien and Dix, now she's going to hold them hostage to ensure my compliance.

Just then, Dix slips between us. "You're a ghost whisperer, right, Maman?"

Margot clicks her tongue. "You're a bit slow, sweetie. We already talked about that. Now if you'd be so good—"

Without warning, he grabs her arm and twists it behind her back. Within seconds, he's got his mother pinned down. "Go, Alix. Get out of here."

"What's happening?" Gaby asks, probably wondering why Margot is breathing hard and her body's twisted like that.

I grab her arm. "Dix is holding her down. He's not invisible to her."

She nods sharply. "Let's go."

Marie brings Sébastien, and the four of us hurry towards the exit, Margot shouting after us, "You're making a mistake! If you refuse to work for me, it's not just GoPol that's coming after you. I—"

The doors open and Gaspar steps in, eyes full of thunder. "I'll take care of this."

"Gaspar?"

He walks up to Margot and Dix. After a nod from Gaspar, Dix lets go of his mother. She stumbles forward and is helped to her feet by Gaspar.

"Look, I mean no offence," Margot says. "I'd love to do some experiments on you and I'm sure we can come to an understanding, but it's not you I want."

She thinks he's here to offer himself in my place. But the man standing there isn't my sweet hedgehog boy. He's the other Gaspar, his dark, cold, spiteful side.

My hands fly to my mouth when he grabs Margot's face and slams her head into the desk behind her. There's an ugly crack and blood splatters. Marie screams and covers her eyes. Gaby spins around and throws up. Sébastien, without Marie's support, stumbles and falls to his knees, eyes wide open, while I just stand there, watching in horror as Gaspar smashes Margot's head into the desk again and again.

"Dix!" Sébastien calls.

I assume he's asking him to stop Gaspar, but instead Dix appears in front of me and holds me, effectively shielding me from the gruesome sight.

What he can't take away are the sounds.

Chapter 32

Dix has his arms around me, his own eyes squeezed shut. All I can hear is Marie's crying, Gaby's gagging, and Gaspar's heavy breathing. There are no sounds from Margot. Not anymore.

"She's dead, Gaspar." That's Sébastien. Although he's talking about his mother, there's no accusation in his voice. He sounds like he's calming down a wild animal. "You can stop now."

"Your father's still alive."

"Gaspar, no!" I cry, pulling myself out of Dix's embrace. As soon as his body gives way, I wish I hadn't. The sight of the blood-spattered computer desk, along with some soft grey lumps, makes me throw up in my mouth.

He killed her. He really smashed her head in, like some kind of monster. *My monster.*

And now he's turned his attention to Charles. Gagged and tied to the table, the GoPol commander is completely defenceless. Gaspar stares at him in disgust, then bends down and picks up the gun, which none of us have touched before. "Huh. I've never fired a gun before."

As he points it at Charles' face, I scream in fear. "Gaspar, please."

"Was that how he pointed it at you, Séb?"

"Don't do it," Sébastien says. He's as white as a sheet, but he manages to keep his voice calm. "He's not worth it."

I certainly can't face another death tonight. Although all I want to do is turn around and run away, I force myself to walk over to Gaspar. He may not be my sweet, innocent hedgehog boy, but he came here for me all the same.

"Please, please, don't do this."

"But didn't he say you're too big a risk to keep alive? Same goes for him."

His answer makes me wonder how long he was listening before he made his presence known.

I walk around a workstation and come face to face with an utterly terrified Charles and the bloody remains of his ex-wife. Even her ghost is so incapacitated she hasn't yet figured out how to speak or move. "Maybe, but I'm not a psychopath like him." *Gaspar, on the other hand...* I close my eyes, feeling the flutter of my eyelashes on my cheeks as I take a few deep breaths. "Don't you think enough people have died tonight?"

"All good things are three." He presses the gun to Charles' forehead.

I can still feel the metal biting into my skin and the naked fear of knowing there's absolutely nothing I could've done if he'd pulled the trigger. And as much as I hate Charles Roubert, I cannot let this happen to anyone else. Not if I can stop it.

"Just don't!" I cry as I rush between them and throw my arms around Gaspar's neck.

The force of my intervention sends him stumbling backwards. A shot is fired, but there's no grunt, just a *BANG* as it hits a wall panel instead. Still, I'm left reeling, shaking from head to toe.

Something falls to the floor. Then two arms wrap around me and hold me tight. Gaspar's ragged breathing reaches my ear, cutting through the shock. "You're safe," he whispers, then cups my face to look deep into my eyes. "I won't let anyone—do you hear me?—*anyone* hurt you again."

I'm still too shocked to form a coherent thought. Margot's blood is on my face, courtesy of Gaspar's hands. I can smell the iron in it.

"Do you understand me?"

I nod, still stunned by the coldness in Gaspar's voice and the emptiness in his formerly warm eyes.

He lets go and sighs. "You, Gaby, and Marie have to go home."

"What about you?"

"I'm going to clean up this mess."

My thoughts immediately go to Charles. "You're not going to kill him, are you?"

"Sébastien will restrain me. Unless he changes his mind."

"I won't," Sébastien says hastily, before I can go into shock again. With Dix's help, he's managed to make his way over.

Crying, I let go of Gaspar and run into his arms. "You promised."

Sébastien holds me close, his nose buried in my hair, as if he wants to take in my scent to make sure I'm really there. "I'm so sorry. It was stupid of me. I really thought I could put an end to it. Keep you safe. Instead, I made everything worse."

I don't have the energy to scold him. I'm just glad he's still here with me. Dix, too.

"Go," Sébastien whispers. "I'll keep him straight."

I don't want to let go, but the smell of fresh blood is getting stronger. My legs are shaking as I stumble away from the mess to join Gaby and Marie at the door.

"We need to get you cleaned up," Gaby says, wiping her own mouth.

"I saw a bathroom on the way in," Marie chimes in, focusing on the practical stuff. Neither of them so much as looks in the others' direction.

Together, we turn to leave the lab, when Gaspar calls out to me. "Alix."

Despite myself, I look over my shoulder. My heart skips a beat as I see the terror in his eyes. He stares down at his bloodied hands, then up at me. He looks as if he's wondering what just happened.

The sight of my sweet hedgehog boy covered in blood is unbearable and I flee.

None of us speak as we clean ourselves as best we can in the nearest bathroom. At some point, I must have lost my headband and there's a spot of blood that just won't wash out of the blue fabric, no matter how much I rub. But at last, I feel ready to face the outside world.

When I look into the mirror, I see a familiar face behind us.

I turn around. "You!"

Nostradamus smiles sheepishly. "Ah, the time-honoured greeting for seers."

"What's going on?" Gaby asks, while Marie whispers, "I think it's another ghost."

"Why are you here?" I confront Nostradamus. "Are you going to take revenge for Margot?"

He chuckles softly. "Do you really think any ghost worth his salt would protect her, like they'd protect you? I warned her, too, you know? But like so many before her, she didn't listen. She only cared about the prophecies so long as they served her."

I suppose, after so many centuries, Nostradamus cares little for mortal life. So much for esteemed colleagues.

"Don't make the same mistake, Mademoiselle Alix. Fate comes for all of us, whether we want it to or not. I never lied to you. You will raise the dead and bring about France's darkest hour."

I close my eyes, unwilling to face this cursed prophecy. "So, I don't get a choice in it?"

"Oh, we all make choices. Well, all except me. I'm just a seer. You, my dear, are a catalyst for change that will blur the line between life and death. What you make of it... well, that's your choice." He winks at me and disappears.

Gaby looks at me worriedly. "What was that about? Did someone threaten you?"

Threaten me? Only with the end of the world or something similarly drastic. I shake my head and open my eyes again. "Let's get out of here."

CHAPTER 33

We drive back to the hotel in complete silence, too shocked to talk about what we just witnessed. My mind keeps conjuring up different images—the barrel of Charles's gun, Sébastien strapped in the cabin, Dix's glitching, and always Margot and what became of her—but I can't put a complete thought together. Eventually, I know I have to make sense of Gaspar's recent behaviour, and to figure out what the implications of everything are. But tonight, my brain is too fried for anything else.

We shuffle off to our respective rooms, eager to shower. For me, it's the room I share with a monster.

That's not who's waiting for me, though. Instead, I find Hélène and Cédric sitting on my bed, surrounded by a sea of white lilies.

Grave flowers, yet my favourites. Hélène looks at me with blood-shot eyes, completely oblivious to her whimpering husband.

"Where have you been?"

After everything that happened at the lab, I'd almost forgotten the evening started out with a tragedy for her. While she collapsed, I ran to save Sébastien. "Does it matter?"

She snorts. "Does it matter? I needed you."

Not as much as Sébastien. "Did you?" She had two families and lots of friends to take care of her.

"Wow. Let me guess, you had some ghost business to attend to."

"Please, Alix, you have to find a way to bring me back," Cédric pleads. "I made a mistake."

Oh, yes, huge mistake.

"If you must know, I left to save a life."

"I see," she says, not a hint of sympathy in her voice. "Too bad you couldn't save my husband's life."

"What?" Surely, I must have misheard. Surely, she's not blaming me for Cédric's stupid decision. "I had nothing to do with Cédric's suicide."

Hélène sniffles slightly. "You're probably glad he's dead. You never liked him."

"Please, Alix. Please."

"*He* did this!" I shout at her. "He killed himself, not me."

"I know," the idiot in question keeps whining. "It was a mistake. Please, just bring me back. Let me make it right."

"Shut up!" I shout at him, unable to ignore him any longer.

Hélène's mouth falls open, but then she notices I'm not looking at her. "Who are you talking to?" Her voice is dangerously low.

I don't want to do this. I don't have the mental capacity. "Cédric. He keeps—"

"He's here?" Hélène cries and jumps up. "My husband is here, and you didn't think to mention it?" She's breathing hard now, her nerves at least as frayed as mine. "You're unbelievable! I hate you! I freaking *hate* you."

Crying, she runs from the room, Cédric hot on her heels, asking her to wait.

I remain standing, her words gnawing at me as I stare at all the grave flowers Gaspar must've organised earlier—before he became a monster. It seems I can't do anything right today. Wherever I go, death and misery follow me.

Someone knocks on the door. "We heard shouting." It's Gaby and Marie, each holding a bottle of wine.

Suddenly, all the horrors of the day come back to me. Hélène's grief, Cédric's idiocy, Margot and Charles' cruelty, Sébastien's pain, and Gaspar's darkness—it's all too much to bear. Unable to hold myself together for a second, I fall to the floor and burst into tears.

Within a second, Gaby and Marie are there, their arms wrapped around me and each other, crying, too.

I have no idea how we're ever going to stop.

CHAPTER 34

Gaspar doesn't return to the room, which makes me both glad and angry. After what happened in Margot's lab, I don't think I can ever look him in the eye again. Yet, I mourn him and what he's become. I avoid my family as much as I can over the next few days. They're so busy looking after Hélène they hardly even notice. Instead, I spend all my time with Gaby and Marie, who don't let me out of their sight. The three of us have lived through the same horrors and we'll never forget it. And then there's Malou, the only thing that brings me joy at the moment.

On the last day of our trip, Sébastien invites me for a walk in the countryside. I haven't seen him since that fateful night, so I'm eager to catch up and see how he's doing. We drive out to Saint Victoire and walk along the rivers and valleys of the mountain while he fills me in.

"Gaspar's returned to Paris. He's going underground for a while and will see you when we get back." Much as I know I need to see him again, I don't feel up to it yet. "He was beside himself when he realised what had happened. My father promised to cover everything up and make sure no one ever learns of what went down in that lab."

"And you believe him?" If I know anything about Charles Roubert, he'd like to pin the whole thing on me.

"He doesn't really have a choice," Sébastien admits. "Sure, he could make a lot of trouble, but he'd have to explain what happened in the room before and what he was doing there. Besides, there are *four* of us who could cause him a lot of trouble. We agreed it was best to keep this quiet. It'll keep Gaspar safe."

That's probably a good thing. I don't want Gaspar to go to prison or worse, some other secret government lab when they find out he was buried five months ago.

"I know it's not what we wanted, and I promise it won't be the end of it." Sébastien takes my hand. "We'll do it your way. Together."

"My way." I snort and roll my eyes. "My way apparently leads to chaos and destruction, and France's darkest hour."

"Nostradamus?" Sébastien asks with raised eyebrows.

"Yeah, he doubled and tripled down on his prophecy."

"You know what I think of them."

I can't help laughing. It's not a pretty sound. "Problem is, he was right. Cédric *did* die on his wedding day. And your mother died, too. Apparently, he warned her, but she didn't believe in prophecies, either."

I regret my words as he winces. I never meant to compare him to that woman.

With a deep sigh, I calm my nerves. "How are you feeling?"

"I'm okay."

"Stop lying!" I know it's all an act. Sébastien is far from okay, maybe even less so now than ever before. "You're not okay. You can't be. So, stop pretending you are when you're clearly hurting."

"I don't want to worry you. None of this would've happened if I hadn't dragged you into it. I feel guilty for introducing you to my parents. To all their shit and lies." His voice starts to break, a clear sign the last few days have taken their toll on him as well.

Without a word of warning, I pull him into a hug. "It's not your fault, okay? None of this is your fault."

Sébastien breathes hard, fighting for his precious composure, but there's the child who blamed himself for his mother leaving. Who believed his father's lies because he wanted to be a good boy. Someone to be proud of. The boy who was betrayed and used by his parents so many times, and still hoped one day they'd turn around and love him. Only they didn't, and he thinks it's his fault.

"I've got you," I tell him, in lieu of his parents. "To me, you're perfect."

Hot tears fall on my shoulder as his mask finally cracks. His fingers tighten in my hair and his whole body shudders as sobs rip through his throat. As heartbreaking as his tears are, they're necessary. My own eyes fill with tears as I mourn the boy he was never allowed to be.

Finally, he pulls back, quickly wiping away the tears. "I'm sorry."

"Don't be. I've cried a lot more since then."

"I'm sorry for that, too."

"Not your fault."

He cracks a small smile. "Noted."

We walk on, both of us trying to catch our breath before facing our future again.

"I've been thinking," I say, after a while. "Maybe your father was right all along."

Sébastien looks at me as if I've lost my mind. "About what?" I love how little he believes Charles has ever done anything right.

But it doesn't change the way I feel about myself. "About me being a ghost whisperer. Sometimes, I think..." The words catch in my throat. "Sometimes... I..." Those damn tears threaten to come back. "I think it would be better if I weren't a ghost whisperer." There, I finally said it.

"Are you kidding?"

"Listen. It's not that I don't like it or anything, but..." Nostradamus' words keep swirling around in my head. "I just keep making a mess of everything. And it doesn't just hurt me, it hurts everyone around me. I almost got my father killed, then the whole mess with Cédric, and Gaby and Marie are traumatised because of me, too. My sister hates me. And Gaspar…"

Sébastien stops and cups my face. "Shh, shh. Easy, Alix."

I blink hard, trying to fight back the tears. "It's just that I keep making things worse, dragging more and more people into it. And if Nostradamus is to be believed, it's going to get a *lot* worse. I'll be responsible for the downfall of this country or something."

Sébastien's lips curl upwards. "You alone?"

I roll my eyes. "I don't want to be the next one who didn't listen to Nostradamus."

He throws up his hands in defeat. "Well, I don't believe him. Or rather, I don't think he's telling the whole truth. He didn't with that other prophecy either. Alix, you're not going to suddenly turn into some monstrous sorceress who rains death and destruction on us. That's not you."

"It could be." After all, Gaspar was a sweet, innocent boy who loved music and exploring the catacombs. And now he's a cold-hearted revenant and a murderer.

"Nah, there's no chance of that. Come, I want to show you something."

He takes my hand, ignoring my protests, and pulls me along the path until we reach a small bridge. A river flows below us. Boys are playing in the water, although it's much too cold for that. They're sixteen or seventeen and, like many of their age, have little to worry about. There are three of them; a blond one who always keeps a bit of distance, a tall dark one with a grim face even when he's smiling, and a little feisty one who's clearly the leader of the pack. He jumps on the big one's back and crows, then laughs when they both fall into the water, and he gets a scolding.

"Are those…"

"Les Trois Insèperables." Sébastien nods, a warm smile on his face. "They've come here every day since you reunited them."

"You've seen them before?" Every day, if he's to be believed.

He nods again. "I found them when I needed to clear my head on Cédric's wedding day. Before I went to my mother's. Then afterwards… I had to see them to believe in the good in the world. The good you brought to it." He turns to me and bathes me in that warm smile. "You did this, Alix. This is what you do. This is why you're a ghost whisperer. And if you're going to be a catalyst for change, this is how you'll do it. One ghost at a time. Who said chaos and destruction were necessarily bad things?"

I can't help laughing. It's a ridiculous perspective, but I'm grateful for the optimism. I slip my arm through his and lean my head on his shoulder as I watch the three ghost boys below us, reliving the kind of boyhood Sébastien should've had. No wonder he's come here so often, looking for comfort.

As I begin to make peace with my fate, I can't help but think of Gaspar. The boy I loved is no more, or is he? His behaviour has been so erratic since his return. As Sébastien once said, on his good days he's pretty great. On his bad days, though, I don't think he can get much worse.

"I've been thinking," I admit. "About Gaspar."

"Me, too."

Sébastien knows. He's been trying to tell me, but I've been too blind to see it until now. It's time to rip the Band-Aid off. "Something went wrong with his resurrection. This isn't him anymore." I suddenly remember the glimpse of him I saw in the mirror at the gallery exhibition in the catacombs. "He's turned into a monster."

My monster.

AFTERWORD

Wow! What a ride! When I was planning this book, I told my husband it would be the sweetest book in the series (thanks to our inseparable ghost special guests) and also the goriest (you know what I mean). I don't know how that went together, but it was a rollercoaster for sure.

I hope you enjoyed this little trip to Provence. I've been there twice before. Once to Cannes when I was a kid with my grandparents, and once to Marseille as a young adult. At the time, I was fascinated by the beautiful, rugged coastline. After researching this book, I want to go back and experience the beauty of Saint Victoire, the lavender fields, and the little villages. Maybe those museums will be open again when I get there.

I definitely had a lot of fun with Émile Zola's and Paul Cézanne's story in this book. Were they really lovers? Not according to history, but damn if they didn't have an extremely close relationship up until the publication of that cursed book (which is totally sitting on my TBR now). We know how reluctant history is to paint anyone queer who wasn't openly so, but reading about them and the letters they wrote, plus Cézanne's reported reaction after Zola's death, I think there's some room for a story like mine.

Now for the less wholesome storylines. I know no one will be sad about the people who died in this book. They both kind of deserved it, but I hope they shocked you a bit and we'll definitely feel the repercussions of their deaths in future books. It also hurt my heart to write Gaspar in this book. I love him dearly, but something had to go wrong with his resurrection. I promise this isn't the end of his love story with Alix—and Sébastien.

The three of them definitely have their work cut out for them in the next book, and it's going to be a doozy. Stick around as we reckon with Charles and GoPol, get back to the Chevalier (sorry for his near absence these last two books), and meet a certain squishy hedgehog in *Ghosts of the World Fair*.

A huge thanks to Perri for her Provence insights and my other beta readers. Paula, who's the fastest and most supportive reader I could have. Jojo, who writes these wonderful, longform critiques I simply live for. And Tina, who was finally won over by Sébastien. I honestly couldn't have done it without you.

Thanks to Jackie, my favourite writing buddy and proofreader. I can't thank you enough for all the hours we spend on Zoom (not nearly enough lately) and for taking such good care of my books, even when your life is a whirlwind. I can't wait to see you in person again when this book comes out.

Last but not least, thank you to my children, who are Malou's biggest fans, and to my husband, who listens to all my woes and joys as I cobble these books together.

As nice as this trip south has been, it's time to return to Paris and the catacombs!

Love, Janna

I've trusted nature spirits with my life, until the storm king decided I had to die.

.

Did you ever wonder what living on the streets of Berlin is like? My name is Rika and I've been homeless for eight years. It's not too bad, since I've got salamanders to warm me in winter and dryads to protect me from stragglers. People say I'm crazy, because to everyone else, those nature spirits are invisible. But they're real. Real and *dangerous*, as I learn when I accidentally cross the plans of the Erlking, an ancient and hate-filled spirit. Now he and his deadly storm are after me.

My only chance are the Spirit Seekers, an elite group of soldiers trained to battle nature's wrath. Since their precious commander is missing in action, they need me to be their eyes. Signing up with the Spirit Seekers is the opposite of run and hide, but they offer me protection and the tools to fight for my survival. All I have to do is betray my old spirit friends and try not to die.

.

Join Rika and the Spirit Seekers in this action-packed stormy urban fantasy adventure and start your supernatural trip to Europe today!

.

Read here

ASHUAN (PRINT)

A Drop of Magic (Ashuan Greed 1)

Magic, Demons and High School Drama

About Janna Ruth

Once upon a time, Janna Ruth studied the plate boundaries of this world. Now, she's creating her own worlds. Born in Berlin, Germany, Janna lives in Wellington, New Zealand, writing both English and German books.

Janna's writing career kicked off when she won a writing competition for German publisher Ueberreuter. Her first self-published novel "Im Bann der zertanzten Schuhe" (Melody of Curse, coming in June 2022) went on to win the 2018 SERAPH for "Best Independent Title". She debuted in English with her witchy novella "Witching with Dolphins" in 2020 and has since published urban fantasy, YA sci-fi, and contemporary coming-of-age novels and series.

When Janna isn't writing, she has a plethora of hobbies, such as aerial acrobatics, cake decorating, drawing, reading, and anything crafty you can throw her way.

Find out more about Janna and her books here:

Website: www.janna-ruth.com

BookBub: www.bookbub.com/authors/janna-ruth

Facebook: www.facebook.com/authorjannaruth

Reader Group: www.facebook.com/groups/storyseeker

Goodreads:

www.goodreads.com/author/show/16513923.Janna_Ruth

BlueSky: https://bsky.app/profile/janna-ruth.bsky.social

Instagram: www.instagram.com/janna_ruth

TikTok: www.tiktok.com/@jannaruthwrites

Pinterest: www.pinterest.com/jannaruthwrites